TELL
THE
MACHINE
GOODNIGHT

TELL
THE
MACHINE
GOODNIGHT

Katie Williams

RIVERHEAD BOOKS • NEW YORK • 2018

RIVERHEAD BOOKS
Published by the Penguin Group
An imprint of Penguin Random House LLC
New York, New York 10014

Library of Congress Cataloging-in-Publication Data

Names: Williams, Katie, author.
Title: Tell the machine goodnight : a novel / by Katie Williams.
Description: New York : Riverhead Books, 2018.
Identifiers: LCCN 2017039824 | ISBN 9780525533122 (hardcover) | ISBN
9780525533146 (ebook)
Subjects: LCSH: Self-realization—Fiction. | Happiness—Fiction.
Classification: LCC PS3623.I558265 T45 2018 | DDC 813/.6—dc23
LC record available at https://lccn.loc.gov/2017039824
p.   cm.

International edition ISBN: 9780525537366

Printed in the United States of America
1   3   5   7   9   10   8   6   4   2

BOOK DESIGN BY LUCIA BERNARD

For Uly and Fia

CONTENTS

TELL
THE
MACHINE
GOODNIGHT

1

The Happiness Machine

Apricity (archaic): the feeling of sun on one's skin in the winter

The machine said the man should eat tangerines. It listed two other recommendations as well, so three in total. A modest number, Pearl assured the man as she read out the list that had appeared on the screen before her: one, he should eat tangerines on a regular basis; two, he should work at a desk that received morning light; three, he should amputate the uppermost section of his right index finger.

The man—in his early thirties, by Pearl's guess, and pinkish around the eyes and nose in the way of white rabbits or rats—lifted his right hand before his face with wonder. Up came his left, too, and he used its palm to press experimentally on the top of his right index finger, the finger in question. *Is he going to cry?* Pearl wondered. Sometimes people cried when they heard their recommendations. The conference room they'd put her in had glass walls, open to the workpods on the other side. There was a switch on the wall to fog the glass, though; Pearl could flick it if the man started to cry.

"I know that last one seems a bit out of left field," she said.

"Right field, you mean," the man—Pearl glanced at her list for his name, one Melvin Waxler—joked, his lips drawing up to reveal overlong front teeth. Rabbitier still. "Get it?" He waved his hand. "Right hand. Right field."

Pearl smiled obligingly, but Mr. Waxler had eyes only for his finger. He pressed its tip once more.

"A modest recommendation," Pearl said, "compared to some others I've seen."

"Oh sure, I know that," Waxler said. "My downstairs neighbor sat for your machine once. It told him to cease all contact with his brother." He pressed on the finger again. "He and his brother didn't argue or anything. Had a good relationship actually, or so my neighbor said. Supportive. Brotherly." Pressed it. "But he did it. Cut the guy off. Stopped talking to him, full stop." Pressed it. "And it worked. He says he's happier now. Says he didn't have a clue his brother was making him *un*happy. His *twin* brother. *Identical* even. If I'm remembering." Clenched the hand into a fist. "But it turned out he was. Unhappy, that is. And the machine knew it, too."

"The recommendations can seem strange at first," Pearl began her spiel, memorized from the manual, "but we must keep in mind the Apricity machine uses a sophisticated metric, taking into account factors of which we're not consciously aware. The proof is borne out in the numbers. The Apricity system boasts a nearly one hundred percent approval rating. Ninety-nine point nine seven percent."

"And the point three percent?" The index finger popped up from Waxler's fist. It just wouldn't stay down.

"Aberrations."

Pearl allowed herself a glance at Mr. Waxler's fingertip, which appeared no different from the others on his hand but was its own aberration, according to Apricity. She imagined the fingertip popping off his hand like a cork from a bottle. When Pearl looked up again, she found that Waxler's gaze had shifted from his finger to her face. The two of them shared the small smile of strangers.

"You know what?" Waxler bent and straightened his finger. "I've never liked it much. This particular finger. It got slammed in a door when I was little, and ever since . . ." His lip drew up, revealing his teeth again, almost a wince.

"It pains you?"

"It doesn't hurt. It just feels . . . like it doesn't belong."

Pearl tapped a few commands into her screen and read what came back. "The surgical procedure carries minimal risk of infection and zero risk of mortality. Recovery time is negligible, a week, no more. And with a copy of your Apricity report—there, I've just sent that to you, HR, and your listed physician—your employer has agreed to cover all relevant costs."

Waxler's lip slid back down. "Hm. No reason not to then."

"No. No reason."

He thought a moment more. Pearl waited, careful to keep her expression neutral until he nodded the go-ahead. When he did, she tapped in the last command and, with a small burst of satisfaction, crossed his name off her list. *Melvin Waxler. Done.*

"I've also recommended that your workpod be reassigned to the eastern side of the building," she said, "near a window."

"Thank you. That'll be nice."

Pearl finished with the last prompt question, the one that would close the session and inch her closer to her quarterly bonus. "Mr. Waxler, would you say that you anticipate Apricity's recommendations will improve your overall life satisfaction?" This phrasing was from the updated training manual. The question used to be *Will Apricity make you happier?* but Legal had decided that the word *happier* was problematic.

"Seems like it could," Waxler said. "The finger thing might lower my typing speed." He shrugged. "But then there's more to life than typing speed."

"So . . . yes?"

"Sure. I mean, yes."

"Wonderful. Thank you for your time today."

Mr. Waxler rose to go, but then, as if struck by an impulse, he stopped and reached out for the Apricity 480, which sat on the table between them. Pearl had just last week been outfitted with the new model; sleeker than the Apricity 470 and smaller, too, the size of a deck of cards, the machine had fluted edges and a light gray casing that reflected a subtle sheen, like the smoke inside a fortune-teller's ball. Waxler's hand hovered over it.

"May I?" he said.

At Pearl's nod, he tapped the edge of the Apricity with the tip of the finger now scheduled to be amputated in—confirmations from both HR and the doctor's office had already arrived on Pearl's screen—a little over two weeks. Was it Pearl's imagination or did Mr. Waxler already stand a bit taller, as if an invisible yoke had been lifted from his shoulders? Was the pink around his eyes and nose now matched by a healthy flush to the cheek?

Waxler paused in the doorway. "Can I ask one more thing?"

"Certainly."

"Does it have to be tangerines, or will any citrus do?"

PEARL HAD WORKED AS A CONTENTMENT TECHNICIAN for the Apricity Corporation's San Francisco office since 2026. Nine years. While her colleagues hopped to new job titles or start-ups, Pearl stayed on. Pearl liked staying on. This was how she'd lived her life. After graduating college, Pearl had stayed on at the first place that had hired her, working as a nocturnal executive assistant for brokers trading in the Asian markets. After having her son, she'd stayed on at home until he'd started school. After getting married to her college boyfriend, she'd stayed on as his wife, until Elliot had an affair and left her. Pearl was fine where she was, that's all. She liked her work, sitting with customers who had purchased one of Apricity's three-tiered Contentment Assessment Packages, collecting their samples, and talking them through the results.

Her current assignment was a typical one. The customer, the up-and-coming San Francisco marketing firm !Huzzah!, had purchased Apricity's Platinum Package in the wake of an employee death, or, as Pearl's boss had put it, "A very un-merry Christmas and to one a goodnight!" Hours after the holiday party, a !Huzzah! copywriter had committed suicide in the office lounge. The night cleaning service had found the poor woman, but hours too late. Word of the death had made the rounds, of course, both its cause and its location. !Huzzah!'s January reports noted a decrease in worker productivity, an accompanying increase in complaints to HR. February's reports were grimmer still, the first weeks of March abysmal.

So !Huzzah! turned to the Apricity Corporation and, through them, Pearl, who'd been brought into !Huzzah!'s office in SoMa to create a contentment plan for each of the firm's fifty-four employees. *Happiness is Apricity.* That was the slogan. Pearl wondered what the dead copywriter would think of it.

The Apricity assessment process itself was noninvasive. The only item that the machine needed to form its recommendations was a swab of skin cells from the inside of the cheek. This was Pearl's first task on a job, to hand out and collect back a cotton swab, swipe a hint of captured saliva across a computer chip, and then fit the loaded chip into a slot in the machine. The Apricity 480 took it from there, spelling out a personalized contentment plan in mere minutes. Pearl had always marveled at this: to think that the solution to one's happiness lay next to the residue of the bagel one had eaten for breakfast!

But it was true. Pearl had sat for Apricity herself and felt its effects. Though for most of Pearl's life unhappiness had only ever been a mild emotion, not a cloud overhead, as she'd heard others describe it, surely nothing like the fog of a depressive, none of this bad weather. Pearl's unhappiness was more like the wisp of smoke from a snuffed candle. A birthday candle at that. *Steady, stalwart, even-keeled*: these were the words that had been applied to her since childhood. And she supposed she looked the part: dark hair cropped around her ears and neck in a tidy swimmer's cap; features pleasing but not too pretty; figure trim up top and round in the thighs and bottom, like one of those inflatable dolls that will rock back up after you punch it down. In fact, Pearl had been selected for her job as an Apricity technician because she possessed, as her boss had put it, "an aura of wooly contentment, like you have a blanket draped over your head."

"You rarely worry. You never despair," he'd gone on, while Pearl sat before him and tugged at the cuffs of the suit jacket she'd bought for the interview. "Your tears are drawn from the puddle, not the ocean. Are you happy right now? You are, aren't you?"

"I'm fine."

"You're fine! Yes!" he shouted at this revelation. "You store your happiness in a warehouse, not a coin pouch. It can be bought cheap!"

"Thank you?"

"You're very welcome. Look. This little guy likes you"—he'd indicated the Apricity 320 in prime position on his desk—"and that means I like you, too."

That interview had been nine years and sixteen Apricity models ago. Since then Pearl had suffered dozens more of her boss's vaguely insulting metaphors and had, more importantly, seen the Apricity system prove itself hundreds—no, *thousands* of times. While other tech companies shriveled into obsolescence or swelled into capitalistic behemoths, the Apricity Corporation, guided by its CEO and founder, Bradley Skrull, had stayed true to its mission. *Happiness is Apricity.* Yes, Pearl was a believer.

However, she was not so naïve as to expect that everyone else must share her belief. While Pearl's next appointment of the day went nearly as smoothly as Mr. Waxler's—the man barely blinked at the recommendation that he divorce his wife and hire a series of reputable sex workers to fulfill his carnal needs—the appointment after that went unexpectedly poorly. The subject was a middle-aged web designer, and though Apricity's recommendation seemed a minor one, to adopt a religious practice, and though Pearl pointed out that this could be interpreted as anything from Catholicism to Wicca, the woman stormed out of the room, shouting that Pearl wanted her to become weak minded, and that this would suit her employer's purposes quite well, wouldn't it, now? Pearl sent a request to HR to schedule a follow-up appointment for the next day. Usually these situations righted themselves after the subject had had time to contemplate. Sometimes Apricity confronted people with their secret selves, and, as Pearl had tried to explain to the shouting woman, such a passionate reaction, even if negative, was surely a sign of just this.

Still, Pearl arrived home deflated—the metaphorical blanket over her head feeling a bit threadbare—to find her apartment empty. Surprisingly, stunningly empty. She made a circuit of the rooms twice before acknowledging that Rhett had, for the first time since he'd come back from the clinic, left the house of his own volition. A shiver ran through her and gathered, buzzing, beneath each of her fingernails. She fumbled with her screen, pulling it from the depths of her pocket and unfolding it.

"Just got home," she spoke into it.

k, came the eventual reply.

"You're not here," she said. What she wanted to say: *Where the hell are you?*

fnshd hw wnt out came back.

"Be home in time for dinner."

The alert that her message had been sent and received sounded like her screen had heaved a deep mechanical sigh.

Her apartment was in the outer avenues of the city's Richmond District. You could walk to the ocean, could see a corner of it even, gray and tumbling, if you pressed your cheek against the bathroom window and peered left. Pearl pictured Rhett alone on the beach, walking into the surf. But no, she shouldn't think that way. Rhett's absence from the apartment was a good thing. It was possible— wasn't it?—that he'd gone out with friends from his old school. Maybe one of them had thought of him and decided to call him up. Maybe Josiah, who'd seemed the best of the bunch. He'd been the last of them to stop visiting, had written Rhett at the clinic, had once pointed to one of the dark bruises that had patterned Rhett's limbs and said, *Ouch,* so sadly and sweetly it was as if the bruise were on his own arm, the blood pooling under the surface of his own unmarked skin.

Pearl said it now, out loud, in her empty apartment.

"Ouch."

Speaking the word brought no pain.

To pass the hour until dinner, Pearl got out her latest modeling kit. The kits had been on Apricity's contentment plan for Pearl. She was nearly done with her latest, a trilobite from the Devonian period. She fitted together the last plates of the skeleton, using a tiny screwdriver to turn the tinier screws hidden beneath each synthetic bone. This completed, she brushed a pebbled leathery material with a thin coat of glue and fitted the fabric snugly over the exoskeleton. She paused and assessed. Yes. The trilobite was shaping up nicely.

When it came to her models, Pearl didn't skimp or rush. She ordered high-end kits, the hard parts produced with exactitude by a 3-D printer, the soft parts grown in a brew of artfully spliced DNA. Once again, Apricity had been correct in its assessment. Pearl felt near enough to happiness in that moment when she sliced open the cellophane of a new kit and inhaled the sharp smell of its artifice.

Before the trilobite, she'd made a *Protea cynaroides*, common name king protea, the model of a plant that, as Rhett was quick to point out, wasn't actually extinct. She could have grown a real king protea in the kitchen window box, the one that got weak light from the alley. But Pearl didn't want a real king protea. Rather, she didn't want to grow a king protea. She wanted to build the plant piece by piece. She wanted to shape it with her own hands. She wanted to feel something grand and biblical: *See what I wrought?* The king protea had bloomed among the dinosaurs. Think of that! This blossom crushed under their ancient feet.

The Home Management System interrupted Pearl's focus, its soft librarian tones alerting her that Rhett had just entered the lobby. Pearl gathered her modeling materials—the miniature brushes, the tweezers with ends as fine as the hairs they placed, and the amber bottles of shellac and glue—so that all would be put away before

Rhett reached the apartment door. She didn't want Rhett to catch her at her hobby because she knew he'd smirk and needle her. *Dr. Frankenstein?* he'd announce in his flat tone, curiously like a PA system even when he wasn't imitating one. *Paging Dr. Frankenstein. Monster in critical condition. Monster code blue! Code blue! Stat!* And while Rhett's jibes didn't bother Pearl, she also didn't think it was especially good for him to be given opportunities to act unpleasant. He didn't need opportunities anyway. Her son was a self-starter when it came to unpleasantness. No, she hadn't thought that.

The sound of the front door, and a moment later, there Rhett was, each of the precious ninety-four pounds of his sixteen-year-old self. It had been cold outside, and she could smell the spring air coming off him, metallic, galvanized. Pearl looked for a flush in his cheeks like the one she'd seen in Mr. Waxler's, but Rhett's skin remained sallow; his visible cheekbones were a hard truth. Had he been losing weight again? She wouldn't ask. After all, Rhett had arrived in the kitchen without prompting, presumably to say hello. She wouldn't annoy him by asking him where he'd been or, to Rhett's mind the worst question of them all, the one word: *Hungry?*

Instead, Pearl pulled out a chair and was rewarded for her restraint when Rhett sat in it with a truculent dip of the head, as if acknowledging she'd scored a point on him. He pulled off his knit cap, his hair a fluff in its wake. Pearl resisted the impulse to brush it down with her hand, not because she needed him to be tidy but because she longed to touch him. Oh how he'd flinch if she reached anywhere near his head!

She got up to search the cupboards, announcing, "I had a horrible day."

She hadn't. It'd been, at worst, mildly taxing, but Rhett seemed relieved when Pearl complained about work, eager to hear about the secret strangeness of the people Apricity assessed. The company had a strict client confidentiality policy, authored by Bradley Skrull himself. So technically, contractually, Pearl wasn't supposed to talk about her Apricity sessions outside of the office, and certainly many of them weren't appropriate conversation for a teenage boy and his mother. However, Pearl had dismissed all such objections the moment she'd realized that other people's sadness was a balm for her son's own powerful and inexplicable misery. So she told Rhett about the man, earlier that day, who'd been unruffled by the suggestion that he exchange his wife for prostitutes, and she told him about the woman who'd shouted at her over the simple suggestion of exploring a religion. She didn't, however, tell him about Mr. Waxler's amputated finger, worried that Rhett would take to the idea of cutting off bits of himself. A finger weighed, what, at least a few ounces?

Rhett grinned as Pearl laid the office workers bare, a mean grin, his only grin. When he was little, he'd beamed generously and frequently, light shining through the gaps between his baby teeth. No. That was overstating it. It had simply seemed that way to Pearl, the brilliance of his little-boy smile. "Moff," he used to call her, and when she'd pointed at her chest and corrected, "Mom?" he'd repeated, "Moff." He'd called Elliot the typical "Dad" readily enough, but "Moff" Pearl had remained. And she'd thought joyously, fool-ishly, that her son's love for her was so powerful that he'd felt the need to create an entirely new word with which to express it.

Pearl went about preparing Rhett's dinner, measuring out the chalky protein powder and mixing it into the viscous nutritional shake. *Sludge*, Rhett called the shakes. Even so, he drank them as promised, three times a day, an agreement made with the doctors at the clinic, his release dependent upon this and other agreements—*no excessive exercise, no diuretics, no induced vomiting.*

"I guess I have to accept that people won't always do what's best for them," Pearl said, meaning the woman who'd shouted at her, realizing only as she was setting the shake in front of her son that this comment could be construed as applying to him.

If Rhett felt a pinprick, he didn't react, just leaned forward and took a small sip of his sludge. Pearl had tried the nutritional shake herself once; it tasted grainy and falsely sweet, a saccharine paste. How could he choose to subsist on this? Pearl had tried to tempt Rhett with beautiful foods bought from the downtown farmers' markets and local corner bakeries, piling the bounty in a display on the kitchen counter—grapes fat as jewels, organic milk thick from the cow, croissants crackling with butter. This Rhett had looked at like it was the true sludge.

Many times, Pearl fought the impulse to tell her son that when she was his age, this "disease" was the affliction of teenage girls who'd read too many fashion magazines. *Why?* she wanted to shout. Why did he insist on doing this? It was a mystery, unsolvable, because even after enduring hours of traditional therapy, Rhett refused to sit for Apricity. She'd asked him to do it only once, and it had resulted in a terrible fight, their worst ever.

"You want to jam something inside me again?" he'd shouted.

He was referring to the feeding tube, the one that—as he liked to remind her in their worst moments—she'd allowed the hospital to use on him. And it had been truly horrible when they'd done it, Rhett's thin arms batting wildly, weakly, at the nurses. They'd finally had to sedate him in order to get it in. Pearl had stood in the corner of the room, helpless, and followed the black discs of her son's pupils as they'd rolled up under his eyelids. After, Pearl had called her own mother and sobbed into the phone like a child.

"'Jam something'?" she said. "Really now. It's not even a needle. It's a cotton swab against your cheek."

"It's an invasion. You know the word for that, don't you? Putting something inside someone against their will."

"Rhett." She sighed, though her heart was hammering. "It's not rape."

"Call it what you want, but I don't want it. I don't want your stupid machine."

"That's fine. You don't have to have it."

Even though he'd won the argument, Rhett had afterward closed his mouth against all food, all speech. A week later he'd been back in the clinic, his second stint there.

"School?" she asked him now.

She fixed her own dinner and began to eat it: a small bowl of pasta, dressed with oil, mozzarella, tomato, and salt. Anything too rich or pungent on her plate and Rhett's nostrils flared and his upper lip curled in repulsion, as if she'd come to the table dressed in a negligee. So she ate simply in front of him, inoffensively. The ascetic diet had caused her to lose weight. Pearl's boss had remarked that she'd been looking good lately, "like one of those skinny horses. What are they called? The ones that run. The ones with the bones." Fine then. Pearl would lose weight if Rhett would gain it. An unspoken pact. An equilibrium. Sometimes Pearl would think back to when she was pregnant, when it was her body that fed her son. She'd told Rhett this once, in a moment of weakness—*When I was pregnant, my body fed you*—and at this comment he'd looked the most disgusted of all.

But this evening, Rhett seemed to be tolerating things: his nutritional shake, her pasta, her presence. In fact, he was almost animated, telling her about an ancient culture he was studying for his anthropology class. Rhett took his classes online. He'd started when he was at the clinic and continued after he'd returned home, never going back to his quite nice, quite expensive private high school, paid for, it was worth noting, by the Apricity Corporation he disdained. These days, he rarely left the apartment.

"These people, they drilled holes in their skulls, tapped through them with chisels." There was fascination in Rhett's flat voice, a PA system announcing the world's wonders. "The skin grows back over and you live like that. A hole or two in your head. They believed it made it easier for divinity to get in. Hey!" He slammed down his glass, fogged with the remnants of his shake. "Maybe you should suggest *that* religion to that angry lady. Tap a hole in her head! Gotta bring your chisel to work tomorrow."

"Good idea. Tonight I'll sharpen its point."

"No way." He grinned. "Leave it dull."

Pearl knew she must have looked startled because Rhett's grin snuffed out, and for a moment he seemed almost bewildered, lost. Pearl forced a laugh, but it was too late. Rhett pushed his glass to the center of the table and rose, muttering, "G'night," and seconds later came the decisive snick of his bedroom door.

Pearl sat for a moment before she made herself rise and clear the table, taking the glass last, for it would require scrubbing.

PEARL WAITED UNTIL an hour after the HMS noted Rhett's light clicking off before sneaking into his bedroom. She eased the closet door open to find the jeans and jacket he'd been wearing that day neatly folded on their shelf, an enviable behavior in one's child if it weren't another oddity, something teenage boys just didn't do. Pearl searched the clothing's pockets for a Muni ticket, a store receipt, some scrap to tell her where her son had been that afternoon. She'd already called Elliot to ask if Rhett had been with him, but Elliot was out of town, helping a friend put up an installation in some gallery (Minneapolis? Minnetonka? Mini-somewhere), and he'd said that Valeria, his now wife, would definitely have mentioned if Rhett had stopped by the house.

"He's still drinking his shakes, isn't he, dove?" Elliot had asked, and when Pearl had affirmed that, yes, Rhett was still drinking his shakes, "Let the boy have his secrets then, as long as they're not food secrets, that's what I say. But, hey, I'll schedule something with him when I'm back next week. Poke around a bit. And you'll call me again if there's anything else? You know I want you to, right, dove?"

She'd said she knew; she'd said she would; she'd said goodnight; she hadn't said anything—she never said anything—about Elliot's use of her pet name, which he implemented perpetually and liberally, even in front of Valeria. Dove. It didn't pain Pearl, not much. She knew Elliot needed his affectations.

Ever since they'd met, back in college, Elliot and his cohort had been running around headlong, swooning and sobbing, backstabbing and catastrophizing, all of this drama supposedly necessary so that it could be regurgitated into art. Pearl had always suspected that Elliot's artist friends found her and her general studies major boring, but that was all right because she found them silly. They were still doing it, too—affairs and alliances, feuds and grudges long held—it was just that now they were older, which meant they were running around headlong with their little paunch bellies jiggling before them.

The pockets of Rhett's jeans were empty; so was the small trash basket beneath his desk. His screen, unfolded and set on its stand on the desk, was fingerprint locked, so she couldn't check that. Pearl stood over her son's bed in the dark and waited, as she had when he was an infant, her breasts filled and aching with milk at the sight of him. And so she'd stood again over these last two difficult years, her chest still aching but now empty, until she was sure she could see the rise and fall of his breath under the blanket.

After Rhett's first time at the clinic, when treatment there hadn't been working, they'd taken him to this place Elliot had found, a converted Victorian out near the Presidio, where a team of elderly women treated the self-starvers by holding them. Simply holding them for hours. "Hug it out?" Rhett had scoffed when they'd told him what he must do. At that point, though, he'd been too weak to resist, too weak to sit upright without assistance. The "treatment" was private, parents weren't allowed to observe, but Pearl had met the woman, Una, who had been assigned to Rhett. Her arms were plump and liver-spotted with a fine mesh of lines at elbow and wrist, as if she wore her wrinkles like bracelets, like sleeves. Pearl held her politeness in front of her as a scrim to hide the sudden hatred that gripped her. She hated that woman, hated her sagging, capable arms. Pearl had sat here in this apartment, imagining Una, only twenty-two blocks away, holding her son, providing what Pearl should have been able to and somehow could not. Once Rhett had regained five pounds, Pearl had convinced Elliot that they should move him back to the clinic. There he'd lost the five pounds he'd gained and then two more, and though Elliot kept suggesting returning him to the Victorian, Pearl had remained firm in her refusal. "Those crackpots?" she said to Elliot, pretending this was her objection. "Those hippies? No." *No*, she repeated to herself. She would do anything for her Rhett, *had* done anything, but the thought of Una cradling her son, as he gazed up softly—this was what Pearl couldn't bear. She would hold Una in reserve, a last resort. After leaving the Victorian, Rhett was back in the hospital again and then the terrible feeding tube. But it had worked, eventually it had. Pearl had eked out her son's recovery pound by pound. Was that where Rhett had been this afternoon? Had he gone to see Una? Had he needed her arms?

A subtle shift of the bedcovers as Rhett's chest rose, and Pearl slipped out of the room. If she were to sit for Apricity again, she wondered if there'd be a new item listed on her contentment plan: Watch your son breathe. Though, in truth, this practice didn't make her happy so much as stave off a swell of desperation.

THE NEXT MORNING, the web designer was late for their follow-up appointment. When she finally arrived, she entered in a huff, which Pearl mistook for more of yesterday's outrage. But once the woman had taken her seat and unwound a long red scarf from her neck, the first thing she did was apologize.

"You probably won't believe this," she said, "but I hate it when people yell. I'm not one to raise my voice."

The woman, Annette Flatte, made her apology in a practical manner with no self-pity or shuffling of blame. She wore the exact same outfit she had the day before, a white T-shirt and tailored gray slacks. Pearl imagined Ms. Flatte's closet full of identical outfits, fashion an unnecessary distraction.

"Did they tell you about what happened after the Christmas party?" Ms. Flatte said. "Why they brought you in?"

Pearl made a quick calculation and decided that Ms. Flatte

would not be the type of person who would consider feigned igno-
rance a form of politeness. "Your coworker who killed herself? Yes.
They told me at the outset. Did you know her?"

"Not really. Copywriting, Design: different floors." Ms. Flatte
opened her mouth, then closed it again, reconsidering. Pearl waited
her out. "Some of them are joking about it," Ms. Flatte finally said.

Pearl was already aware of this. Two employees had made the
same joke during their sessions with Pearl: *Guess Santa didn't bring
her what she wanted.*

"It's tacky." Ms. Flatte shook her head. "No. It's unkind."

"Unhappiness breeds unkindness," Pearl said dutifully, one of
the lines from the Apricity manual. "Just as unkindness breeds unhappiness." She reached for something else to say, something not in
the manual, something of her own, but the landscape was razed,
barren. There was nothing there. Why was there nothing there?

"They're scared," she finally said.

"Scared?" Ms. Flatte snorted. "Of what? Her ghost?"

"That someday they might feel that sad."

Ms. Flatte stared at the scarf in her lap, combing its fringe.
When she spoke, it was in a rush: "She wrote something for me
once, a little line of copy, or actually poetry. She left it on my desk
my first week here."

"What did it say?"

Ms. Flatte bent down to the bag at her feet. Pearl could see the
bones of her skull through the close crop of her hair, could see the
curve and divot where spine and skull met. Pearl pictured fitting
these pieces together, turning the tiny screws. Ms. Flatte came back

up with a pocketbook, and from its coin compartment she extracted a slip of paper. Pearl took the slip carefully between two fingers. It was printed with a computer font designed to imitate hasty cursive.

You will take a long trip and you will be very happy, though alone.

"I looked it up," Ms. Flatte said. "It's from an old poem called 'Lines for the Fortune Cookies.' And see? Doesn't it look like the little paper you get inside the cookie? Apparently she did it for everyone on their first week, chose a different line from a different poem. To welcome them. No one else told you about how she did that?"

"They didn't say."

Ms. Flatte pressed her lips together.

"The truth is, you were right," Ms. Flatte said. "Or your machine was anyway. I do need *something*." She laid heavily on the last word. "I don't know about religion. I was raised to distrust it. But . . . something. This morning—" She stopped.

"This morning?" Pearl prompted.

"The bus takes me through Golden Gate Park, and there's always these old people out on the lawn doing their tai chi. Today I got out and watched them for a while. That's why I was late to meet you. Do you think . . . could that be it? For me, I mean? Do you think that's what the machine could have meant?"

Pearl pretended to consider the question, already knowing she would deliver the standard reply. "Try and see. With Apricity, there's no right and wrong. There's just what works for you."

Ms. Flatte smiled suddenly and broadly, her whole face changed by it. "Can you imagine?" She laughed. "All those old Chinese people . . . and me?"

She thanked Pearl, apologizing once more for her outburst the day before, before bending to gather and rewind her long red scarf.

"Ms. Flatte," Pearl said as the woman stood to go, "one more thing."

"Yes?"

"Would you say that you anticipate Apricity's recommendations will improve your overall life satisfaction?"

"What's that?"

"Will you be happier?" Pearl asked. "Will you . . . will you be happy?"

Ms. Flatte blinked, as if surprised by the question; then she nodded once, curt but sure. "I think I will."

Pearl was surprised to feel a flare of . . . was it disappointment? She watched the gentle nape of Ms. Flatte's neck as the woman walked from the conference room, and she felt a sudden and ferocious wish that Ms. Flatte would turn around and, as she had the day before, begin to shout.

WHEN SHE RETURNED HOME, Pearl wondered if she'd find the apartment empty again. But no, there was Rhett, in his room at the computer, doing schoolwork, just as he was supposed to be.

"Hey," he said without turning around.

Pearl was so focused on the delicate wings of his hunched shoulders that it took her a moment to spot the half-finished trilobite set out on his desk.

"Is it okay I took it?" He'd turned and followed her gaze.

"Of course. But it's not finished yet. It still needs its details: antennae, legs, a topcoat of shellac." Then, on impulse, "You could help me finish it."

"Yeah, maybe." He'd already turned back around.

"This weekend?"

"Maybe."

Pearl lingered. She wished she could make her departure now, on this promising note, but they had to get it done before Rhett ate (drank) his dinner.

"Rhett? It's weigh-in day."

"Yeah, I know," he said tonelessly. "Just let me finish my paragraph."

He met her, minutes later, in the bathroom, where he shrugged off his sweatshirt and put it into her waiting hand.

"Pockets," she said.

He gave her a look but obliged without comment, turning them inside out. It had been his trick in the past to load his pockets with heavy objects. When Pearl nodded, Rhett stepped on the scale. She was not tall, but he was taller than her now, taller still as he stood on the scale. Taller, but he weighed less than her, and she was not a large woman. Rhett stared straight ahead, leaving Pearl to gaze at the number on her own. She felt it, that number. Higher or lower, she felt it every week, as if it affected her body in reverse, lightening her or weighing her down.

"You've lost two pounds."

He stepped off the scale without comment.

"That's not good, Rhett."

"It's a blip."

"It's not good."

"You've seen me. I'm drinking my shakes."

"Where were you yesterday?"

He closed his mouth slowly, defiantly. "Nowhere that has any-thing to do with that number."

"Look. I'm your mother—"

"And I'm sorry for that."

"Sorry? Don't be sorry. I just want you to—" She stopped. What was she saying? She just wanted him to what? She sounded as if she were reading from some sort of script. "We'll do an extra weigh-in. On Saturday. If it's just a blip, it'll be back to normal then."

"Okay."

"If it's not, we'll call Dr. Singh and adjust the recipe for your shake. He may want us to come in."

"I said okay."

DINNER WAS SILENT, except for the deliberate sound of Rhett slurping his shake. Pearl comforted herself by thinking that this was the exact sort of thing teenage boys did, acted purposely ob-noxious to get back at you for scolding them. After dinner, she got out a new modeling kit, this one for a particular species of wasp, and began the armature, twisting the wire filaments with her pli-ers. As usual, Rhett had disappeared to his room directly after din-ner. To study for a test, he'd said. Pearl was lost in her work with the wasp, only emerging when she heard a scrape on the tabletop to find Rhett there, returning the trilobite. He stood, as if waiting, his hand still on the model. She couldn't read his expression.

"It's fine if you keep it in your room," she said. "I mean, I'd like you to."

"But you need to finish it? You said that."

On impulse, she reached out and grabbed his wrist. It was so thin! You didn't really know until you'd touched it. She could have circled it with her thumb and finger easily. There was still a bit of the fur on his skin, the silky translucent hair that his body had grown to keep him warm when he'd been at his skinniest. *Lanugo*, the doctors had called it. They both stared down at her hand on Rhett's wrist. She knew he was probably horrified; he hated being touched, especially by her. But she couldn't make herself release it. She stroked the fur with her finger.

"It's soft," she murmured.

He didn't speak, but he also didn't pull away.

"I wish I could replicate it on one of my models." She'd spoken without thinking, a bizarre and horrible thing to say.

But Rhett stayed and let her stroke his wrist for a moment longer. Then, something more, he touched it—improbably—to her cheek before extricating himself.

"Goodnight," he said, and she thought she heard him add, "Moff." Then he was gone; again, the sound of his bedroom door. Pearl stared at the unfinished trilobite, imagined it swimming through the dark oceans without the benefit of its antennae to guide it, a compact little shell, deadened and blind. Surely he hadn't said "Moff."

Pearl stayed up late again, pretending to work on the wasp, but really making unguided twists in the wire, ending up with an improbable creature, one that had never existed, could never exist; evolution would never allow it. She imagined that the creature existed anyway, imagined it covered with fur, with feathers, with scales, with cilia that reacted to the slightest sensation. When the light to Rhett's room finally shut off, she went down the hall and got a cotton swab from her bag.

Rhett slept on his back with his lips slightly parted, the effect of the sleeping pill she'd crushed into his shake when fixing his dinner. It was easy to slip the swab into his mouth, to run it against his cheek without causing a murmur or stir. Easier than perhaps it should have been, this act that Rhett and the company, both, would consider a violation. The Apricity 480 sat on the kitchen table, small and knowing. Pearl approached it, the cotton swab in her grip. She unwrapped a new chip, the little slip of plastic that would deliver her son's DNA to the machine.

You will take a long trip and you will be very happy, though alone.

She loaded the chip, fit it into the port, and tapped the command. The Apricity made a slight whirring as it gathered and tabulated its data. Pearl leaned forward. She unfolded her screen and peered into its blank surface, looking to find her answer there, now, in this last moment before it began to glow.

2

Means, Motive, Opportunity

CASE NOTES 3/25/35

SUSPECT	MEANS	MOTIVE	OPPORTUNITY
LINUS	deals zom	none known	at party
JOSIAH	friends w/ Linus	Saff won't say	at party
ASTRID	none known	revenge for scapegoat	at party
ELLIE	caught on zom last October	she's Ellie	at party

Saff says it's funny to think of someone hating her enough to do what they did. She says it's funnier to think that she herself was there while they were doing it, that she already knows the solution to this mystery; she just can't remember what it is. She says that her body must remember—that the person's fingers are printed on her skin, their voice in her eardrums, their reflection on the backs of her eyes—and maybe her body could tell her, if only she could get her brain to shut up and let it. She lifts her bracelets to her elbow and lets them drop back down to her wrist, where they fall against each other, chiming. "You think I'm crazy, don't you, Rhett?" she says, adding, "Tell me the truth."

"I don't think you're crazy," I say. "But then most people wouldn't consider my sense of what's crazy to be particularly reliable."

Saff crinkles her nose. Does she think we're flirting? If she does, I let her go on thinking it because it's less trouble that way.

And I *don't* tell Saff the truth: that my body knows more than my brain does, too, that that's why I starve it. Instead, I tell her a lie. I tell her that I can help her.

CASE NOTES 3/26/35

The Crime

On the night of 2/14/35, Saffron Jones (age 17) was dosed with "zom," short for "zombie," so named for the drug's effects of short-term memory loss paired with extreme suggestibility. Basically, if you're on zom, you'll do whatever anyone tells you to and you won't remember any of it afterward, won't remember much of what came before it either, which is the nastiest part because you won't remember who dosed you. While on zom, Saff was told to strip naked and recite conjugations of the French verbs dormir, manger, *and* baiser *(respectively, "to sleep," "to eat," and "to fuck"). She was told to shave off her left eyebrow and to ingest half a bar of lemon soap. These events occurred in the basement of Ellie Bergstrom (age 18) during a party at Ellie's house and were recorded on Saff's screen. No one besides Saff is visible or audible in the video. As is typical with zom, Saff woke up the next morning with no memory of the previous night. She remembered leaving her house for Ellie's party, that's it. She thought she'd gotten drunk. She didn't realize anything more had happened until she accessed Facebook and discovered the video posted to her account. It had 114 dislikes, 585 likes.*

"IT COULD HAVE BEEN A LOT WORSE," Saff tells me.

We're sitting in her car in Golden Gate Park, pulled over on one of the access roads behind the flower conservatory. I can almost see the white spires of the conservatory through the treetops, but my clearest view is of the dumpster in the back where they throw out the flowers that have wilted and gone to rot.

"Saff. They made you eat soap."

Saff showed me the video. (I don't go on Facebook anymore.) In it, she took bite after bite of the thick bar of soap like it was a tea cake. Her pupils were huge and lavender in the dim basement light. (So were her nipples.) Her eyes weren't dead, though, not zombified like you'd think. She has big, dark eyes, Saff does. And in the video, they glittered. Also, she smiled as she chewed. We think she must have been told not just to eat the soap, but to *like* eating it. I stared at her mouth so I wouldn't look at her breasts, all too aware that the clothed Saff was sitting across from me, watching me as I watched her. In the video, the tip of her tongue darted out to collect a stray flake of soap from her bottom lip. Her lips parted, and a bubble formed between them, quivering like a word you can't speak. Then she threw it all up, a foamy yellow torrent. After that, the video cut out.

Saff shrugs. "At least my eyebrow is growing back. Can you tell?" She's penciled in the missing brow with care, but I *can* tell because it's a slightly different shade of brown from the real one. "It could have been worse."

"Are you sure it wasn't? Are you sure you weren't . . . ?" *Raped* is what I'm not going to say.

"I think I could tell. It would have been . . . new." *I'm a virgin* is what she's not going to say.

Saff is sneaking looks at me, but this time it's not because she's trying to flirt. She's embarrassed, either to tell me she's a virgin or maybe just to be one. I want to tell her not to bother being embarrassed, not around me. When I left school last year, all the kids in our class had started declaring themselves straight, gay, bi, whatever. Me, I had nothing to declare. Because I was nothing. I am nothing. I'm not interested in any of it. The doctors say I would be if only I ate more, but they think every true part of me is just another symptom of my condition. What they don't understand is that my condition is a symptom of *me*. That I am a stone buried deep in the ground, something that will never grow, no matter how good the dirt.

"You were, though." I decide I'm going to say the word this time. "Raped." And when I do, Saff's breath hisses out. "Even if you weren't actually. They made you do those things. They forced you. I know how it is."

"Yeah. Well. Everyone knows how it is because of that damn video."

"No. I mean I know how it feels. To be forced."

"Oh, Rhett," Saff whispers. "Oh no." And she's misunderstood me. She thinks I mean that *I* was raped. What I mean is that the doctors shoved a feeding tube down my throat when I was too weak to resist. That my parents told them it was okay. That it felt like I was drowning. I let Saff misunderstand, though. I let her clasp my hand and stare at me with her big, dark eyes. Because I know that when people comfort you, they're really just comforting themselves.

CASE NOTES 3/27/35, LATE MORNING

OPPORTUNITY

Opportunity holds no clues for us. Everyone in the class had the opportunity to dose Saff. Zom is taken transdermally. It's loaded on a see-through slip of paper, like a scrap of Scotch tape. You press the paper to your bare skin—your arm, your palm, your thigh, your anywhere—and it dissolves into you. You can take it on purpose for the side effects: slowed time, heightened sense of smell, euphoria. Even though you won't remember much of any of it the next day. Or you can get dosed without knowing it. A stranger's hand on your bare shoulder as you push through the crowd, on your cheek pretending to brush away a stray eyelash, on the back of your hand in a show of sympathy.

At the clubs, everyone stays covered up: full-length gloves, turtlenecks, pants, high boots, even veils and masks. In fact, the more covered you are, the more provocative, because you're saying that you might let a stranger touch you anywhere there's cloth. Some kids will let bits of skin show through, peeks of upper arm, ankle, and neck. Not too much skin, though, just enough to stay vigilant over. You have to protect what you show.

Saff wasn't covered up when she left her house. She was wearing a T-shirt and jeans and had left her sneakers at the door: bare arms, bare hands, bare neck, bare feet. So many vulnerabilities. But Saff wouldn't have thought she was vulnerable. This was a party at Ellie's, just like a hundred other parties at Ellie's going back to her platypus-themed fifth-birthday party, an event all the same kids had attended, add me. Seneca Day School is exclusive, meaning tiny, designed for kids with parents in big tech. There are only twelve students in each graduating class. (Eleven in mine, since I left.) We've all known each other forever. We all trust each other.

Except of course we don't. After all, where is there more distrust than in a small group of people trapped together for eternity? Old grudges; buried feelings; past mistakes; all those former versions of you that you could, in a larger school, run away from. Trust? You'd be safer in a crowd of strangers.

I EXPLAIN TO SAFF that we'll solve her mystery by looking for three things: means, motive, and opportunity. I tell her that every-thing everyone does can be predicted by this trinity of logic: Are they able to do it? Do they have a reason to do it? Do they have the chance to do it?

"Everything everyone does?" Saff repeats with a raised eye-brow, her real eyebrow. "What if I did something, like, totally spontaneous?"

Her hand whips out and knocks over the saltshaker. We're meeting in the diner across from school in Pac Heights. Salt cascades across the table, over the edge, soundlessly to the floor. The waitress glares at us.

"You've just proved my point," I tell her. "Your arm works. That's means. You wanted to challenge my theory. That's motive. The saltshaker was right there in front of you. That's opportunity."

Saff considers this. "You helping me then. How is that means . . . whatever?"

"Well. I have the means because I've read about a thousand detective novels and because I'm smart. Opportunity is that you asked me to help. Also, I'm in school online, which means I don't have adults watching over me all day."

"And motive?" she says.

Because they forced a feeding tube down my throat, I could tell her. *Because when I saw you again, you didn't say how healthy I looked,* I could tell her. *Because kid-you knew kid-me, before all of this shit.*

Instead I say, "Because I feel like it."

Saff screws her mouth to one side. "For it to be an actual motive doesn't there have to be, like, a reason?"

In response, I reach out and knock over the pepper shaker.

She laughs.

There's movement in the diner window. Ellie and Josiah are there across the street, beckoning to Saff. They're both on our list. Ellie is an obvious suspect. Because she would. That there is a true sentence: *Ellie would.* Whatever your proposition, Ellie would do it without hesitation. But Josiah? Josiah wouldn't hurt anyone. He might stand there with his hands in his pockets and say, *Hey. Come on, guys. Stop it.* (And that's almost worse, isn't it?) But he wouldn't actually *do* anything to anyone.

I haven't seen Josiah in almost a year. He looks the same. Taller. That stupid thing adults always say, *You look taller,* as if that's an accomplishment, and not just something your body does on its own, without your permission.

"Gotta go." Saff leans forward like she's going to kiss me on the cheek.

Across the street, Josiah squints, trying to make out who it is Saff is sitting with. I slouch down in the booth, and so Saff's kiss is delivered to the empty space where I just was.

"Don't tell them you saw me," I say.

CASE NOTES 3/27/35, AFTERNOON

MOTIVE

The Scapegoat Game started as a unit in Teacher Trask's junior English. She assigned "The Ones Who Walk Away from Omelas," "The Lottery," The Hunger Games, Lord of the Flies, *and other classics with a scapegoat theme. They even watched a Calla Pax movie,* The Warm-Skinned Girl, *where Calla Pax is sacrificed to a god living in an ice floe to stop planet heating and save the world. Saff says everyone got really into it, so much so that the class decided, without Trask's knowledge, to test the scapegoat concept in real life. My former classmates charted out eleven weeks, for the eleven of them, each one signing up for a weeklong turn as scapegoat.*

Like in the stories, the scapegoat had to take everyone else's abuse without comment or complaint. For that one week, ten were free to vent all their anger, frustration, pain, whatever, on the eleventh, knowing that the next week someone else—maybe you yourself—would become the scapegoat. They decided that made it fair.

SAFF COMES OVER AFTER SCHOOL to continue our conversation from the diner. When I swing open the door, she looks upset. Her eyes are pink. The inner edge of her penciled brow is smeared like she's been rubbing at it. I have the impulse to reach up and touch it, that bare little arc of skin. I shove my hands in my pockets.

"Are your parents home?" she says.

I tell her no, that my mom is at work. And that my dad doesn't live here anymore.

"Okay," she says.

And I'm grateful she doesn't say, *I'm sorry*, because then I don't have to say, *It's okay*. Or, *I see him on weekends*. Or, *It's better this way*. Or any other of that divorce-kid bullshit.

"We have until six," I say. "My mom usually gets home around then."

Not that it's against the rules to have Saff over. In fact, I'm pretty sure Mom would be delighted, which is precisely why I don't want her to find Saff here. It's too hard to have Mom hoping things about me. She got home before me yesterday, when I was at the park with Saff. Now she keeps looking at me, but she won't ask where I was, and I won't tell her. Not just out of stubbornness.

I've bought a tube of cookies and a couple sodas from the corner store in case Saff is hungry. There's plenty of food in the kitchen, of course, but Mom will notice if any of it is missing, and she'll think (hope) that I'm the one who's eaten it. I offer the snacks to Saff like I haven't bought them special. I even left them in the kitchen so that I can pretend to go in and get them from the cupboard. We take the food into my room.

Saff turns in a slow circle. I picture my room through her eyes: twin bed, rag rug, desk-chair–screen setup. No bullshit band posters or Japanese mech figurines to announce my unique store-bought personality. I threw all that stuff in a box last year. Now the room is simple (*bare*, Mom says), pure (*monkish*, Mom says). The walls are its only distinction. Today they're set to Victorian wallpaper, an exact replica of the wallpaper in the old BBC show *Sherlock*. On one wall there's even the image of a fireplace, complete with ashtray and curling pipe.

I wait to see if Saff gets the joke, but she sinks down on the floor by my bed without comment. She slides out a couple cookies, then shakes the tube at me. When I say, "No thanks," she doesn't push it, doesn't study me with meaningful eyes, doesn't say, *Are you sure?* So I return the favor and don't ask why she's been crying.

Instead, I say, "Tell me more about the game."

"Game?"

"The Scapegoat Game."

She rolls her eyes and bites off half a cookie in one go. "Oh. That fucking thing."

"Whose idea was it?"

"Whose do you think?"

"Ellie's."

She nods.

Popularity—who's cool, who's not, jocks, nerds, whatever—is, for Saff and me, something that exists only in movies about high school. When you have a class of twelve people, there really aren't enough of you to divide up into cliques. Sure, there are some best friends, like Ellie and Saff, or like Josiah and me (used to be). There're some couples, Ellie and Linus for a while, then Brynn and Linus, basically every girl and Linus. Except Saff. She's never been with Linus. Though maybe she has this past year; I wouldn't know, I've been gone. My point is, mostly everyone hangs out with everyone else.

There is one role, though, one rule: Ellie is always the leader. It's been that way from our first year, back when Ellie would whip the dodgeball at you and then, when you cried over the burn it'd left on your leg, explain how that was just part of the game, explain it so calmly and confidently that you found yourself nodding, even though the tears were still rolling down your cheeks. That makes it sound like I think Ellie is a bad person. I don't. In fact, the older I get, the more I think that Ellie's got it right, that she knew at five what the rest of us wouldn't figure out until our teens: the world is tough, so you'd better be tough right back.

"And so?" I say to Saff, because there's always more to the story when Ellie is involved.

"*And so*, after Ellie comes up with the scapegoat idea, she even volunteers to go first. Which, if you think about it, is pretty smart because at first everyone is, you know, gentle. Warming up to it. Also, if you go first, you haven't scapegoated anyone else yet, so they don't have anything to pay you back for." Saff pauses. "Do you think she actually plans this stuff out ahead of time?"

"I think Ellie has an instinct for weakness."

"Well, that first week we didn't do much—tugged Ellie's hair, kicked the back of her chair in class, made her carry our lunch trays. Nothing really. I think she had *fun*. Actually, I know she did. The last day, she dressed up as Calla Pax, from that sacrifice-on-the-ice movie we watched. In, like, a sexy white robe. She looked great. Of course. Then, the next week, Linus went. The guys were rougher on him, but not in a *mean* way, if that makes sense? And you know how Linus is. Easy with it all. It felt like a game. Fun even. Like free. When you have permission to . . . if you can do whatever . . . sometimes it's like . . ." She taps a thumb against her chest, then gives up trying to explain and takes another cookie. Her third. (I can't help counting other people's food.)

"But then it got bad. Each week, each new person. We kept upping it. Meaner. Rougher."

"When did you go?"

"Last," she says, smiling bitterly. "Like a fucking fool."

She looks like she's going to start crying again. I type some notes into my screen to give her a chance to get ahold of herself.

"'An instinct for weakness,'" she mutters.

I look up from my screen. "I didn't mean that you're weak."

"I don't know. I feel pretty weak."

"You're not, though. That's why they gave you zom. They had to *make* you weak. Which proves you're not. See?"

She bites on her lip. "I haven't told you about Astrid yet."

"Astrid is weak."

"Yeah, I know. She was scapegoat just before me."

Astrid's parents both work as lawyers for big tech, her mom for Google, her dad for Swink. For them, arguing is sport, which maybe partway explains the way Astrid is. If you're someone who needs to explain why people are the way they are. In second grade Astrid used to brush her hair over her face. Right over the front of it until it covered everything right down to her chin. The teachers were constantly giving her hair bands and brushes and telling her how nice she looked in a ponytail. At Seneca Day, there's a certain style the teachers are all supposed to use, "suggesting instead of correcting." But finally one day, Teacher Hawley lost it and shouted, "Astrid, why do you keep *doing* that!" And all the rest of us looked to the back row where Astrid sat and here comes this little voice, out from behind all that hair: "Because I like it better in here."

I still think about that. *Because I like it better in here.*

"We got carried away," Saff says. "We thought because we're such good friends that we could say anything, *do* anything, and it was safe."

She goes quiet, so I prompt her: "Astrid."

"I just rode her, Rhett. All week. I didn't let up." As she talks, she pushes up her sleeves like she's preparing for hard work. "I knew it was bad, too. I knew she was going into the bathroom to cry during break. And *that* made me even harder on her. Talk about an instinct for weakness."

"You're saying Ellie put you up to it?"

"That's the thing. She didn't. It was me. All of it. I was way worse than the rest of them. Even Ellie probably thought I was going too far. Not that she'd ever stop anyone from going too far." Saff shakes her head. "I didn't know I could *be* like that."

"And you think Astrid wanted to get back at you?"

Saff shrugs. "I'm the one crying in the bathroom these days, aren't I?"

She looks so beyond sad. Which is maybe why I make the mistake of saying, "It's been pretty bad, huh?"

And Saff starts crying right there in my room.

"It's not the soap," she says, through sobs, "though I still gag every time I have to wash my hands. It's not the stupid eyebrow." She touches it, rubbing away more of the pencil. "It's not even that I was naked. It's that everyone *saw* me. All the seniors. All the *middle graders*. The teachers. My friends' parents. My parents' friends. When they look at me now . . . well, mostly they *won't* look at me. That, or they look at me really intensely, and I can practically hear them thinking to themselves, *I'm looking her in the eye. I'm looking her in the eye.*"

She puts her face in her hands. I watch her cry. I know I'm not going to hug her, know I'm not even going to pat her arm. But I feel like I should do something. So I take a cookie from the tube. So I bite it. It's the first solid food I've had in over a year, and chewing feels funny. Saff looks up at the *crunch*. Her eyes are wide, like it's some big deal, which makes me want to spit out the bite. Instead I take another bite. Then I pass it to her. She takes a bite and passes it back to me. We finish the whole cookie that way, bite by bite.

CASE NOTES 3/27/35, EVENING

MEANS

Any of our suspects could have found the means to dose Saffron Jones.

Linus Walz (age 17) deals recreational drugs, primarily LSD, X, and hoppit, but it wouldn't be difficult for Linus to get zom, either for his own use or for a classmate. Ellie never confessed where she got the zom she was caught with last year, but it's common knowledge that Linus got it for her.

Josiah Halu (age 16) is Linus's close friend, and like Ellie, he could've asked Linus to get him the zom or even stolen it from Linus's stash.

Of the four suspects, Astrid Lowenstein (age 17) seems the least likely to have been able to secure the drug, though she shouldn't be ruled out on these grounds.

At this point, none of them can be ruled out. Any of them could have done it, even if it's difficult to imagine any of them having done it. It's difficult because they used to be my friends. I can't allow my bias to blind me. One of them did do it. Sentimentality must be starved.

THAT WHOLE NIGHT, I keep thinking about Saff crying in my bedroom. For the first time since I left school, I almost wish I could be back at Seneca Day so that Saff would have someone there to, I don't know, trust. Except, if I'd stayed at Seneca, I would've played the Scapegoat Game with the rest of them, I would've gone to Ellie's party that night, and then I would've been just another one of Saff's suspects. I'm only able to help her because I'm here, on the outside.

I ask myself why I even care about helping Saff. Ask myself why I keep picturing her blotchy one-eyebrowed face. I mean it's not like Saff cared about me. None of them did. After I left, a few emails, a handful of texts, a "get well" card some teacher undoubtedly bought and made them all sign. Linus and Josiah came by the apartment a few times, then just Josiah, then no one. Not that I wanted anyone to visit. Not that I answered any of their emails or texts. Then just last week, almost a year to the day that I'd left school, Saff texted me: *I think you're maybe the only person who hasn't seen it yet. I need you to tell me you haven't seen it yet. Please don't have seen it.*

It was the video. And, no, I hadn't seen it yet. Saff and I met at the bus stop outside my building. We sat in the plastic rain shelter, even though it was sunny, and let bus after bus go by. She looked the same, Saff did, short crinkly hair; round face; sleeve of metal bracelets, like her own personal wind chimes. I'd never thought much about Saff; she was always Ellie's friend, daffy and harmless, a sidekick, a tagalong. Ellie wasn't here now, though. Saff had come to meet me by herself. And maybe she looked different after all. Maybe she looked harder. Braver.

She sat on the bench next to me and said, "Hey, Rhett."

She didn't say, *You look better,* or *You've gained weight.*

Which meant that I didn't have to say, *Yeah, I got fat again.*

Which meant that I was able to say, "Hey, Saff." Like we were just two normal people waiting for the bus.

I told Saff that she didn't have to show me the video if she wanted there to be one person who hadn't seen it. She said it was different because she was *choosing* to show it to me. She unfolded her screen and told me to check that the projection wasn't on, then she watched me while I watched it. When I handed her screen back, I made sure not to glance at her body, made sure not to *not* glance at her body. What Saff said about the way everyone looks at her, I know about that. People do it to me, too.

The idea for how to help Saff comes to me that night in the middle of a calculus exam, and I'm so excited about it that I get the last question wrong on purpose because it's taking too long to work out the numbers. I hit *Submit* on my screen and jump out of my seat. Mom is due back from work any minute, and if I don't get it now, then I'll have to wait until morning. Mom's work just upgraded her machine a few weeks ago, and so if I'm lucky, the old model will still be in the hall closet waiting to be returned to the office. And it turns out that I *am* lucky because there it is sitting next to her rain boots: the Apricity 470. I pick it up and weigh it in my hand, that little silver box. And I forget that I hate it, hate Mom's belief in it and its so-called answers. I ditch all my moral qualms. Because this is how I'm going to do it. This is how I'm going to figure out who dosed Saff.

CASE NOTES 3/28/35, AFTERNOON

FROM *GROVER VS. THE STATE OF ILLINOIS* CONCURRING
OPINION

*"Whether or not the Apricity technology can truly predict our deepest
desires is a matter still under debate. What is certain, however, is that this
device does not have the power to bear witness to our past actions. Apricity
may be able to tell us what we want, but it cannot tell us what we have done
or what we will do. In short, it cannot tell us who we are. It, therefore, has
no place in a court of law."*

SAFF AND I DECIDE TO SPRING IT ON THEM, spring *me* on them.
There's a class meeting after school to come up with a proposal for
the end-of-the-year trip. The only adult there will be Teacher
Smith, a.k.a. "Smitty," the junior class adviser, and Smitty insists
on "student autonomy," which means that during class meetings he
sits across the hall in the teachers' lounge grading papers. We can
sneak in, me and Apricity, with no one the wiser.

"Let's go through it again," I say. We're sitting in Saff's car at the
far edge of the parking lot waiting for the meeting to start. "We're
focusing on four people: Linus."

"Because he has access to zom," Saff fills in.

"Ellie."

"Because she could get zom and because she would do it."

"Astrid."

"Because I was a monster to her," Saff says.

"And Josiah?" I phrase it like a question.

"Yeah. Josiah," she agrees, but nothing else. She won't tell me why she suspects him.

Is it because you two were together? I want to ask. The thought has been in my head all week. But I can't ask, because then Saff might think that I care. Though maybe that's why she's not telling me. I should tell her not to worry about it, me caring. I should tell her that I don't care. About her and Josiah. About her. About anything. I should tell her that.

Instead I say, "Have you ever thought it could be all of them? I mean, the whole class together?"

Saff turns to the window, blows on it, then erases the mark her breath has left. "Sure. But I don't think about it for long. It's too shitty to contemplate."

"Sorry."

She looks over, surprised. "Why are you sorry?"

"I don't know. For saying it could be all of them."

"But you're right. It could be."

"It won't be all of them," I say, though of course I don't know that this is true.

"The only thing I'm sure of is it wasn't you," Saff says, holding my eye.

"Yeah. It wasn't me."

She flashes a smile, fleeting as the jangle of her bracelets. There and gone.

The meeting is about to start, so we go in.

Smitty does us one better than the teachers' lounge. He actually goes out to sit in his car and (not-so-) secretly smoke. Saff enters the classroom first, while I wait in the hall. It turns out that I'm nervous. My heart is going at about a million. A few months ago, I would've had to sit down and put my head between my knees, but now I'm strong enough to keep standing. I guess that's something anyway. The doctors would say that's something. To stand when you need to stand. Strength. I count to thirty, then step into the room.

"Rhett!" Linus shouts, and suddenly, it's a year ago, and I never left them. "My man!" He's smiling big, his arms stretched wide in welcome. A couple of the girls, Brynn and Lyda, rush over to fuss at me. ("You look *so* good, so much better." "Yeah, there's, like, color in your cheeks.") These two would make a project out of me if they could. Astrid gives a half wave, and Ellie calls out, "Hey, skinny," causing a couple of the others to shoot her looks, which she ignores. Josiah doesn't say anything until I catch his eye. As usual, his bangs are in dire need of a cutting. "Hey, man," he says so softly I only know what the words are because I can read them on his lips.

The classroom is seminar style, so instead of desks there's a conference table and swivel chairs. Brynn and Lyda guide me to the head of the table, where the teacher usually sits.

"Are you back?" Linus asks.

And it occurs to me that I could be. I could say *yes* and, just like that, be back with my class at Seneca Day just in time for my senior year. The school would let me. The doctors would, too. Mom would be overjoyed. But I look around at them, these too-familiar eleven faces, and I just can't. I don't know how to explain it. It's nothing that any of them did, and it's nothing that I think they would do. I just know that if I came back I'd stop eating again. And, look, I'm not saying I want to eat. But for the first time, I maybe want to want to.

Josiah is staring down at his lap. All the others are watching me. Saff has her lips parted like she'll step in for me if I can't answer.

"No. I'm doing a project for school," I say. "*Cyber*school," I amend. And if there's any disappointment that I'm not returning to Seneca Day, it's whisked away by their excitement over the Apricity I set out on the table.

No one resists taking the Apricity. Everyone is willing to be, as Mom would say, swabbed and swiped. The only hint of hesitation comes from Ellie, who announces, "I don't need to be told what makes me happy," though she sucks on her cotton swab along with the rest of them. Ten times, I brush the cotton on a computer chip and fit the chip into the side of the machine, just like I've seen Mom do. And Saff and I lie to the class a second time, saying that my screen battery just ran out and that I'll have to take it home to recharge it before I can get their results from the machine.

"So we'll see you again?" Josiah says, a little stiffly. I can't tell if this means that he wants to see me again or that he doesn't.

Before I can answer, Smitty pops his head into the room, making a surprised face at seeing me there. "Rhett! What a surprise! If

I'd known you were coming I would've baked you . . ." He trails off, embarrassed.

"A cake?" I finish the sentence for him. "Sorry, Smitty. Not hungry. Haven't you heard? Never hungry." And after an awkward pause, everyone laughs. Even me.

CASE NOTES 3/28/35, LATE AFTERNOON

SUSPECT APRICITY RESULTS

> Linus: *arrange fresh flowers, visit Italy, sing out loud*
> Josiah: *put a warm blanket on your bed, spend time with your sister,*
> Astrid: *take the night bus, drop math class, get a tattoo*
> Ellie: *run ten miles a day, write poetry, don't listen to your father*

"I DON'T SEE ANYTHING SUSPICIOUS," Saff says. "Do you?"

I shuffle through the results again, reluctant to tell her that I don't see anything suspicious either. We're sitting on the floor in my room, Saff with the tube of cookies again. She's eating so frenetically I've lost count.

"I was hoping someone's might say, *Tell the truth*, or *Apologize to Saff*," she says through a mouthful of crumbs. "Isn't that stupid?"

"No. That's actually the kind of thing that happened when the police used Apricity in interrogations, you know, when that was still legal. It's like the person's guilt is what's keeping them from being happy."

"Well. I guess whoever did it must not feel guilty then," Saff murmurs. "They must think I deserved it."

"Yeah, maybe. But then again, whoever did it is pretty fucked up."

She sighs. "What'd you get?"

"'Get'?"

"On the Apricity?"

"I didn't take it."

"Yeah, but when you have?"

"I've never taken it."

"What? Never? But your mom," she says. "It's, like, her job."

I keep my eyes on the results. "Uh-huh. So?"

"So you've never even been curious?"

"I'm just not interested."

"You're not interested in happiness?"

"Yeah." I look up at her. "Exactly."

She narrows her eyes. "I'd think sad people would be the ones most interested in happiness."

"I'm not sad."

"Yeah," she says, deadpan. "Me neither."

We look at each other for a minute, but what is there to say? We're both sad. So what.

"You know what's funny?" I push our friends' results at her. "What's the first thing you think of when you look at this?"

"That I can't imagine Linus arranging flowers?"

"Okay, but in general, looking at all of them, what do you think?"

She flips through the pages. "I don't know. They don't make much sense."

"That's what I mean," I tell her. "Apricity results sound random. They don't make sense. 'Take the night bus.' 'Arrange fresh flowers.' 'Drop math class.'" I pause, then say, "'Recite French verbs. Shave your eyebrow. Eat a bar of soap.' The things you did on zom, it's like someone made you do a reverse Apricity."

"Oh." Saff raises her hands to her mouth, and her bracelets clang. "I think maybe I took one."

"An Apricity?"

"Yeah. Maybe."

"You mean that night? You remember something?"

"Maybe," she repeats, her eyes tracking back and forth as she tries to remember. "Maybe in an arcade?"

They have those remakes of the old fortune-teller machines with the papier-mâché Gypsy. You press your finger to a metal panel and the machine prints out a contentment plan. It's not a real Apricity, though. There's no DNA involved, no computing. It's just a game.

"There's an arcade on Guerrero, isn't there?"

"Yeah. The Tarnished Penny."

"Isn't it just a couple blocks from Ellie's house? Do you think you went there that night?"

"I told you. I don't remember that night." She brings her hands up higher, over her face, and I think of Astrid saying, *I like it better in here.* From behind her hands, Saff says, "Rhett. What did I do?"

CASE NOTES 3/29/35

Josiah's Apricity results (in full):
Put a warm blanket on your bed.
Spend time with your sister.
Tell someone.

SO MAYBE I LIED TO SAFF. Because maybe it's a clue, and maybe it's nothing. *Tell someone.* This was Josiah's last Apricity recommendation. I deleted it from his results before showing her. I rationalize the omission because the Apricity said, *Tell someone*, not *Tell everyone*. I rationalize it because I know I'll do what's right when it comes to Saff. And I know that sounds like some stupid hero-with-a-moral-code bullshit or whatever, but I also know that it's true, that I'll do right by her.

The pattern of the carpet in Josiah's building gives me that taffy-stretch feeling of familiarity. It's a deep purple geometric pattern—octagons within octagons within squares. We used to play out here, Josiah and me, building miniature cities out of the shapes, setting up our pewter men. When Josiah answers the door, that's familiar, too. Though when I'd come here before, he'd open it and already be partway back to his room, knowing I'd follow him there. Today he leans in the doorway, filling the space, and I wonder if he's going to tell me to go away. After a second, though, he swings the door open, and we go into the living room together, sitting across from each other in the two stiff decorative chairs I've never seen anyone in the Halu family actually sit in before.

"They're out," he says, nodding toward the rest of the apartment. "Rosie has a game."

"How's Rosie?" I ask. She's his little sister. I like Rosie.

"Yeah, she's good. Um." Josiah flips his bangs out of his eyes, but they fall right back to where they were. His eyes, for the second I can really see them, look nervous. "So what did it say?"

"The Apricity, you mean?"

"I'm guessing that's why you're here."

"Or maybe I came because I missed you."

I don't plan on saying this. It just comes out of my mouth, and when it does, I realize that I *have* missed Josiah. Also, that I'm angry at him for staying away. I know this isn't fair, to not return his texts or calls and to expect him to keep trying. But there it is. The truth. The truth is I thought he'd keep trying.

Josiah leans forward. "Really?" He sounds genuinely curious.

"Nah," I lie.

He smiles and leans back. "Yeah. Nah. It's that damn machine."

"It said you have something to tell someone. I thought maybe"— I shrug, suddenly embarrassed—"you could tell me."

He bows his head, fingers playing at his lips. This is Josiah thinking.

"The machine thinks you'll feel better if you tell me," I say. "Happier."

"I don't know if I want to feel happier," he murmurs.

"Why wouldn't you want to be happy? If you could?" It is, I realize, a different version of the same question Saff asked me.

He raises his head. "I don't know if I deserve it. You know?"

And I do know. Oh man, do I know.

"It's about Saff, isn't it?" I say. "It's about that night."

Josiah looks at me for a second, then he just gets up and leaves the room. I wonder if I'm supposed to follow him or maybe leave the apartment altogether. He comes right back, though, and drops something in my lap, a slip of paper. At first, I think maybe it's a dose of zom, but it's too big for that, and opaque. It's just regular paper.

HAPPINESS AWAITS!

IF YOU DO THESE THREE THINGS:

1. LEARN A FOREIGN LANGUAGE

2. TAKE CARE OF YOUR PRETTY FACE

3. USE FRANGESSE™ LEMON BEAUTY BAR

Except that's not exactly it. Each of the recommendations has been doctored in silver pen.

HAPPINESS AWAITS!

IF YOU DO THESE THREE THINGS:

1. RECITE ~~LEARN~~ A FOREIGN LANGUAGE NAKED

2. ~~TAKE CARE OF YOUR PRETTY FACE~~ SHAVE OFF YOUR LEFT EYEBROW

3. ~~USE~~ EAT A FRANGESSE™ LEMON BEAUTY BAR

The handwriting isn't familiar, but then it doesn't need to be. I already know whose handwriting it is. Josiah is watching me through the brush of his overgrown bangs, waiting for me to finish reading and figure it all out. And I do. Saff's mystery. I solve it.

"She did it to herself," I say.

Josiah nods.

"She dosed herself and asked you to tell her what to do when she was under," I continue. "She made you promise."

I don't have to ask why Saff would choose Josiah to help carry out her punishment. If she could get him to make a promise, Josiah would keep it. He's a good guy. That's why he was my friend. Josiah is a hero with a moral code, no bullshit. Except he doesn't look so heroic just now. He looks pale and pretty much terrible.

"I didn't know she was going to dose herself like that," he says. "She waited until I promised and then stuck the zom on *her collarbone*. That close to the neck, you go *out*."

"She doesn't remember any of that night."

"On her collarbone," he repeats. "I'm surprised she remembers any of that *week*. I almost didn't go through with it, Rhett. I really almost didn't. But we were playing this stupid game—"

"I know. She was the scapegoat."

He stares at his hands like he's just discovered them lying there in his lap. "I didn't do it because she was the scapegoat. Kind of the opposite. I did it because she asked me to. And I thought the scapegoat deserved a moment of . . . of respect. She explained it to me. Why she wanted to do it."

"Because of how she treated Astrid?"

"She said she needed to know how it felt. How she'd made Astrid feel. She said she was afraid of becoming someone who couldn't feel things."

"So you did it," I say.

"Yeah. I did it. But I took the soap away from her when she got sick. It was enough. I got Ellie. We cleaned her up, got her dressed and home."

I ask one more question, though I already know the answer to this one, too. "Why didn't you tell her? After, I mean. Why didn't you and Ellie tell Saff that it was her all along?"

"She made me promise that, too: not to tell her. She said it'd ruin it. That it'd make it feel, like, noble or something. And that the whole point was to feel like Astrid did. Like a victim." He shakes his head. "I didn't know she was going to get you to—you're trying to find out what happened that night, right?"

"She asked me to help her," I say, but the sentence doesn't have the same power as it did before, when I would think it to myself.

"I kind of figured that out when you showed up together at school." Josiah shakes his head. "I should've known she'd go to you."

"Wait. Why?"

"Well, because of the Apricity. Because deep down she must remember taking it." He gestures at the paper in my hand. "And she knows your mom works for the real thing."

"I guess that makes sense."

"And because she always talks about you."

"She does?" It's a stupid question, but that's what I ask: *She does?*

"Yeah. Out of the blue, she'll say, *I wish Rhett was here*, or *I wonder how Rhett is doing*. She's the only one of us who actually says . . ." He shakes his head again. "But we're all thinking it, man. I hope you know that."

"Yeah, I know," I say, and suddenly it's true: I do know it.

A little while later, when Josiah walks me out, he says, "So I'll see you again?"

"Yeah," I say.

"Soon?" he says.

"Yeah," I agree. "Soon."

CASE NOTES 3/30/35

The Solution

I can now conclude with reasonable certainty that Saffron Jones commit-ted the perfect crime. She built a machine of revenge and set it to run, con-cocting a series of unsavory tasks, eliciting the help of Josiah Halu to carry them out, giving herself an amnesiac dose of zom. She did this to assuage the guilt she felt over bullying Astrid Lowenstein during the Scapegoat Game. Because of the effects of the drug and the promise of secrecy she ex-acted from Josiah, Saff doesn't remember that she was not just victim but also culprit. Cruelest are the punishments we visit upon ourselves.

I MEET UP WITH SAFF, ready to tell her that I've done it. I've solved her mystery. Even if I don't know how I'm going to tell her the truth, even if I don't know how she'll react when I do. We drive to Golden Gate Park again, to that same road behind the flower conservatory where we met to figure things out right at the beginning. Six days and a thousand years ago. The whole way there, I'm thinking about how I should say it, what the best words would be. I'm thinking that if she cries I'll go ahead and pat her arm. Or hug her? But before I can say anything, Saff cuts the engine, looks at me level, and says, "You know, don't you?"

"It was you," I say, all my careful words gone from my head. "You did it to yourself."

I see her take the news. I see it change the smallest things about her face. She doesn't cry, even though her eyes are big like she might. She breathes in shakily through her nose, then out again.

"Okay," she finally says in a small voice. "Okay. I remember now. I mean, I remember enough."

"Do you want me to tell you the rest?"

"Don't."

She turns and looks out through the windshield. I watch her profile for a second, but I hate people staring at me, so I turn and look where she's looking, which is up. I remember how you can see the spires of the conservatory through the treetops. I search for them there among the green.

We're quiet for a minute, just looking. Then Saff says, "I thought maybe it was the Apricity that told you to stop eating."

"What?" I say. "No."

So many people have asked me why I refused to eat, my parents, my doctors, my therapists, my nurses, Josiah, and that's just naming the headliners. But Saff doesn't ask me why. I mean, she *does*, but she asks it in a way that I can understand.

"Motive?" she says.

I glance over at her, and she's looking straight back at me.

"Come on: motive?" she repeats.

And I do something all the Apricities in the world could never have predicted. I go ahead and answer her.

"It felt strong. Denying myself something I needed to feel strong. Not giving in when I was hungry felt strong."

"Okay." She nods. "Yeah, okay. I get that."

But somehow I'm still explaining. Because suddenly there's more. "I think it's that I wanted to be what's essential. I wanted to be, like, pure."

"Shit, Rhett." She smiles, her eyes big and bright and sad. "Me too."

And I want to tell her that her smile is what's essential, that her smile is what's pure. But I could never say something like that out loud.

So I do what I can. I lick my thumb, reach for her face, and rub the eyebrow pencil away. There are little hairs in an arc, just starting to grow back. Then I do something more. I lean over and kiss her, there above her eye, where her eyebrow used to be.

Means: I am brave.

Motive: I want to kiss her.

Opportunity: She bends her head forward to meet my lips.

3

Brotherly Love

arter heard the stories before he met the man: Thomas Igniss, the new contentment technician manager for Apricity's Santa Clara office. The position was a top spot, a notch above Carter's job as manager for the San Francisco office. Santa Clara was where it *happened*, down there in Silicon, working shoulder-to-rump with the boys in R&D. Carter hadn't even known the job was opening up, not until after it had already been filled. And Igniss an outside hire! Skrull's people must have tapped the guy, like the recruit for a secret society. Carter imagined a whiff of cigar smoke, the feel of a stately finger on his own shoulder, a *tap, tap* that spelled out, *Yes. You.* Carter's own shoulder remained unfingered, the air around him disappointingly clear of smoke. It crossed Carter's mind that he should feel envious of Igniss, but since the promotion had been lost before it'd even been coveted, his envy came out miniaturized, not a punch in the gut, more a pimple on the earlobe.

Shortly after Igniss's arrival followed the lore. That Thomas

Igniss hadn't come gimlet-eyed from the East Coast, like most managers, but had been forged deep in the Midwest, from the twang, from the heartland. That Thomas's people (not his "family" or "relatives," but his *people*) worked livestock, going back three generations. That Thomas himself had hay-bucked through college. (Carter had looked this up, this bucking of hay, to see what it entailed and had found pictures of leaning, heaving men, the sun pitching spears of light across their broad shoulders.) That even with his salt-of-the-earth background Thomas Igniss was no bumpkin. That his Adam's apple rested on a perfect four-in-hand knot of jacquard silk tie. That he spoke fluent Italian; that he spoke fluent Korean (and which language was it? Did the man speak both?); that he'd carpentered the office conference table himself out of sustainable wood; that he'd briefly dated Calla Pax before she was famous; that he was currently dating a burlesque-dancer-cum-bike-messenger named Indigo.

Carter had no such stories. He was the son of an electrical engineer (father) and a kindergarten teacher (mother). He'd grown up an hour away in Gilroy, notable only for its garlic stink. His childhood had been a pastiche of evenings watching popular sitcoms, the couches the actors sat upon in their fake living rooms a nicer version of his family's own couch. Carter's mother collected cow figurines, Holsteins and heifers on every table and shelf, and for no reason the woman could articulate. *Have you ever even touched a cow?* Carter had recently asked her. She'd looked so confused. *Why would I touch a cow?* she'd said. That was his mother all over, and his father with his tatty books of Sudokus. But that wasn't Carter.

Carter had made it into a top B-school, made it out of a lingering childhood pudge, and, in quick succession, scored Angie and a job at Apricity. From there it had been up and—to Carter's simultaneous astonishment and vindication—up some more. Carter considered himself a self-made man, not that it'd been easy when he'd been given such shit materials to work with.

CARTER AND THOMAS FINALLY MET at the spring team-builder in Napa. The "TB," everyone called it. It was supposed to have been just Carter's office at the Napa TB, but then two days before go-time, Santa Clara's TB had fallen through (a foible with the required waiting period for hang-glide certification), and it was decided that the two TBs should merge.

"It's a regular TB outbreak," Carter said to Pearl, who someday was going to laugh at one of his jokes.

In reply, Pearl coughed. Carter couldn't tell if she was continuing the TB joke or if she simply had a tickle in her throat. They were standing in a Napa winery tasting room. He tried and failed to catch her eye, but she'd turned her head, so he could only see the back of her neck. She'd cropped her short hair even shorter than before; now the ends curled around her earlobes. He wanted to tell her it'd looked better long, but he'd wait for the right moment so as not to offend her. Pearl swished her wine and spit in the barrel.

The spit barrels were the only things Carter liked about the wineries, which made the flimsiest attempts at refinement—the sommeliers' blouses a shiny acrylic, the words *Tasting Room* in big brass letters over the door, the branding absolutely everywhere. At the last one, they'd been selling polo shirts with the winery's name embroidered over the tit. "Something-or-other & Sons." Carter didn't understand why you would wear that on your chest unless you were either the Something-or-other or one of his sons.

He was already regretting the wine tour, which had been whose idea? Not Carter's. Owen's? Izzy's? Not Pearl's. Pearl had, in fact, tried to get out of the TB, something vague about her teenage son. Carter had told her no dice. After all, wasn't he leaving Angie alone with their baby daughter, and she barely three months old? The TB was only two nights, he'd told Pearl. Required.

At this point in the afternoon, it was certainly feeling required. The group was at its third winery, and the grapes, both literal and figurative, were withering on the vine. There'd been a campaign in San Francisco that year asking people to drive north and support the wineries, which were struggling because the weather had become too hot to harvest the traditional grapes. Instead of Pinot Noir, the wineries were now bottling something approximate and calling it, with a wink, El Niño Noir. Carter called it Pi-*not* Noir. (Pearl hadn't laughed at that one either.) The new wine tasted thin and sweet and awful, like the saliva of someone who'd been sucking on a grape lollipop. Pi-*not*.

By the middle of their fourth, and final, winery of the day, Carter wasn't sure if he was disappointed or relieved that the Santa Clara office had yet to show up. He posted himself by one of the barrels, watching his employees swish and spit. He kept an eye on

Pearl, the only one out of the group sticking to white wines. He wanted her to try a red. He wanted her teeth to stain purple and for her not to know it. Why couldn't she so much as smile at him?

Just then an arm wrapped around Carter's neck in a way that simultaneously unsteadied and stabilized him. A voice murmured in his ear, "Let's taste this swill."

Carter turned to find Thomas Igniss's grinning face inches from his own, looking exactly like the picture on the company website. Who looked as good as their company headshot? No one, that's who. Thomas Igniss, that's who.

"Swill we will!" Carter rejoined, a line of Angie's that he'd never liked, but it must have been decent after all because Thomas Igniss's grin cracked wider and he slapped Carter on the back, pushing him forward.

Carter stepped up to the counter. "Miss? Two glasses please. We'd like the opportunity to spit in your barrel."

Behind him, Carter heard Thomas chuckle.

Thomas and Carter spent the rest of the trip together. They partnered for the useless trust and communication exercises that the dithering HR women forced upon them. They hobnobbed in the hotel bar, the center of a spinning pinwheel of employees vying for their favor. They stayed up late in Carter's room, allowing room service to drain the last of their per diems. They were thick as thieves. They were thick as good wine. They had legs.

Here, after hours at the TB, Carter became privy to the real stories about Thomas Igniss. The truth of the man. He verified that Thomas could indeed speak both Italian and Korean, though the

Korean was something that Thomas dismissed as "tourist's Korean." The conference table, Thomas had built it, true story. Carter even heard the dirty details of the burlesque-bike-messenger girlfriend, whose name was not Indigo, after all, but Martha. Which made her all the sexier somehow.

In return, Carter told Thomas that he'd had a thing going with Pearl (which wasn't true, but *might* have been), but that he'd called it off when Angie told him she was pregnant. He explained how he felt that the affair had actually been a good experience because it had helped make him into a better father than he otherwise would've been. Thomas nodded at this; he understood.

The two men talked about work as well, about how difficult it was to manage people, their endless needs and complaints, how you could never really *be* with your subordinates.

"But then who'd want to be, right?" Carter said.

Thomas gave a nod. "We're where we are for a reason."

"We are!"

"It's an act of courage," Thomas went on, "to admit that you are indeed better than other people."

At these words, Carter felt a frisson down his spine. *Yes. You*, it said.

When he got home from the TB late on Friday, he repeated the sentiment to Angie, who wrinkled her nose and said, "An act of courage. What does that even *mean*?"

Carter took his fussing daughter from his wife's arms. Angie smelled sour, like something the baby had left behind. But he was grateful to her, after all, for suffering the indignities of pregnancy. Carter held the baby above his head, where she balled her little fists triumphantly at the ceiling.

"Really, Carter, what's that supposed to mean?"

Carter didn't bother answering. He had known she wouldn't understand.

THE CALL CAME ON THURSDAY, Thomas asking Carter if he could come to the Santa Clara office that night. The time Thomas named was after hours, after dinner even. "Once the grinds and scolds have fled the premises," he said, adding cryptically, "Bring an Apricity."

Carter wound through the dark campus and thumbed himself in at the door Thomas had specified. He walked down a long, empty hallway, the security lights like a corridor of heralds, flaring at his arrival and dousing in his wake. There were voices up ahead, a bright chirrup of group laughter. When Carter finally found the occupied room, the placard on the door read *Lab 7A*.

Thomas was inside the lab, seated at a table with four other men. Two of them were coders; Carter could tell by their age (younger) and their dress (whatever was on the floor by the bed), though these metal-studded, smirking specimens seemed superior to Carter's own coders, who carried the oily nocturnal look of stale coffee. The third man had to be in communications, and senior at that; you could see it in the rubber of his smile and in the graying temples of his faux-hawk. And the fourth man was, improbably, a custodian. Coveralls and the whole shebang. Had the fellow been invited? Or had he simply wandered in and sat down?

"Carter!" It was, bizarrely, the custodian who greeted him by name.

The others all turned as one, and Carter knew how he must have looked to them: wide-eyed and half-crouched in the doorway, as if about to bolt.

"Carter!" Thomas Igniss echoed. "This man here!" he said of Carter, and the others nodded, though the sentence was left unfinished. *This man here . . .* what?

Thomas waved Carter in. There was a spare seat, next to one of the coders and across from the custodian.

"Did you bring an Apricity from your office?"

Carter slid the machine from his bag and set it on the table. Thomas nodded to the coder seated next to Carter, who got up and unlocked a cabinet in the corner of the room, returning with a second Apricity. Carter looked between the identical machines. Well, almost identical. Theirs had a tiny dent in the upper-right corner of the casing.

Carter said the obvious. "Two 480s."

Thomas and the others grinned around at one another. The coder spoke up: "This one's only a 480 on the exterior. The interior has certain modifications."

"You made it better?"

"Not 'better,'" he said. "Just different."

"Noooo." Thomas wagged a finger at the coder. "Carter's right. We made it better!"

"How?" Carter asked. "Accuracy? Processing?"

Thomas gestured at the machines. "Try it and see. Yours first, then ours."

"What? Me?"

The custodian pointed at him. "Yes. You."

The men were all watching him.

"Go on," Thomas said. "This is why I invited you."

Carter complied. Of course he did. He swabbed the inside of his cheek and swiped his cells on the computer chip, and the Apricity gave him the same contentment plan it always did:

- STAND UP STRAIGHT.
- DON'T WORRY ABOUT STANDING UP STRAIGHT.
- ADOPT A DOG.
- SMILE AT YOUR WIFE.

"Project it!" the custodian shouted. Sheepishly, Carter did, the dratted list floating at the center of the table for everyone to see. He'd always felt embarrassed by his contentment plan. Apricity tested what the company called *deep happiness*; its recommendations did not speak to the daily annoyances of an empty stomach or a traffic jam, but to the depths of self and soul. So while your contentment plan wouldn't change frequently, it would change over time, as you changed. Except Carter's plan never did. Maybe because he'd never tried to follow it.

"'Stand up straight' *and* 'Don't worry about standing up straight'?" Graying Faux-hawk read loudly. "I find it perpetually surprising that people buy into this shit."

"It's your job to sell it to them," one of the coders snorted.

"Aw, man, that last one?" the other coder said. "That sounds like it belongs on your wife's con-plan, not yours."

Carter shrugged. "It's never made much sense to me either."

"And *that's* why you're here," Thomas said. "We around this table share your skepticism."

"You mean . . . you think Apricity is wrong?" Carter nearly whispered it. After all, it was sacrilege. And from the mouth of a manager!

"Not wrong per se," Thomas said slowly. "More wrong*headed*. This here is correct." He reached out and dragged a finger through the projection so that it wavered in the air. "If you did these things, you'd likely be happier. But let me ask you this: just because it's *correct*, does that mean that it's *right*? What I'm saying is: is happiness what *you* want, Carter?"

"Well. Sure. What else is there?"

Thomas Igniss raised his eyebrows. "Luke," he said, and the custodian passed Carter a fresh cotton swab.

Carter wheeled the cotton along the inside of his cheek, thinking of the wine tasting, thinking of the spit barrels. One of the coders put his hand out for the swab, dabbed it on a chip, and slid the chip into the machine: the same process as always. Except it didn't feel the same. Around the table, the men had all, ever so slightly, leaned forward. Carter found that he was leaning forward, too, his mouth suddenly dry, as if the swab had absorbed more than his saliva and a few cheek cells, had sucked up something from deep within him.

When the screen lit, the coder didn't project it, but handed it to Thomas first, who read it and nodded once in approval. He passed the screen around the table in the direction that meant Carter would see it last. The other coder chuckled; Faux-hawk murmured, "That would do it"; the custodian smiled beatifically. When the screen came around to Carter, he saw that there was only one recommendation listed:

REMOVE ALL CHAIRS FROM YOUR OFFICE EXCEPT YOUR OWN.

"What is this?" Carter said. "I always get the same thing. I always do! Stand up straight, don't worry about standing up straight, smile at Angie, adopt a dog."

"It's not a con-plan," one of the coders said.

"Yeah, it's no 'con,'" the other repeated. And how had Carter not noticed before that the two coders were twins, identical but for their slightly different constellations of facial piercings?

Thomas spoke. "It's not telling you what will make you content."

"Then what's it telling me?"

"You're a smart guy," Faux-hawk said. "What do *you* think it's telling you?"

"I don't know."

Thomas smiled. It was a different smile than the one in his picture on the website, than the one he'd thrown at the other men at the table, a smile just for Carter. "What's more important than happiness?"

Carter knew that there was an obvious answer, and he also knew that he didn't know it. An image came into his head, his baby daughter, her fists pounding the air.

"Power, Carter. The machine is telling you how to be powerful."

CARTER DID EXACTLY what the machine instructed. He removed the two chairs that faced his desk, leaving only his leather swivel. His employees would enter and spin in a slow circle.

"Where are the chairs?" some would ask.

Carter decided a simple response was best. He patted his own chair. "Right here. Here's the chair."

Others stood precariously, not daring to ask for a seat. Sometimes Carter took pity and told them they could perch on the edge of his desk, which was even better. Grown men in suits, haunches hoisted like 1950s secretaries! Pearl, of course, refused to perch, though Carter offered her the surface multiple times. Well, her choice.

At first, it was difficult to carry out the machine's plan. Carter had always striven to be well liked. But that hadn't worked, had it? And when he thought of the sly looks he sometimes caught his employees sharing when he spoke, it became a lot easier to watch them teeter and shift in the middle of his office. By the next week, Carter noticed a change. No more covert tapping on screens during the Monday meetings, no faint sniggers from the workpod he'd just visited; instead, dropped eyes and reports handed in on time. The chair directive was simple. It was elegant. It was managerial jujitsu.

When Carter came home from work, he spun Angie around, her hair whirling. "Carter!" she squawked. He took the baby and threw her in the air, catching her back giggling. "Not so high!" Angie called out. Both of them, him and the baby, shaking with giggles.

THOMAS INVITED CARTER to Lab 7A again the following Thursday, where the dented Apricity announced the new tactic Carter would use.

TELL YOUR EMPLOYEES WHAT COLOR THEY'RE WEARING.

"Like their shirt color?" Carter said.

"Hmmm," Faux-hawk's lips buzzed.

Thomas Igniss nodded thoughtfully.

Carter surveyed the faces around the table. Blank. Watchful.

"Look. The chair thing has been great. Surprisingly effective."

"Has it?" Thomas sounded pleased.

"What were people's reactions?" one of the coders asked, swapping a glance with his twin.

Carter explained how instead of being upset, like you'd think, the office workers had become deferential, apologetic, obedient. "It was like they wanted it," he said. "Needed a little spanking. But this?" He gestured at the screen. "This—I'm sorry—I just don't get."

"Apricity's recommendations may seem strange at first—" Faux-hawk began, and the others all booed him down.

"We told you," one of the coders said, "don't quote your own copy at us."

Faux-hawk shrugged comically, like, *Hey, I tried!* Carter realized he didn't know the man's name, any of their names, actually, except for Thomas's. Though they all seemed to know his.

"Hey," Thomas said, "Apricity has had me do some strange things, too."

"*You're* doing it, too?" Carter asked.

"Carter! Of course!" He paused, then leaned in and whispered, "How do you think I got the Santa Clara position?"

"Really?"

Thomas winked.

"Can I . . . can I see?"

"See what?"

"Your Apricity." Carter indicated the dented machine. "See you do it."

"I can just tell you."

"Sure. I know. But I feel like if I could *see* . . ."

"Let him see!" the custodian shouted.

Thomas shot the custodian a look, then raised his eyebrows at one of the twins, who nodded slightly in return.

"Okay, Carter. Sure. You can see me do it."

"But we have to reset the machine," the other twin said.

It didn't take long. A minute of silent negotiation between the twins, conducted entirely in screen taps, and they handed the machine back to Thomas. The custodian produced the cotton, and Thomas swabbed and swiped. When the screen lit up, he read it swiftly, glanced at the twins, but passed it to Carter first.

GIVE UNCOMFORTABLY LONG HUGS TO EVERYONE YOU MEET.

"Uncomfortable is right," Thomas said with a chuckle. "You think your color thing is wacky. See what I have to endure?"

Carter's first thought had been that Thomas hadn't given *him* a hug when he'd come in the room, hadn't even given him a handshake. For a moment he imagined Thomas's hug, a brotherly hug, the arms around him strong from the years of hay-bucking, protective, approving. Carter sank into the imaginary embrace.

"Seriously, Carter, all this damn hugging! I think I may be on the verge of a sexual harassment complaint."

"Should you maybe scale back, then?"

"Scale back? I only know how to push forward! Give the color thing a try," he said. "Who knows? You may find yourself surprised."

And once again, and as ever, Thomas Igniss was right. The color directive turned out to be even more effective than removing the chairs. Carter did exactly what the machine instructed. When an employee entered his office, he told them what color they were wearing, delivering his line with an even tone and expression.

"You're wearing purple."

"You're wearing black."

"You're wearing turquoise."

The employees' reactions were invariable. They looked down at their clothes, as if they'd forgotten what they'd put on that morning, then they looked back up at Carter, waiting for the inevitable compliment, a "You look good in that!" or an "It brings out your eyes!" When no compliment was forthcoming, the statement curdled. Carter wouldn't have predicted that they'd all react with the same startled look, their mouths quivering in weak laughter, their eyes blinking at him vulnerably, like a child's. Most interesting of all, once he'd commented on an employee's clothing color, Carter noticed, the employee never wore that color again.

This time even Pearl seemed discomfited when Carter observed that her blouse was orange.

Like the others, she looked down, fingering the collar self-consciously, murmuring, "I got it on sale."

THE NEXT THURSDAY, Carter told Angie that he was going to his weekly poker game, that he'd joined a league.

"Aren't leagues for bowling?" she said absently.

"A whatever . . . a cabal then."

"Aren't cabals for plotting government overthrow?"

"A circle then," he said, peeved. "Call it a circle. And don't say what it's for. The purpose is to play a game."

"Sure, sure. A circle. A game. Like ring-around-the-rosy," she said, smiling down at the baby and beginning to sing the song. The thought rose into Carter's mind, like it did sometimes, coiling bitterly: *You wouldn't have loved me if we'd met when I was fat.* This time, though, the thought was answered by a chill response: *But you love me well enough now, don't you.*

At the "poker game," Carter recounted the results of the color directive to the table, smiling humbly as the men congratulated him.

"We've started hearing about you over here," Faux-hawk said.

"You have?" Carter's exhilaration faltered along with his voice. "Is that . . . I mean, what have you heard?"

"That there's a real ballbuster over in the SF office!" Thomas said.

"Yeah," one of the coders echoed. "A ballbuster."

"Well," Carter said, shrugging, "technically, they don't all have balls."

"No, *they* don't," Thomas said. "*You* do."

Next, Apricity told Carter to randomize employee lunch breaks. And it told Thomas to come to work dressed in velvet loungewear, the poor fucker.

Though Carter's screen had a randomizing app, he didn't bother with it. Rather, he preferred to walk through the office and tap someone's shoulder decorously, announcing, "Eat!" Soon Carter was getting murmurs of the "ballbuster" rumors that Graying Faux-hawk had alluded to. He heard the whispers, saw the glances, noted the hush when he entered a room. Carter felt the power course through him. He woke with a smile. He woke with a *growl*.

"These days, you're so . . ." Angie searched for the word.

"Virile?" Carter said.

"Loud," she decided upon.

The baby squealed.

"Both of you," she amended. "Both loud."

WHERE, EXACTLY, does one locate the beginning of the end? Was it the day Carter made Pearl stand in his office for over an hour delivering her monthly report? Toward the end of the meeting, her hands had begun to shake and her voice, too. She dropped her screen, came up with accusing eyes.

"What did I ever do to you?" she said.

And she *had* done something to him, hadn't she? He felt that she had, that she'd wounded him, but he couldn't remember precisely how.

"At this level, you should be able to handle different types of managerial styles," he told her as she fled the room.

The next day, the call came from Skrull's office. Carter's screen was on the blink, so he got the message an hour after it was left. VP Molly Danner needed to talk with him about some concerns with his managerial style.

Carter strode over to Pearl's workpod, grabbed her by the shoulder, and spun her chair around. He held up his screen as if it were Exhibit A. "Are you going to say it wasn't you?"

Her voice didn't shake this time. "I'll say it wasn't *just* me."

Carter looked up across the landscape of workpods and became aware of all the eyes upon him.

WHEN CARTER ARRIVED AT SANTA CLARA, the offices were empty, even though it was still early on a Wednesday afternoon. He found everyone eventually. They were all packed into a lounge, with hurrahs and plastic glasses of wine. Carter spied Thomas at the center of the scrum; Carter waved, trying and failing to get his attention.

"What's the celebration?" he asked the man next to him.

"Mr. Igniss has been named VP! We just heard."

"Oh," Carter fumbled, wondering if he should go. He didn't want to ruin Thomas's good news. "Congrats."

"Of course, we all knew it was coming," the man added smugly.

"You did?"

"Yeah. It was between him and some other manager. But come on! Who could best Igniss? Here." He pressed something into Carter's hand. A glass of wine. "Have some. It's the good stuff."

Carter brought the cup to his lips. The rich flavor cut through his numbness. Yes. An achingly good ferment.

He backed out of the lounge and wandered the corridors until he found Thomas's office, in the same location as Carter's own actually. He decided to settle in and wait for his friend. The party wouldn't last forever, and when it was over, Thomas would come back here and help Carter, tell him where he'd gone wrong. It was then that Carter saw it, the dented Apricity on a shelf near Thomas's desk. And, well, *it* could tell Carter, couldn't it?

He fumbled in Thomas's drawers until he found a sample kit.

Then he swabbed and swiped and, with shaking hands, fitted the chip into the machine.

A voice interrupted him. "What are you doing in here?"

It was one of the coding twins.

"Hi . . . there!" Carter said awkwardly. How did he still not know the man's name?

"Carter. Hey." The coder forced a smile. His eyes darted to the machine. "Does Thomas know you're in here?"

"He's celebrating," Carter said. "Did you hear? About his promotion?"

"I . . . yeah, I heard."

"There's a party in the lounge. Wine. The good stuff." Carter still had his glass, he realized; he raised it in a little mock toast. "I just need a minute in here. Thomas won't mind."

The coder was backing away, hands raised. "I'll just get him, man. You just wait here." His eyes darted again to the Apricity. Carter saw that the screen had lit up with its report.

"You stay right there and wait," the coder said. "Just don't . . . don't . . ." He didn't finish, turning and heading in the direction of the celebration at a jog.

Carter looked at the screen.

COME TO WORK DRESSED IN VELVET LOUNGEWEAR.

It was the directive Thomas had gotten at the end of their last meet-up. Maybe the machine hadn't registered the new chip. Carter unwrapped another chip and swabbed and swiped again.

The same sentence lit the screen. He stared at it, suddenly tasting rotten grapes at the back of his tongue. He could feel the imaginary finger tapping him on the shoulder. *Yes. You.* But it wasn't choosing him after all. It was trying to get his attention, trying to get him to see. But Carter didn't want to turn around and look. He touched the little dent in the corner of the machine, ran his finger across it, and felt it was himself. He was the dent.

"Carter." Thomas stood in the doorway. His lips were stained pink with wine. He wore a different smile now, a new one; it didn't fit right. "You didn't . . . ?" He gestured at the machine.

"It told me to do what you did," Carter said.

"Did it?" Thomas ran a hand through his hair. "Yeah. See. The thing's been on the fritz."

"I tried it twice. The same directive. Both times." There was— he heard it only as he spoke—a pleading note in his voice.

"I'm gonna have the guys look at it. Nascent technology and all that."

Carter opened his mouth. He had come here to tell Thomas about the call from Skrull's office, about Pearl's betrayal, about the goddamn fuckery of it all. *Betrayal*: the word stayed stuck in Carter's mind, a thumbtack affixed to his chest. Thomas Igniss licked his wine-stained lips, looking like a vampire from a low-budget TV show. He was wearing his usual tailored gray suit, not, Carter noticed, velvet loungewear. *Betrayal.*

"Congrats on the VP thing," Carter said weakly.

"Thanks," Thomas breathed. He looked again at the Apricity, his lips screwing to one side. "Hey, look, man, I'm sorry." When

Carter didn't answer, Thomas tried again, extending his arm for a handshake, or maybe a hug.

Carter pushed past him out the door.

CARTER RETURNED HOME TO FIND ANGIE deep in one of her midday naps, not-so-gently snoring. The baby, however, was wide awake, on her back in the side-along, staring up at him. Carter lifted her gently, then, on impulse, extended his arms, holding her above his head. Her eyes gleamed, dark and depthless, whole galaxies stretching out behind them. She pounded her fists in the air as she always did when she was airborne. Carter lowered her, pressing her fat belly to his face, then he lowered both of them until he was curled over her in the middle of his bedroom carpet.

"What do I do now?" he murmured, his shoulders starting to shake.

Her tiny fists battered the sides of his head. She let him have it.

Such a Nice and Polite Young Man

Pearl waited until Rhett wasn't looking; then she lifted the cup and freed the spider. A breath. Rhett leaned back in his chair, feet up on the table, eyes fixed on his screen. The upside-down cup tilted under Pearl's hand, the crescent of space between its lip and the tabletop just enough room for the spider to escape. Pearl imagined how the spider must have seen it: The dark circle of the world shifting. The horizon unfastening. Light. Another breath and the spider skittered out from under the cup and across the kitchen table, but it moved in the wrong direction, circling away from Rhett and back toward Pearl. Her shriek was only partly feigned.

Rhett's eyes ticked up from his screen. "That's a big one."

It *was* a big one. It was a big one because Pearl had waited for a big one, for weeks tipping smaller specimens into the flower box outside the kitchen window. The other spiders had been whispers of gray and motes of dust compared to this one: a spider so large you could distinguish the joints of its legs, poised at delicate angles.

Pearl had found the spider that morning as she was stepping into the shower. It was worse, finding it while naked. She'd felt the thing crawling all over her bare skin, even as she could see it sitting there motionless in the bottom of the tub, even as she lowered the cup over it, trapping it. Strangely, this was when she felt its touch the most, when she knew it couldn't get to her.

"Get it!" Pearl urged.

"You get it. It's over by you."

By now the spider had made it to the edge of the table. Pearl shuffled back, hands raised helplessly. The creature disappeared over the edge of the table and drew its descent, an invisible line from tabletop to floor.

"There it goes!" Pearl pointed. "Right there!"

Rhett watched her with curiosity.

"Rhett! Please!"

He sighed, scraped back his chair, and took two long strides, the last of which landed square on the unfortunate spider. They both stared at Rhett's sneaker, the truth of the matter beneath it. He lifted his foot and inspected the underside, making a face. The tile bore a dark smear.

He raised his eyebrows. "Happy now?"

It felt wrong to say yes.

"I'll clean off your sneaker."

Rhett made a noncommittal noise and pried the shoe from his foot, letting it drop over the stain. He limped back to the table. "I didn't know you were scared of spiders."

Pearl's exhalation became, halfway through, a shudder. "I just couldn't stand it."

IT HAD BEEN FIVE WEEKS since Pearl had drugged her son and stolen a sample of his cells to run through the Apricity machine. What exactly had she expected the machine to tell her? To buy him a puppy? To make sure he ate his vegetables and played outdoors every once in a while? The platitudes of motherhood crowded her head, bangs trimmed, sweaters knotted at their waists, smiles benign. Fucking useless, the lot of them. When Rhett's contentment report came back, Pearl thought, at first, that it was blank. That he, like his father, was one of the rare few that Apricity couldn't test. Then she saw it crouching there, small and black at the edge of the screen: an asterisk.

The asterisks were one of the reasons Apricity was so tightly controlled, the tests delivered by trained contentment technicians, such as Pearl, to highly vetted, high-end clients, and the machines kept out of the hands of the general public. Bradley Skrull had been adamant that Apricity would be a pure technology, that it would invite joy, not malice, into the world. And so the Apricity machine had been designed with safeguards in place—"angels in the programming" was the in-house term for it—that redacted any violent or illegal actions from a person's contentment plan. These bad ideas were blanked out and replaced on the list with asterisks, with stars. About one out of ten plans Pearl ran for work would include, couched among its recommendations, a star. Every once in a great while, a person's list would contain multiple stars, and Pearl would have to look up from her screen and smile at the recipient as if nothing were amiss.

Pearl stared at the asterisk for days, calling up Rhett's report on her screen time and again to verify that it was indeed there, that bristle of ink. She began to see the asterisk elsewhere, in the drop of coffee on the tabletop, in the glob of mascara on the end of her eyelash, in the spots that flared when she closed her eyes and tilted her face toward the sun. True, she'd seen, at times, a meanness in Rhett, but she'd told herself it grew out of sadness, not cruelty. If he was going to hurt someone, it'd be himself. At his next weigh-in, he'd lost another pound. Pearl looked down at the black specks on the scale, each one signifying a pound. She blinked and they became asterisks, all.

"Mom?" Rhett said. "Can I step off now? Can I step off the scale?"

That's when Pearl had decided: she would help him.

The item that the machine had redacted from Rhett's report could have been anything from shoplifting a pair of sneakers to spraying gunfire at a school playground. So Pearl cast a wide net, giving herself a general directive: *Do harm.* Well, to make Rhett do harm.

The spider under the cup was not Pearl's first attempt. She hadn't started with animals. Of course not. She'd started with harm done upon inanimate objects, among them: a ruined blouse (purposely bumping into Rhett so that his protein shake spilled down her front), a crumpled fender (insisting during Rhett's driving practice that he had still more room to back up), and a broken model of a tule shrew (balancing it behind Rhett's elbow so that when he shifted, it fell and shattered). After the model of the shrew had broken, the glass bead of its eyeball rolled on the floor, the pupil wheeling, until it finally came to rest, staring up at Pearl.

And?

Nothing. No effect. Rhett had remained sullen, biting, unhappy. He'd lost another pound. Then another. Pearl knew she'd have to call Dr. Singh's office soon, had gone so far as to hang up on the receptionist. She'd felt a small, mean stirring of pleasure at cutting off the woman's bewildered *Hello?*

Pearl gritted her teeth and moved on from objects, reasoning that true harm must be felt by its recipient. She laced the watering can with bleach and watched as, under Rhett's oblivious ministrations, the plants in the window box whitened and curled up on themselves. She'd waited until Rhett was in a terrible mood before thrusting the phone in his face—"Your father wants to talk to you"—then listened in the hall for the inevitable explosion. She'd sacrificed not only plants and sweaters and her ex-husband's feelings, but her own body, slipping into Rhett's clumsy teenage path, darting her toes under his footfalls, placing her face in front of a door just as he was about to open it.

And?

The trouble was that Rhett seemed stricken by the harm he caused her, Pearl's trod-upon toes and dinged forehead. No, the trouble was that it was *her* intent, Pearl's; she was the one doing harm, not Rhett. No, the trouble was that it started working. Rhett was happier.

This was not a matter of interpretation. He was. At his next weigh-in, he was up three whole pounds, his best gain yet. He was hanging out with his friend Josiah again. Just yesterday, she'd spied crumbs on his bedroom rug. She got on all fours to inspect, took one up on her finger, and tasted it. The crumb had come from a cookie. A *cookie*. A year earlier she had begged Rhett, to the point of tears, to swallow a spoonful of vegetable broth. How could she possibly stop now?

Pearl promised herself that the spider would be it, the largest sacrifice. Or maybe a goldfish. Certainly nothing larger than a fish.

PEARL WISHED SHE COULD TALK to someone about Rhett's report. Not her parents, who, in a surprise move five years ago, had retired to a sustainable community up in Oregon. They had let age buff away all concerns and would tell her she was overreacting, a verbal pat on the head. Ditto Elliot. She had never been close to her sisters, who were over a decade older and, therefore, more like pleasant aunts than siblings. Her friends had drifted off during Rhett's illness and were now only available for the odd lunch or overly exuberant birthday wish. Gone were the days of intimacies and confidences. Pearl felt like an asterisk herself, alone on the page.

Besides, Pearl wanted to talk with someone who knew about Apricity and the asterisks. But even at work, discussion of the asterisks was frowned upon. The public didn't know about them, and the Apricity Corporation didn't want them to know. It did not suit the slogan. *Happiness is Apricity.* Stepping into work the next morning, Pearl saw the empty office across from her workpod and realized that there was, in fact, one person who might talk to her. She located her former boss, Carter, lurking in the break room.

Recently Carter had been "repositioned," as the company liked to call it, from contentment technician manager to a plain old humble technician, like Pearl herself. He'd taken the demotion like a sulking teen, too prideful to show hurt, but too pissed off to hide it. Pearl had yet to see him sit in his newly designated workpod; he'd only skate by it to drop off or collect an item, as if he were assigning work to an invisible employee. He never so much as glanced at his old office, which remained empty and unlit, the position yet to be refilled.

Even now, he leaned against the break-room counter with his screen balanced on his forearm like he was only passing through. And Pearl felt what she often felt in his presence, a divergence of emotion—annoyance and amusement, disgust and pity—all twisted up into one ratty braid.

She busied herself with the coffeemaker. "Want a cup?"

"Oh!" he said, as if only now realizing Pearl was there, though he could hardly have missed her in the small room. "You're asking if I want a *cup* of *coffee?*"

He was suspicious of her offer, and no wonder. When he was her manager, he would call her into his office and there'd be two cups sitting out on his desk. He'd gesture at them and say something like: *I know we should have you fetching the coffee, but that's just the kind of guy I am!* Pearl never took so much as a sip, a matter of principle.

"Dark roast, right?" She held up a capsule.

"Blacker than pitch." He watched her carefully. This was the thing you had to remember about Carter: as foolishly as he behaved, he was not, in fact, a fool.

She nodded at his screen. "Doing the P&Ps?"

His eyes narrowed. Now he thought she was rubbing it in. *P&P* stood for "Parole and Probation," Apricity's long-standing government contract and the technicians' least-favorite job. Usually they passed it around among themselves week to week. However, along with his demotion, Carter had been assigned to six months straight of P&P.

Pearl handed him the coffee with what she hoped was a sympathetic smile. "You should see what they've got me doing over at Cal. Psychology majors." She made a face. *"And* the professors. I bet they have more stars than your criminals do."

She held her breath, waited. Would he scold her for mentioning the asterisks? He wouldn't miss the opportunity to chastise her. But no:

"Bet they have more stars than *the sky* does," Carter replied gamely. He took a drink, then lifted the cup in a toast. "This is good. I can see why you never liked mine." And Pearl felt guilty and irritated, both at once. It was capsule coffee, for god's sake; it was all the same.

"How does the Apricity even do it?" She turned back to the coffeemaker, trying to make it seem like a nothing question.

"Do what?"

She lowered her voice, glanced at the door. "Know what recommendations to make into stars?"

"How does the Apricity know anything?" he said, not bothering to lower his. "How does it know what will make us happy?"

"But that comes from us. From DNA. The stars are . . . a judgment. A moral judgment."

He shrugged. "It's just programming."

"Angels in the programming," she said, repeating the phrase. She went over and closed the door, though he didn't seem concerned that they might be overheard.

"Angels?" Carter stuck out his tongue and blew a raspberry. "Don't be silly. Not angels. People. It's like this: The company gives the coders a list of phrases, and they write a little line of code for each thing on the list. When the machine gets one of those phrases, the code tells it to replace the words with a star."

"And the phrases are—"

"Bad things."

Pearl took her cup and perched on the edge of the table. "But that's someone's *job*? To sit in a room and think of all the horrible things people might do?"

"Sure. 'Kick a dog.' 'Steal a car.' 'Strangle your wife.' Simple."

Pearl winced.

"I've never had a star myself," he added, then peered at her. "Have you?"

She shook her head.

"You sure?" He raised his hands. "No judgments!"

"Yes, I'm sure."

"Because you never can tell who'll get one. Ever notice that? Once I had this little old lady, wispy hair, flowers on her dress. Movie grandma. *All* stars. Her entire list!"

"What did you do?"

"I told her the machine had malfunctioned." Carter paused, took a sip, and then said, "He always seemed like such a nice and polite young man."

Pearl tensed. "Who did?"

"No one. Like on the news. What the next-door neighbors say: 'He always seemed like such a nice and polite young man.'" Carter shook his head ruefully. "And then they find the bodies in the basement."

PEARL STOPPED BY THE PET STORE on the way home from work. She was planning on picking up a goldfish, but that was before she'd set foot in the reptile room with its damp ionized air and eerie violet light. An hour later, she came out with an eighteen-inch monitor lizard and all the associated equipment. Terrarium, heat rock, heat lamp, branch shelter, shallow bath, mulch to spread on the bottom of the tank—there was so much stuff that the salesguy had to help her carry it to the car. The salesguy had a remarkably long beard clasped every few inches with a different rubber band, like the tail of a circus pony. His beard had dipped in surprise when Pearl had chosen the monitor lizard. And in fact, Pearl was surprised with herself, but she liked the lizard with its river-pebble skin and fluted ridges above its eyes. It reminded her of one of the models she made, extinct creatures motivated by ancient and vicious instincts, the closest thing they had to wisdom.

"They can count, you know," the salesguy told her, nodding at the lizard.

"Maybe I'll teach it arithmetic."

"You could. And it's a her, actually."

"Okay. Her."

"At least we think so."

"The mice she eats, they're alive, right?"

"Could do. Some people say it's more natural. But you don't have to worry about that. You can buy frozen. For her size, you'll do pinkies."

"Pinkies?" Pearl lifted her hand and indicated her smallest finger.

"'Pinkies' is baby mice. They're, um, pink."

"I see. Because they don't have their fur yet."

He rubbed the back of his neck. "I know. It's a toughie."

"I'll take a box of them. Live ones."

PEARL LEFT THE LIZARD in the car.

"Just a minute, girl," she said, feeling slightly ridiculous speaking to it.

She'd texted Rhett from the pet store saying she was coming home with a surprise. No reply, but the HMS said he was there. In the mailbox, another surprise, Pearl found brochures for three different nearby universities. She'd mentioned applying to college to Rhett months ago but had not gone so far as to request literature, not after the sulfurous look he'd given her. Could Rhett have ordered the brochures himself? That was too much to hope for. The schools must have automatically sent them to households that had kids at the right age. Pearl tucked the mail under her arm, the paper slick and glossy, the faces of smiling teenagers pressed flat against the skin of her arm.

Rhett stood in the foyer, his breath quick, as if upon hearing her key, he'd run from the other side of the apartment and planted himself in front of the door.

"Oh! Hello!" she said.

His cheeks were flushed, too. A strange thought came into Pearl's head: *If my son were a vampire, I would find blood for him to drink.*

"Why are you smiling like that?" he asked her.

"Am I smiling?"

"Your mouth is."

She touched the corner of her lips.

Pearl set the mail on the table, the brochures on top. Rhett took a step toward them, then stopped himself.

"Did you . . . request those?" she said lightly, oh so lightly.

He frowned. "Don't make a big deal."

"Santa Cruz has a beautiful campus. If you wanted, we could visit."

"Mom."

"All right. Okay."

Rhett glanced back toward his bedroom door, a frequent tic of his, as if he were a wild creature caught out in the open looking for the route of escape.

"Before you go," she put in quickly, "I need your help carrying something up from the car."

"Your surprise?"

"*Your* surprise actually."

"What is it?" He followed her back out into the corridor.

"Remember when you said you wanted a puppy?"

"I was seven. That's before I knew that dogs eat their own yack."

"Well. It's not a puppy."

"I JUST DROP it IN?" Rhett said.

"The same as last time," she told him.

Rhett held the pinkie mouse above the terrarium. It squirmed sightlessly in his grip, a vivid pink nubbin. It looked more like a crawfish or a grub than a mouse, Pearl thought, something dug up from the mud. The monitor lizard, sensing a meal, swiveled her neck out from under the branch shelter and then stilled, the movement and the stilling both so sudden, it seemed as if she had flickered from one posture to the next.

Rhett wrinkled his nose. "I don't think I can do it."

"You did it before."

"I don't think I can do it *now*."

"You don't have to *do* anything. Just open your fingers."

"Yeah, right. *I* don't do anything. Just open my fingers and then a monster comes and eats it."

In the silence between their words was a soft fleshy sound, skin rubbing against skin—the other pinkies in the straw-lined box. *Do it*, Pearl thought. *Go on and do it.* But Rhett turned his palm upward, cupping the mouse safely in his hand.

"Hey. Look." He presented his hand to her. "It's like that story."

"Story?"

"'The Mouse and the Mollusk.'"

Pearl shook her head.

"You don't know it? I thought it was an old myth or something. Una told it to me."

Pearl flinched inwardly at that name. Una the hugger. She pictured her son gathered in the woman's embrace, his limbs a bundle of sticks, kindling for the fire. The bills the insurance sent had coded the treatment, guttingly, as "hospice." Pearl didn't like to think of this time, and until now, Rhett had never spoken of it.

"Una told you stories?" she breathed.

"Sometimes," Rhett said, his eyes on the mouse. "Sometimes I dreamed them. Can't always remember which."

No surprise. Rhett had been emaciated, wracked with fevers and chills. Pearl couldn't help but reach out now to touch him, a teenage boy, solid and whole. He didn't flinch or pull away, just lifted the mouse in his palm to eye level, staring at it.

"So it goes like this: There was this kid," he said, and it took Pearl a moment to realize that he was now telling her Una's story, "who was training to be an oracle . . . like to give people their fortunes? And part of the training was to stand in the temple, totally still, and hold a mollusk in one hand and a mouse in the other. And then people would come to ask the kid questions. But the people had a choice. They could turn to his right hand and ask the mollusk for a truth they did want to know. Or they could turn to his left and ask the mouse."

He paused, waiting until she asked, "And what did the mouse tell them?"

"A truth they *didn't* want to know." He glanced at her. "You really never heard that story?"

"No."

"Guess Una made it up."

With that, Rhett turned his hand over, and the pinkie dropped to the mulched floor of the terrarium, where it lay squirming. It was only there an instant before the monitor's head snapped forward. Pearl and Rhett both leaned in. You couldn't help it. It was like witnessing a magic trick: the little mouse there and then gone. The monitor receded under her branches.

"Nice pet you got there." Rhett got up, wiping his palm on the leg of his pants. "It didn't even chew."

He'd been poking at Pearl the entire week, as was his habit. He'd named the lizard Lady Báthory after a sixteenth-century Hungarian countess who'd slaughtered servant girls and bathed in their blood. He'd also named the feeder mice, watching Pearl slyly as he'd done so, each one after a different shade of pink: Rose, Carnation, Flamingo, and so on. Still, every evening when she'd called him to the living room, he'd chosen a mouse from the box and, with her urging, dropped it down to the lizard. The mice that remained filled in the empty spaces left by their sacrificed brethren, wriggling together in the center of the box for heat or, perhaps, comfort.

At Rhett's next weigh-in, he was up 1.4 pounds. He'd started listening to music while doing his homework. He'd been out with friends twice in the past week. The other night at dinner, he'd reached over to Pearl's plate and plucked up a cube of potato. Pearl had kept her eyes fixed on the tabletop, but she could hear it, the near-silent sound as he chewed and swallowed. She imagined the starches and the sugars of that little cube softening, dissolving, feeding him.

Even now there was a lightness to Rhett, a buzz, a hum, a (say it) happiness. He took sliding backward steps across the living room, a quirk to his mouth. "Got a paper due tomorrow," he said, not even making her have to ask what he was doing with his evening. And in return, she did not remark that she'd never seen him so pleased about homework, and later when she heard the murmur of his voice from behind his closed door, she did not allow herself to pause and listen. Instead, she sat on the sofa and watched the terrarium for small stirrings between the leaves.

THE COMING WEEKEND WAS ELLIOT'S. Pearl dropped a kiss on the top of Rhett's head before she left for work; he would be at his father's when she returned. Rhett was already up and sitting in front of his screen, still in his pajamas. The college brochures had moved from the hallway table to the corner of his desk, but Pearl didn't make mention of this. Rhett's head smelled faintly of their laundry detergent, from his pillowcase, the familiar scent altered slightly by the oils of his hair. She lingered; he hadn't yet shrugged her hand off of his shoulder.

"I'll get to take the car out, right?" he asked.

"'Out'?"

"You know. With friends."

"Maybe with *a* friend."

"Okay. One friend."

"Josiah?" she asked.

"Josiah. Sure."

She squeezed Rhett's shoulder. "And you have to get your license first."

"Check."

She thought of the asterisk again, a blot, a birthmark, a cancer on the otherwise pure screen of her mind. It could be nothing, the item the star stood for. It could be a minor infraction. Except . . . the spider, the mice.

"And the city is busy," she went on. "Lots of pedestrians. We'll have to practice looking out for them."

Rhett craned up at her and said, with a whiff of accusation, "You think I'm going to hit somebody!"

"Accidents—"

"—happen?" He cut her off.

"They do, though."

THIS TIME, Carter wasn't in the break room. Pearl found him in the smaller of the second-floor meeting rooms, which was in the middle of a redecoration. The table and chairs had been taken out and the carpet yanked up. Carter was sitting on the padding next to a mound of carpet swatches, his screen balanced upon his knees.

"She's back," he said, not even glancing up. "Still stargazing?"

Pearl stepped inside the room and leaned against the wall just next to the doorway. "I was wondering if you could get me . . ." She pressed her lips together, suddenly unsure.

"What?"

"The list."

"List?"

"The one they make and give the coders. The phrases to redact."

"Oh. That. It's more like a book than a list."

"The book then."

He set his screen down on the floor. "It's actually a file."

"Whatever it is, could you get it?"

"Me?"

"I thought you might have access, since . . ." She didn't want to say the rest, *Since you used to be my boss.*

Carter began piling the carpet swatches into small stacks. "I could get it."

Pearl closed her eyes, trying to quell her irritation. "*Will* you get it?"

"I'm not supposed to. Restricted info. Restricted to"—his lip curled—"management."

"Oh. Okay. I under—"

"But I'll get it for you." He arranged the swatches around himself like tiny battlements. "Because . . . fuck 'em." His eyes flashed to hers.

Pearl paused, then echoed, "Fuck 'em."

He nodded in satisfaction and put another carpet swatch on the stack.

She wondered if he actually *would* get the file for her. He was more than a little pathetic, hiding out in a room that stank of carpet glue, his chin sinking into his neck fat, his haircut expensive and tacky. Surely he hated her for her part in his demotion. He'd probably give her the file and then report that she had it. She'd be fired.

And if he did? Pearl found she didn't care, not as long as she got the file first. It was powerful and painful both, this realization that she would do whatever was necessary to get what she needed. It was like sprouting wickedly sharp claws that then cut into your palms each time you made a fist.

"I could take the P&Ps," she said, "in exchange."

Carter raised his head slowly, his eyes slits. "Do you *want* to give me something in exchange?"

"Um. No. Not really."

"Then why are you offering?"

"Because I thought you'd expect it."

He lifted his palms in the air, showing them to her.

"Hey," he said. "Why can't I just be a good guy?"

———

THE LIZARD WAS TORPID. Pearl could barely see it beneath its branches, and from what she could see, its scales and eyes were dull. She looked up the symptoms on her screen and discovered that she and Rhett had been feeding it too many mice. The lizard needed a balance of mice and insects. Pearl had a vague memory of the salesguy telling her precisely this. She returned to the pet store and came back with a bag of colorless crickets, a few of which she shook into the terrarium, where they flitted and twinkled like antennaed confetti. The lizard appeared wholly uninterested.

Pearl took out her Apricity machine, called up Rhett's contentment report, and eyed the star. She felt as if her entire life had been denoted with an asterisk, the instructions simple enough until you scanned down to the bottom of the page and found the long list of exceptions and addendums.

Rhett had been such a good boy, such a sweet boy, glimmering eyes and a puckish tuft of hair atop his head. He'd been the kind of child even complete strangers had doted on, and not out of politeness. It had been just the two of them at home for the first six years of his life, before he started school and Pearl started work at Apricity. Pearl and Rhett. Mother and son. Devotee and small god. Pearl couldn't run an errand without being stopped every few steps by some new person with the same flat toothy smile as the last one. *Can I say hi to the baby?* This had continued as Rhett entered elementary school, where more than one teacher had leaned across the desk during parent conferences to confide in a phlegmy whisper,

Your son is my favorite in the class. Elliot and Pearl routinely discussed how they would need to counterbalance this glut of adulation to keep Rhett from growing up to be an egoist.

"It's not like he's something we made," Elliot once marveled. "It's like he's something that was visited upon us. Like freak weather."

And like weather, Rhett had changed. His sudden sullenness could be explained away as typical teenage behavior, but then the withdrawal, the truancy, and finally the starvation. Inexplicable. It hadn't been the divorce, which Elliot and Pearl had made sure was amicable, donning their mutual politeness like flak jackets. Or maybe it *had* been the divorce? Or maybe something at school. Or brain chemistry. Or societal messages. Bullying? Molestation?

"Kids. You give them life so they can kill you," Pearl's dad had said with a chuckle one time she'd called her folks, panicked and exhausted after a day at the hospital with Rhett.

"Dad!" she'd cried.

"What?"

"*I'm* your daughter, you know."

Over the years, Pearl had tried and failed to identify the cause of Rhett's unhappiness. Always, even now, a small part of her brain was scanning and assessing, weighing and rejecting possible explanations, a machine that never ceased its calculations. Except she could now, couldn't she? She could cease. She could stop trying to understand the cause. Because the type of poison doesn't matter. Not if you already have the antidote, a cold little bottle curled in your hand.

Pearl stirred from her thoughts with the awareness that something in the room had changed. It was the chirping. Or, rather, its lack. The living room had fallen silent. Pearl looked to the terrarium. The crickets were gone.

ON SUNDAY NIGHT, the HMS announced that both Rhett and Elliot were ascending from the lobby. Elliot didn't usually come up when he dropped off Rhett, not because he and Pearl avoided each other, but because parking in Pearl's neighborhood was a nightmare. Here Elliot was now, though, bustling through the door with Rhett's duffel thrown over his shoulder, the two of them deep in an animated conversation about—Pearl decoded the jargon—a VR game. Both father and son played. It seemed that they'd been to a VRcade together over the weekend.

Rhett broke off mid-sentence, turning to Pearl. "How's Lady?"

"Lady?" Pearl repeated.

"Lady Elizabeta Báthory," he said impatiently.

"You mean the lizard? I thought we were calling her Báthory."

"'Lady' is prettier."

"*Lady* is fine," Pearl said. "In fact, she's due a mouse."

"Dad, come on, I'll show you. It's pretty sick."

As he passed Pearl on his way to the living room, Elliot paused to kiss her hello on what might be considered her cheek, but would be more accurately described as the corner of her mouth. Even though he'd divorced Pearl and married his mistress, Elliot needed intermittent reassurances that Pearl was still in love with him. She didn't know what he'd do if she ever had a serious boyfriend. Probably kiss him on the corner of his mouth, too.

Pearl watched from the doorway as Rhett got out the mice and urged Elliot to select one. Elliot's hand hovered here and there over the open box.

"I feel like I'm picking a chocolate," he said.

"All of them have the same filling," Rhett said.

"Yuck."

"What yuck? You and Val eat your steak bloody."

"Fair point."

Pearl watched, fascinated. It was a role reversal, Rhett now in Pearl's place, urging the kill. Elliot glanced at Pearl, the reluctance in his face like ripples in a puddle. Behind him, behind the glass, Lady emerged silkily. Her head was turned to the side, but she didn't fool Pearl; the lizard watched them all with one eye. Elliot selected his mouse, held it over the tank, and with a grimace, dropped it down. Lady tipped up her head and caught the morsel before it hit the ground. Elliot made a noise of disgust.

"I used to feel that way, too," Rhett said, folding down the corners of the box. "But then someone pointed out that she's got to eat in order to live. It's not cruelty. It's life."

Had Pearl told Rhett that? She couldn't remember doing so.

"After that I was okay with it." Rhett stood and turned from them, putting the box back in its place on the shelf. "I don't want to watch her starve."

He didn't say this with any particular feeling, but the sentence skewered Pearl. And it must have skewered Elliot, too, because he sought out her eyes.

Rhett, oblivious, was already halfway out of the room. "I gotta check my classes. We played *way* too much VR this weekend. I did, like, zero work."

"You're going to get me in trouble with your mother," Elliot said woodenly. "Tell her I'm not to blame."

Rhett disappeared into the hall, calling back, "It was all Dad's fault!"

The second they heard his bedroom door close, Elliot rose and moved so swiftly across the room that, for a preposterous moment, Pearl thought he was going to sweep her into his arms. But he stopped an inch away, tilting over her. Elliot had a rare quality, the ability to tower over people without seeming looming or intimidating. Val called Elliot "the friendly lamppost."

If Elliot was a lamppost, the bulb, his face, was now aglow.

"What?" Pearl whispered.

"He ate dinner with us."

"You mean food?"

Elliot nodded.

"Not the horrible shake?"

Elliot kept nodding. "A Mediterranean salad. Rice. A couple bites of lamb."

"Lamb? You're kidding."

"I'm not."

"The salad—?" she said, and didn't need to ask more because

Elliot knew what she wanted to hear and was already listing the ingredients.

"Tomatoes, zucchini, eggplant, onions, olives, parsley, an oil dressing."

A feeling rose in Pearl that was too big for her chest. She put her hands to her cheeks, then moved them to Elliot's cheeks. He was still nodding. She kept her hands there, lifting and lowering with Elliot's nods, until she realized she was crying. She brought her hands back to her own cheeks, pressing her tears flat.

Elliot glanced toward Rhett's room. "We didn't make a big deal of it."

"No, no. That's good."

"And he was back to the disgusting shakes the rest of the weekend."

"Of course."

"But he ate."

She exhaled, her breath hitching on its way out. "I've been trying something, and perhaps—"

"Val says he's in love."

"What?"

Elliot nodded with new vigor. "She's convinced of it."

"Did Rhett tell her that?"

"She says she knows the signs."

"I'll bet," Pearl said, and regretted it immediately, for Elliot was already moving forward to take her hands, ready to capitalize on any sign of jealousy. And Pearl wasn't jealous, not of young, brash, pink-haired Val, not of her marriage to Elliot, not anymore.

"Dove," Elliot said, charming and chiding.

"It's just that he doesn't go out much," she said. "So I don't see how he'd have the opportunity."

"Maybe it's online love."

"And when he does go out it's only with Josiah."

Elliot raised his eyebrows. "Maybe he's in love with Josiah."

Pearl plucked her hands out of his. "I don't know where Val gets her ideas."

Elliot chuckled. "Yeah. Me neither."

Pearl looked back at the terrarium, the lizard nowhere to be seen.

"It's a nice thought, though, isn't it?" Elliot said from behind her. "That after all we've tried, the cure was love."

"You're being a romantic," she said softly.

"Can't help it." He snuck in another kiss, this time on the soft place beneath her jawbone. She resisted the urge to turn and bite him.

PEARL DIDN'T HAVE TO SEEK OUT CARTER; this time, he found her. He caught her coming out of the bathroom and, sidling by, tried to surreptitiously press the memory tab into her hand. Pearl jerked her wrist away, startled by his grab at it, and the tab bounced across the carpet like a coin. When Pearl realized what he was trying to do—*like a spy movie*—she had to stifle her laughter. Besides, maybe it was like a spy movie. She didn't know the risk he'd taken in getting the file, but she knew the repercussions if they were found in possession of it.

"You seem to have dropped something," Carter said, snatching up the tab and handing it to her.

"Thank you."

"What is it?" he said.

She looked around to find that they were the only ones in the hallway.

"Just a coin," she said, uncertain of this game.

"Is it antique? It looks antique." His eyes betrayed no twinkle, no smile.

"No," she decided to say. "It's a regular coin. Like any other."

"Better put it in your pocket then," he said.

"Um. I will." She slid the tab into her pocket. "Thank you for telling me I'd dropped it."

Carter half smiled, half shrugged. "No need to thank me. It's what any decent person would do."

THE FILE WAS HORRIBLE. Of course it was horrible, and in all the ways you would expect. Firstly, its size. Pearl waited until she got home to open it—she didn't want to do it at work—to find that the file was over a thousand pages of dense tiny text. She kneeled on the couch, not allowing herself to sit, and began to scroll through. The phrases themselves were horrible, too. The variety was horrible, the cruelty, the knowledge that someone had thought of each one. Horrible. Horrible. Also horrible? Knowing that Rhett's phrase was here somewhere. Not knowing which it was.

The file was also punishing in ways she didn't expect. The

tedium of it, and then how she became inured to it, deadened. *Yes, that. Sure, that. Of course. Why not that?* She started feeling strange in her head, like her thoughts were being spoken, not by her own voice, but by a faraway announcer. She breathed thinly between her teeth and was overly aware of each time she blinked. Then the HMS chimed, announcing Rhett in the lobby. *Stop,* she said, the thought in her own voice now.

She made herself get up from the couch and circled the room, ending at the terrarium, but instead of bending down to peer into the glass, she reached for the little cardboard box on the shelf. She held it in her hands for a moment, then loosened its flaps. Movement from below: Lady gliding out from under the branches, eyes keen. She must have learned that the sound of the box opening meant a meal was coming. Pearl peered into the box. The mice were repulsive, a blind undulating knot of flesh. Steeling herself, she picked one out and set it in her palm, where it lay flat on its belly, its legs splayed. Then it gathered itself and began to crawl forward, nosing, and Pearl could see the little knobs where its ears would be. Below her, Lady's head whipped once, impatiently.

And Pearl knew, as she stood there, that there was a dark mote within herself, expanding with each of her thoughts: Her anger at Elliot. At Val. At Rhett. At herself. Her own stupid helplessness. The chasm of her loneliness. How good it had felt to do something, to do harm, when so much harm had been done to her.

The HMS sounded again as the front door opened, and Pearl looked up to see Rhett in the doorway. There was an oddness in his expression, which she thought, at first, was embarrassment.

Then she blinked and saw that beneath the embarrassment was a giddy pride, was happiness.

"Mom," he said.

The girl stepped into the doorway next to him, leaning to the side ever so slightly so that their shoulders brushed. She had short hair fastened into little twists and a sleeve of thin bracelets from wrist to elbow. She was in love. Pearl could see it on the strange girl only because she could see it on Rhett, whom she knew so well, and it was the same look. They were, both of them, in love.

"Mom," Rhett's voice broke through, "Mom, this is Saff."

"Hey." The girl waved, then thought again and extended a hand, each of her movements accompanied by a metallic scale, ascending or descending as the bracelets slid up or down her arm.

And with that, the dark expanse that had opened up in Pearl shrunk back down to a mote, to a speck on her heart, to a size she could endure.

"Hello, Saff," Pearl said.

She moved forward to take the girl's hand but stopped short, realizing that her own hand still contained the little mouse. Pearl could feel it on her palm, small and struggling.

5

Midas

lliot was on his sixth bowl of honey when he began to vomit. The honey had gone down in perfect orbs, golden bubbles, gleaming and quivering on the end of his spoon. It came back up in gouts, splashing into the bucket at his feet, sticky, brown, and reeking. When his retching finally ceased, Elliot wiped his mouth and straightened to find the entire room of gallery-goers staring at him. Their eyes skated away from his in embarrassment, as if it had been they, not he, who had just vomited on a platform in the middle of an art gallery. Elliot told himself that he felt no shame at being watched while puking. After all, this was the point. Of the piece. Of art in general. That one should stop and look at it. He smiled brightly at the onlookers and thumbed a bit of sick from the corner of his mouth.

Two kids about Rhett's age stepped up to Elliot's platform. Each had a hardback sketch pad clamped under an arm like a single wing. Art students. Elliot had carried an identical hardback when he was in art school and, over that time, convinced a few different girls he'd dated to have sex upon it. Each one had mounted a tiny protest at the suggestion—a skeptical eyebrow, a scoffed breath, a *like hell*—but in the end he'd always managed to coax their round bottoms down onto the cool marbled board. Juvenile as it now seemed, the act still stirred Elliot. There was a word attached to it, one too silly to admit out loud: *transmutation*.

The boy who stepped up to Elliot's platform wore wire-rimmed glasses, the kind a little old man would pick from the case. The girl had her hair wrapped in a bright scarf, a few braids spouting from the top, the tinsel on a party hat. The kids surveyed the objects on Elliot's platform, the glass jug of honey, the spoon, the bowl from which Elliot ate. Their eyes lingered on the reeking bucket.

"You think that jar was full when he started?" the girl asked of the honey jug.

"Well, *that's* fake," the boy said, gesturing at the bucket. He blinked at Elliot through the smudges on his lenses. "He has a tube rigged up or something."

"The barf? Naw, it's real. I can tell."

Elliot took up the bowl of honey and spooned another dose into his mouth, praying his stomach was settled enough to manage it. He had the sudden urge to impress and appall them, these kids.

But the girl only clucked her tongue and said, "Mister. After today, you're never going to be able to eat honey again. Did you even think about that?"

There was something to the set of her expression that reminded him of Val. It was her eyes; they were Val's eyes. All their eyes, he realized, all the eyes of all the people in the gallery were Val's eyes—flashing, opaque, unknowable. Elliot let the spoon fall back into the bowl. He thought again of Val's confession, or rather her confession that there was something she would not confess.

Tell me. Why won't you tell me?

"*Midas*," the boy read off the placard affixed to the platform, then appraised Elliot and the jug anew. "It's about greed. Midas is the story of a greedy king."

"No, it's not," the girl said. "Midas is the story of a guy who killed his family."

At the end of the day, a man who could have been Elliot's double—pleasant parakeet features, carefully tousled hair, tallness made agreeable by a stoop—stepped forward and squinted at the placard. When he'd finished reading it, he gave Elliot a jaunty little salute and said, "Everything I touch turns to puke, too."

Elliot smiled; his stomach roiled.

APRICITY CONTENTMENT PLAN: Eat honey.

"Eat honey."

That's what my Apricity said. If it was even a real Apricity. Gwen and I had been sitting in the park on the first not-cold day of spring, the dampness from the ground coming up through our blanket, when the man approached us with his slick silver case. Gwen recognized the machine before the guy'd even told us what it was. Some of Gwen's rich clients got their Apricities done, not that any of them seemed happier for it, she said, not even a little bit. The man explained that he was an artist and that he was taking people's Apricities for an art project he was doing. Except he didn't call it an art project. He called it *a piece*.

And I thought, *A piece of what?*

Could he do ours? the guy asked. I was shaking my head no even as Gwen was gesturing for him to take a seat.

The man kneeled and grimaced as the wetness of the grass soaked up from our blanket to the knees of his pants. He told us how it would be just a cheek swab and that he'd keep us anonymous and that we'd get our results out of it, too. Still, it was no small thing to say yes. We knew Apricity results could be embarrassing, life wrecking even. It was always in the tabloids, some story about the humiliating thing this celebrity or that politician had gotten on their Apricity.

But Gwen looked at me and I looked at Gwen, and it was the same look we'd shared before we stole that car someone had left running on the curb and drove it all over the city; the same look as on the day we both agreed to tell our respective asshole bosses at our respective boring office jobs to screw off; the same look as on the night we got drunk on Gwen's roommate's cheap vodka and had sex, which we didn't talk about and hadn't happened since.

So we did it. We let a stranger in the park take our Apricities. And one of the things the machine told me was "Eat honey." So now I have a single spoonful every night before I go to sleep.

Gwen wouldn't show me her results, so I don't know for sure what the machine told her, but a few days after that day in the park, she kicked out her roommate and asked me to move in instead. Now, every so often she reaches over from her side of the bed and runs her hand up under my shirt, saying, "Come on, sweetness. Pass that spoon over here."

VAL HAD SKIPPED THE FIRST DAY of the installation on account of the fact that she was a sympathetic vomiter. Val gagged when Elliot spit a bit of gristle into his napkin. She gagged when the cat hacked up a wad of fur. She gagged when she brushed her own teeth. She'd come by the gallery once Elliot was done, Val had promised, and they could take the train home together. But those plans had been made yesterday afternoon, before Val's confession, which was not a confession, and their fight, which was not a fight. And now a portion of Elliot, a portion that had increased in certainty over the past three hours spent retching upon a stage, had started to think that Val would not show up after all. An unfamiliar worry. Elliot had always taken it for granted that whomever he was meeting would already be there when he arrived, scanning the crowd for his face. So when he heard Val's braying laugh from the front room of the gallery—a wonderfully vulgar laugh for an otherwise delicate woman—the power of his relief surprised him. The feeling came from down deep within him, from the gut, same as the puking.

Elliot located Val at the front desk gossiping with Nita. Before she could turn and see him, he grabbed her around the shoulders and smacked a kiss on the top of her pinkish pageboy. This, too, was a bit of performance, and Val must have known it, though she allowed herself to be tousled. Nita watched them expressionlessly.

"What are you telling my wife this time?" Elliot asked over the top of Val's head.

Nita flashed a smile. "None of your concern."

The women's friendship was founded upon embarrassing stories about Elliot from Elliot and Nita's college days. Nita pretended full disclosure with these stories, but was in truth discreet, scrubbing any mention of Pearl from their plots. Not that Val had ever shown even a twinge of jealousy toward Pearl or any other woman, something Elliot had been proud of, his confident young wife. Today, though, it felt as if insecurity had bypassed Val only to buzz around him.

"This is why gossiping women are compared to hens," Elliot said. "Geese. Partridge. The eating birds."

"*The eating birds?*" Nita repeated.

"You sound like a serial killer, honey," Val told him.

"If you could not mention honey." Elliot grimaced and clutched his stomach.

Val's face creased in concern, and she touched his arm. Elliot noted her fingertips, their tiny pressures. "Was it awful?"

He wondered if she would tell him her secret now. He looked down for the answer on her face but saw only the top of her head, the crooked pink part, the pale path of her skull.

"Don't feel sorry for him," Nita told Val. "He does it to himself."

"And you show it in your gallery," Elliot retorted, leaving out the fact that Nita had only booked his installation in her tiny Civic Center gallery (and then only after it had been rejected at every other gallery in town) because of their long-standing friendship.

Elliot had been going through a creative fallow period—Val's phrase for it—ever since he'd finished the *Valeria* series. In the two-plus years since, he'd filled up notebooks with scribbles and sketches that became stuck on their pages; he'd blathered on in front of attentive classes of young art students; he'd wasted entire fellowships, months of them.

Unlike most of his peers, Elliot had never treated being an artist with any reverence. As a kid he'd had busy hands and would fidget with whatever you put in front of him. When he was a college freshman he'd taken an art class to fill a requirement, and then unceremoniously chosen it as his major. His parents hadn't even minded. His older sister, Mallory, had already done the reasonable thing and become a lawyer. Besides, his parents were wealthy enough that having a child in the arts was a status symbol, like a vacation home in a foreign country. Lo, Elliot was an artist. No crucible of hardship, no spiritual calling. Art was just something he was good at, therefore something he was praised for, therefore something he kept doing. He was good at the business of art, too, the machine of it. He filled himself up with the commissions and group showings, the parties after, the gossip of the scene, filled himself up like he was a glass canister full of dried beans, the kind where you can win a prize if you guess how many. But in the time after *Valeria*, Elliot had begun to believe that he was done, the canister empty, the smart guess zero. And the thing was, it didn't feel as bad as he might have feared. In fact, it didn't feel so different from being full.

Until one day: an idea. He'd gone to Pearl's to pick up Rhett and had seen her Apricity on the front table alongside her gloves. The tagline came into his head, spoken in the voice of the actor from the ads: "Happiness is Apricity." *Midas* was Elliot's first piece in three years.

"You bet your ass I'll show it," Nita said. "You think I'd miss seeing you puke your guts onto the floor?"

BACK AT HOME, Val sat atop the kitchen counter and delivered noodles directly from the takeout carton into her mouth. Elliot was forgoing dinner, his stomach still in a tumult of syrup and acid. He kneeled on the rug below Val, laying out strips of cashmere and vicuna to practice wrapping himself for tomorrow's performance.

Elliot had been working on *Midas* for months. He'd borrowed a decommissioned Apricity machine from Pearl—which had required his signature on dozens of forms, practically promising to sever his left arm if he lost or broke the damned thing—and had collected contentment reports from a few hundred people. It didn't feel like making art so much as canvassing. Elliot had liked talking to the strangers, though, approaching them at the market or on the street, making his pitch, mining their desires. For the actual piece, Elliot had chosen, from hundreds of Apricity reports, seven recommendations to act out over the course of a week, one per day. Today had been honey, tomorrow would be vicuna.

Elliot held one end of a vicuna strip and wound it up the length of his arm, tucking the other end into the wrapping once it reached his bicep. The next strip he wound around his shoulder and neck.

He decided that it made the most sense to work from the bottom up, feet and legs first, then torso, then arms, head last.

"Hey, look. This is the perfect food for what you're doing." Val presented a cluster of noodles trapped between her chopsticks. "See? Like tiny bandages."

"These aren't bandages," he said.

"Well," Val replied in the tone of *Yes they are.*

Val was always noticing patterns. She had an artist's eye; Elliot had told her so, but she seemed indifferent to the compliment. Val worked as a freelance namer. Her job was precisely what it sounded like: companies hired her to choose a name for the department they were forming, the conference they were planning, or the product they were launching. A lot more went into it than one might think—research, linguistics, focus groups. And of course there were also Val's own unerring instincts when faced with such questions as whether a car should be called the Tornado or the Tempest, the new branch of a company referred to as a collective or a department, an antidepressant named with soft syllables or fricatives. So if it seemed preposterous to be paid thousands of dollars for coming up with a word or two, well, it was and it wasn't. In fact, Val had been the one to name Elliot's current piece. *Midas.*

Midas is the story of a guy who killed his family.

"A little help?" Elliot asked. He'd wrapped the strip all the way to his fingers and was having trouble tucking in the end.

"I won't be able to help you tomorrow," Val warned.

"I just need to figure it out."

"You're wrapping your face, too?"

"Of course."

"Hm."

"It wouldn't make sense otherwise."

"Do you think maybe you should do your hands last?"

"I'm figuring it out," he repeated, this time with a tone.

Val sighed and hopped down from the counter. She took the end of the strip, then paused and rubbed her face against the fabric, looking much like their cat.

"This feels like divinity. What is it again?"

"Vicuna."

"That's a rabbit?"

"A sort of camel."

"A *soft* sort of camel."

Her eyes were closed in pleasure, her eyelashes a fringe against her cheeks. For the *Valeria* series, Elliot had cast Val's face in plaster, pressed it into clay, chipped away flecks until it had floated to the surface of a block of marble. He'd used plants to make a landscape of her face, plates of metal and tiny bolts to hammer it out, a synthetic skin replacement to grow it in a saline bath. But as he looked now, he found that his wife's features had become unfamiliar to him, shapes that had been arranged within the same frame but did not otherwise belong to one another. Elliot looked away. The idea that he might not know her after all was painful to him.

And surely this was the wrong time to say, "Are you just not going to tell me?"

Val kept her eyes closed for a moment. Tiny veins branched from the centers of her eyelids, a luminous pink, as if they were lit up by a source of light from within her head. Then her eyes opened, and she watched him silently.

She tucked the end of the fabric into the wrapping on his arm, her fingers a soft scratch against his palm, then scooted back onto the counter and picked out some more noodles.

"What if I said I won't?" she replied, chewing.

"Not ever?"

"Yeah. Never ever."

"Then I'd be left to wonder—" He gestured vaguely with his mummy's hand. "Then I don't know."

"What if I said that last night I was lying? What if I told you I only said it to see how you'd react?"

"Did you?"

She shrugged and peered down into her carton. But he *did* know her after all, or at least he knew her well enough to recognize that the tautness in her neck and mouth meant that she had *not* been lying. Elliot's heart began to pound beneath the strips of fabric that felt not like bandages anymore but like the filaments of a web.

Here is what happened the night before:

Elliot and Val had been up late drinking. Val was young enough that alcohol was still recreation, not yet anesthesia, and their nights too often ended in tumblers of diminishing ice. It was all right to perform the honey eating with a hangover, Elliot had reasoned; in fact, it might help with the regurgitation.

They'd been discussing Elliot's own Apricity test, which was blank. Blank when he'd first sat for the Apricity years ago and blank again now. A little under 2 percent of the population produced blank results, Pearl had explained to him in an apologetic rush, like she was worried the non-result would bother him. It didn't. In fact, Elliot felt it suited him. He liked being the blank slate. The page unwritten. The vampire gazing in the mirror.

"Maybe you're already as happy as you possibly can be?" Val said, swirling her glass so that the ice cubes chased one another round its base.

"*You* make me happy," he replied automatically. When she didn't answer in kind, he looked up to find her eyes full of tears.

"What? Val? What is it?"

"I did something bad," she said.

And she refused to say any more. When he tried to reassure her that it couldn't be *that* bad, she started crying again. When he said that he loved her no matter what, she cried even harder. Still she wouldn't say what it was she'd done. He asked her of course; over and over he asked, and over and over she shook her head. When that didn't work, he guessed, then he acted like he didn't care, and finally he pleaded for her to tell him. What began as concern for Val's tears became disbelief that she wouldn't confide in him, became a game to get her to confess, become an unexpectedly deep well of bitterness. Whiskey and bitterness. He'd left his wife for her. His son. He'd carved her face into metal, marble, wood, and displayed it to the world. What couldn't she tell him? What confidence didn't he deserve to have shared? In the end, Elliot had gone to bed in a huff. When he'd woken in the morning, Val had already left for work. But then, she'd had an early meeting on her schedule.

During his time on the platform that day, Elliot had decided that he would not ask Val to tell him her secret, and in this way, eventually, she would confess it to him. It was like how he stood very still in the alley to coax the cat back after it darted out the kitchen door. But here he was asking again, and here Val was not answering, eating her noodles, and seeming entirely unperturbed.

The moment felt somehow familiar, and Elliot realized with a pang that he'd experienced it before, only from the other side. He recognized in his own voice the desperate lilt of girlfriends past, of Pearl even, when they finally sensed he was breaking things off. At which point a stillness would settle over Elliot as he watched them grapple to retrieve what he knew was already done and gone.

"Are you really never going to tell me?" Elliot asked Val, taking care to hold his tone steady.

She clicked her chopsticks together. "What if I didn't?"

"Well." He considered this: what would it be like never to know? "I would be forced to think the worst."

She pursed her lips. "Or you could choose to think the best."

"Did you have an affair?" And it felt, at first, preposterous to say this; then suddenly it felt like this must be what she'd done. "That's it, isn't it?"

She laughed, but not an actual laugh. She just said, "Ha!"

The *Ha!* meant that Elliot was the cheater and Val knew it. Val knew it because he'd cheated with her while he was still married to Pearl. Thus, it would serve Elliot right if Val turned around and did the same thing to him. Elliot's stomach stirred its sickly brew of honey. Oh, but this was miserable!

"I feel," Val said carefully, "that if I say no to one of your guesses, you'll be motivated to keep guessing. Then eventually you may guess correctly, and I won't be able to say no anymore."

"Answer just this once. I won't ask anything else. If you did cheat, I forgive you," he added impulsively before even stopping to think if this was true.

"That's very generous of you, hon, but I didn't cheat. In fact, it has nothing to do with you."

"So it was something you did before we met?"

"See!" She pointed at him. "What did I say? You're still guessing!"

"You should never have told me there was something if you weren't going to tell me what it was!"

Elliot stood and began unwrapping the strips of fabric from his limbs, casting them off and wishing for them to crash against the floor instead of landing how they did, silently, limply. All day he had been consumed with curiosity and anxiety and insecurity and regret, but that—all of that!—was wrong. Anger. Anger was the appropriate response. Anger poured into Elliot, crackling and righteous, until he looked up and saw Val with her knees pulled up to her chest and her face sunk down between them, a little girl hiding from the world. His anger sloughed away.

"I wasn't going to tell you," she said, her voice muffled. "Not ever. I knew I shouldn't. But." She lifted her head, her forehead marked from the press of her kneecaps. "I wanted you to know—"

"Then tell me! You can tell me."

"—a *little*," she interrupted. "I wanted you to know *a little*. Can you be content with knowing only a little?"

They went to bed together, at least. Elliot knew Val was making a point of staying up with him. Usually she turned in first, and he sailed on into the night with his screen, stumbling into the bedroom after waking at some blue hour, having fallen asleep on the couch. Tonight they lay on their respective sides of the bed, the cat an oblivious lump at their feet. The light from the street lamps pressed into the room with a yellow glow and a low buzz. Sometimes to help himself fall asleep, Elliot would close his eyes and imagine that he was in a giant incubator, a robotic womb that was composing him into being, building one more layer of him each night.

"Maybe it'd be easier to tell me in the dark," he said.

For a second, he thought she might answer him. For another second, he thought she was already asleep. Then, in one large motion, Val turned and curled around him, hooking a leg and arm over him and burying her face in his shoulder. She squeezed herself against him so tightly that it began to hurt in the places where her nose and knee pressed.

"Maybe you stole some money," he said, adding, "Maybe not even because you really needed it, but just because you wanted to."

She neither answered nor slackened her hold.

"Maybe you hit someone with your car."

The buzz of the street lamps seemed to grow louder.

"Maybe you'd been drinking. Maybe that's why you didn't stop to see how hurt they were. Or maybe you did, and he was dead."

"He?" she murmured.

"Maybe he wasn't dead, but you left anyway. Maybe he died

later because help came too late. Maybe you didn't even call because you knew they'd trace your number. Maybe you saw his face in the obituaries. Maybe he was young. Rhett's age. Maybe you tracked down his mother and followed her around the grocery store, always keeping an aisle away."

She said Elliot's name into his shoulder, but when he paused to give her the chance to say more, she didn't.

"Maybe you dropped a twenty-dollar bill on the floor of the grocery store so that his mother would find it. But that made you feel worse because why not a hundred-dollar bill? Then again, what would a hundred dollars matter? It's an insult to even think of a dollar amount. What could ever be enough?"

He paused. In a small voice, she said, "What else?"

"What?"

"What else could it be?"

So he went on into the night, listing different acts of violence and betrayal until he realized that her limbs had become dead weight and her breath even. At some point during his litany, she'd fallen asleep. He examined her face, sweet in repose, then arranged the covers around her chin.

In the morning they moved through their routines without mention of the night before or the night before that. And after lunch, Val accompanied Elliot to the gallery, helping him fold the strips of fabric in an old suitcase so that he could pull them out in the right order when he was on the platform.

Today was easier than yesterday. The wrapping procedure went as Elliot had practiced it, and the only physical discomfort was a bit of sweat. *I'm doing it*, he thought woodenly as he wrapped himself up. *I'm doing it*. Val and Nita came in and out of the room at intervals, picking a vantage point in an unobtrusive corner. While the gallery-goers watched Elliot with a range of interest and bafflement, no one looked at him with disgust, as they had the day before. And after Elliot had wrapped his face, he wouldn't be able to see their expressions at all.

Just before he laid the first strip of fabric over his eyes, Elliot noticed a man at the edge of a cluster of people but seemingly not with them. He was tapping something into his screen. An art critic? It was possible. Nita had sent out invitations to the local papers and blogs. This was how it had begun with the *Valeria* series; positive reviews in a few estimable blogs had led to gallery invitations had led to museum installations had led to a sizable grant. And his next piece would be even better, people had assured him. Or had it been *he* who'd assured *them*? He had never been a starving artist or even a slightly peckish one. Of course, his mother had wired a monthly amount to his account, finally gifting him with a big lump on his twenty-fifth birthday. Beyond that, he'd bobbed along from commission to fellowship to funded retreat with few pauses between. *Of course*, his friends would say when the next thing came through for him. *Of course Elliot got that*. The most difficult part of the last few years had not even been the rejections; it had been not knowing where to place blame. Was it Elliot's own fault for not making good art? Was it the gallery bookers' fault for not recognizing that his art was indeed good? Was it (somehow) *Valeria's* fault for being the only good art he could make?

Through the fabric, the people appeared as shadows passing before Elliot, sometimes pausing and peering so that the blot of them
grew larger in his field of vision. "*Midas*," they read off the card,
adding, "That's the king. The one with the touch." At one point, a
figure came and stood before Elliot, unmoving for many minutes.
Val? he wanted to call through the muffle of his bandages, but he
kept himself from saying her name.

APRICITY CONTENTMENT PLAN: Wrap yourself in softest fabric.

"It sounds like a fortune cookie," I told the guy. Elliot. The guy
with the machine. "'In softest fabric.' Sounds fake. This isn't a real
Apricity, is it? It's a random generator. You set us up, and you see
our reactions. *That's* the art project, isn't it? You can't trick me. I
read about these things."

"No, no, it's real. It'll be in a gallery," the guy with the machine
assured me, and showed me where the company name was em-
bossed on the thing, like *that* couldn't be faked.

He looked slippery to begin with. The machine guy did. Too
tall. That stoop. Like he was deigning to bend down and talk to
me. He'd come from money, obviously. Of course he had if he
could fritter his days away pretending that this was an actual job. A
grown man!

"If you don't believe me, come see the show when it's up," he
said. He held up the "machine" with my "result" displayed on the
screen. "Yours is interesting. I might use it."

"So let me get this straight," I said. "You're going to wrap your-self in fabric and call it art."

"Pretty much. But I'm going to do it to the nth."

"The nth?"

"Overdo it."

"I know what 'the nth' means."

"Like with yours, I'd mummify myself in soft fabric until I can barely breathe. The idea is to make myself sick on happiness."

"And call it art."

"And call it art," he repeated. "I'll order special fabric for it. Cashmere. Or something softer than cashmere if that exists. What-ever's most expensive."

"Whatever's most expensive. Huh. I'm sure you will."

"I could send you the fabric after the show is over. Would you like that?"

"Why would I like that?"

"Because the machine says you would."

"Let's all do what the machine says and see where we end up!" I told him, and then I went home and pricked each of my fingers with a pin until it bled, one after the next, because I damn well could.

ELLIOT LEFT VAL ALONE for the next few days, and this seemed to suit her just fine. If he was hoping that she'd confess her secret, she didn't. She didn't cast him looks of any sort either, not guilty, long-ing, or grateful. She merely went back to being Val, and any strain in their interactions, Elliot knew, came from him alone. At home, he'd watch her out of the corner of his eye, fixing on the articulation of her foot or a lock of hair the dye had frizzed or that little tab of flesh that marked the opening of her ear. Often enough Val would catch him watching her and smile at him. And how was it that as she became more unknowable, more remote, she also became more beautiful, more precious to him?

In the grip of Elliot-didn't-know-what, he hired a private investigator, not to follow Val but to look into her past. He expected a grizzled ex-cop like in the movies, but the PI ended up being an elfin young woman in a sweater knit with blobby shapes that Elliot finally deciphered as rabbits and carrots. When Elliot asked the girl if she had "experience in the field" (a phrase borrowed from the same movies that the grizzled ex-cops populated), she explained that there was no "field"; the investigation would be conducted wholly on the Internet. *Of course*, she clearly wanted to add.

Elliot felt foolish as he answered the young woman's questions. How had he and Val met? Through a mutual friend. No, Elliot didn't think Val was having an affair. No, she wasn't after his money; she'd signed a prenup. No, he didn't know what he was looking for exactly, whether an event or a person, a place or a thing. The girl looked without comment at the picture of Val he sent to her screen, but she didn't need to say it; Elliot knew what she was thinking: *Middle-aged man, pretty young wife. Typical.* He wished he could explain that it wasn't like that.

"So *what* am I looking for?" she asked again.

"You'll know it when you see it," Elliot said, and now *he* was the character in the movie.

That afternoon Elliot took the stage of Nita's gallery. He sat in his chair, face forward, wearing headphones with the volume so loud that even in the far corners of the gallery people kept looking around to locate the tiny, tinny orchestra. A man stepped up onto the platform and lifted an ear of Elliot's headphones to verify the source of the music they were hearing.

Val did not come to the gallery. Elliot had told her not to bother, but he had hoped she would show up even so. He let the sound surround him, enclose him, swallow him up. At the end of the day, when he removed the headphones, ghost sounds rang and whooshed within his ears. He wondered if he'd done permanent damage to his hearing and found that he did not care if he had. Chris Burden had famously shot himself in the arm for a performance piece, after all. If Elliot went deaf, he could just call it art.

PEARL KEPT THE SURPRISE off of her face when she answered Elliot's knock. But then the HMS would have announced him from the lobby. He held up the borrowed Apricity. "See? I didn't break it."

She took it from him. "Rhett's out with friends."

"But you're here." He smiled at her.

After a beat, she stepped aside and he came into the apartment. Pearl's latest biological model was laid out on the table, a moth the span of Elliot's hand. Its wings were made of thousands of tiny luminous filaments. Pearl had started making these models after their divorce. The hobby had surprised Elliot when he first learned of it. As far as he was concerned, Pearl didn't make things; she managed them. But then maybe it was just him she'd managed. Maybe he hadn't known her either.

As part of the *Valeria* series, Elliot had made a replica of Val's face out of real butterfly wings, which had necessitated pulling the wings free from the insects' bodies with tweezers until he'd had an array of vivid colors on one side and a small pile of black twigs on the other.

Elliot reached to touch Pearl's model of the moth.

"Careful," she said. "It's still drying."

He lifted his hands in the air like a criminal in the flashlight beam. Slowly he turned around. "Hey. Pearl. What's the worst thing you've ever done?"

She was still standing at the front door, the Apricity in her hand. She was barefoot, in her pajamas, her hair feathered around her face, her dark eyes wide. She was as pretty as ever, especially when she gave him that weary look and sighed. "What'd you do?"

"Me? Nothing! It's just a mental exercise."

She left the doorway and stepped smartly between him and the moth as if she thought he might ignore her warning and touch it anyway. "A mental exercise for some piece you're working on?"

"No, no. Just for me. For my curiosity."

She smiled, not so nicely.

He lowered his hands and shoved them into his pockets, stooping a bit and smiling in a way he knew was charming. He'd cultivated the look in high school and cleaned up with it at college, Pearl included.

"Come on, dove. You can tell me."

"What's the worst thing I've ever done?"

"Yeah."

Her smile deepened like the joke only got better from here. "Married you."

"Really?"

Her smile disappeared. "No."

Elliot knew then that he loved her still. It wasn't like the love he felt for Val. This was a safe love, polished and put away somewhere, like a stone wrapped in cotton.

He took a step toward her and reached down to touch her cheek.

Pearl flicked a bit of wing at him, the speck landing on his sleeve.

"Get out of here, El, before you get yourself in trouble."

WHEN ELLIOT ARRIVED HOME, he found Val on the couch reading. Without a word, he lifted the screen from her hands, took down her pants, and hoisted her hips to the edge of the couch. He persisted over her laughing questions and moved the hands she laid on his head back down to her sides so that his mouth was the only point where he and she joined. He thought of the honey, how it brimmed above the curve of the spoon while still holding its droplet shape. Val didn't taste like honey of course; she tasted briny and close. He worked at her tenderly, stopping to kiss the folds and scallops of her, tracing them with the tip of his tongue and nose. After she came, she looked down at him, her eyes not opaque anymore but transparent, glass.

Then she saw something in his face that made her push him away, scrambling back on the couch, her eyes becoming stone.

"That was a lie, wasn't it?" she said in a small voice.

"What?"

"That. Just now."

And it had been. The sex wasn't a lie, but the tenderness was. He didn't even have to answer.

"You're not who I thought you were," she said thickly. She fumbled with her pants, her legs and ass pale, the insides of her thighs shining. "I know that's what you're thinking about me, but you should know that I'm thinking it about you, too."

Elliot stayed kneeling on the floor in front of the couch, listening to the sounds of his wife showering and dressing and putting items into a bag. The sounds were at a great distance, then they rushed in close, his hearing still distorted. The hinges squeaked open from a front door miles away. The dead bolt slid closed right next to his ear. And he realized he could hear normally again; the whooshing sounds were gone.

APRICITY CONTENTMENT PLAN: Listen to music.

Now I know what to do.

And I like music, I do! Maybe I'll be a singer. Maybe I'll have a band and they'll play the cymbals every time I jump in the air. I already have eight different albums and twenty-six singles on my screen at home. And I don't have to ask permission to listen to them.

I *did* have to ask permission to have the artist man give me the test, and what was bad is that Mom forgot to sign the permission slip even though she'd had it for an entire week because I'd taken it out of my backpack the day we got them and put it in the place on the table by the door and set the little brass pig on top and that means *Sign this.* I almost cried when I remembered I didn't have it. Mrs. Hinks was going to have me go sit in the library with Risa J. and Matt S., who didn't forget their permission slips but whose parents wouldn't sign them for religious reasons. Everyone can have a different religion, and we respect that. And people can have no religion, and we respect that, too. But even if I respect Risa J. and Matt S. and their religions, that didn't mean I wanted to sit with them in the library while all the rest of the class got their futures told. We were all lined up at the door and everything just waiting for one of the librarians to come walk us over when I saw Mom in the hallway. Her cheeks were pink from running and she had a white paper in her hand. My permission slip! And I was happier than maybe I've ever been.

THE INVESTIGATOR WITH THE BLOBBY rabbit sweater called him that night.

"I found the thing," she told him. "Or at least, I found *a* thing that I think is probably *the* thing."

"How bad is it?" Elliot asked.

"I don't know, man. I don't know your scale. Do you want me to send you my report?"

"Yes. No. Can you send it to me through the mail?"

"Like in an envelope?" He heard her exhale impatiently. "I don't have stamps."

"I'll pay you extra for your trouble," Elliot told her.

And the envelope arrived in the mail two days later, though Val did not arrive with it. Elliot had held out for the first night she was gone but had called her screen the next morning and every few hours thereafter. She never answered, and he never left a message.

If Elliot held the envelope up to the light, he could see the border, a fraction of an inch, that marked the edge of the paper folded within. He didn't open it, though. He left the envelope sealed and went through Val's clothes instead, hanger by hanger, sliding his hands into the pockets of jackets and pants, a curious feeling when there was no body wearing them. Deep in the pocket of a winter jacket, he found an earring Val had thought she'd lost. He held the little gold circle in the cup of his palm. He called her screen but could think of nothing to say beyond, *I found your earring*, so he hung up without saying anything at all.

He drank whatever was left in their bar. He lay on the couch with the cat perched on his chest and one of his feet on the floor to steady the room. He pictured Val snapping the cat's neck, castrating an ex-lover, drinking a goblet of blood. Did he care what she'd done or only that she refused to tell him? Or was it that she had denied him this last inch of her? He rose up from the couch, startling the cat, and made it to the bathroom just in time. He threw up; somehow it still tasted like honey.

He wandered to the gallery and hovered by Nita's desk like a ghoul. *Midas* was over, after garnering a handful of listings, a few middling reviews on lightly trafficked blogs. One blogger thought it was an indictment of capitalism. Another a rejection of the physical body. The only review Elliot had liked was the one where most of the screen was given over to a hand-drawn illustration of a vicuna. So it seemed *Midas* would not be lucrative after all. Irony. It was midday on a Tuesday. The gallery was near empty. Nita gave him a sharp look and did not rise from her seat at the desk to greet him.

"She's staying at Lisette's," she said, adding, "If you were going to cheat on her, at least it could've been with me."

Elliot didn't bother correcting her.

He waited in a coffee shop across the street until he saw Nita leave for lunch, turning the little white sign and locking the door. Elliot let himself in (Nita had thumbed him into the locks long ago), leaving off the lights and walking through the dark to the second display room. Nita hadn't removed his platform yet, the small plywood stage, painted over white. He stepped up onto it and stood facing out into the darkened gallery.

From his back pocket, Elliot took the envelope the investigator had sent him. He tore it in halves, quarters, eighths, sixteenths, until the bits of paper were so small that they escaped his fingers and fluttered to the floor. He closed his eyes and imagined Val standing in front of the platform, watching him make scraps of her secret. Her face turned to canvas, to clay, to papier-mâché, to blown glass, to moss, to marble, to metal. He reached forward into the dark, wishing that his fingertips would find her cheek, that it would turn back to flesh at his touch.

6

Origin Story

My mother didn't get a wink of sleep while she was pregnant with me. The moment she closed her eyes, she would feel me within her, quickening, spinning, a churn of synapse and star matter and amniotic fluid, commanding her to stand, commanding her to get out from whatever ceiling she was under and put the sky over her head. She might catch snatches of sleep, a few minutes slumped in a chair or leaning against a door-jamb, until I noticed that the rhythm of breathing around me had deepened, at which point I would begin to thrash. *I was terrified of you before you were even born*, she used to tell me, and then she'd reach out and press the tip of my tiny nose like she was ringing a doorbell.

The birth was worse than the pregnancy, a horror of labor. My mother vomited, shitted, was wracked when, finally, she expelled me. Under the dim lamp in the recovery room, my skin looked blue, and her blood appeared black against it. She gazed down at me, a live creature balanced there in her own two hands, an infant.

But no matter how intensely she stared, my eyes would not open in return. They remained closed, two little crevices in my tree knot of a face. I was not dead, the doctors assured her, only sleeping. As I was awake within her, I was asleep without her. *You slept. Ah! How you slept!* she sighed. And so she named me Valeria for the valerian root, used to cure insomnia. Others wish their children ten fingers, ten toes. Others wish their children happiness. My mother prayed that I would not stir.

THE TESTING FACILITY is busy today. Wednesdays are when the parole officers have their reports due, so all the last-minute appointments pile up on the bottom of Tuesday. My PO is Georg, and it is Tricia when Georg is on vacation or in court. Though the waiting room is full, the chairs on either side of me remain empty. I am more dressed up than I normally would be for my swab-and-swipe because I have a meeting after with a client. Across the aisle a teenage girl stares at my fine stockings and dress, openly covetous. The girl has an eye tattooed on each of her cheeks. The tattooed eyes are the same size and shape as her real eyes, inked an inch below in sure black lines. They leak fat tattooed tears.

A man slips into the seat next to mine. With a congenial smile, he lifts a strand of my hair, holding it beneath his nose. He inhales deeply. "I wanted to see if it *smelled* pink," he says. When I turn and fix my gaze on him, he drops the lock of hair and moves away with an air of professional courtesy, as if he has recognized that I am not a customer but a colleague.

That man has done something very bad to someone. I know this without needing to read his file. The girl with tattooed eyes has done something very bad to someone, too, possibly to herself. All of us in this room have done something very bad to someone, and so we must sit here and wait. The woman at the window calls my name.

These days, Georg lets me swab my own cheek. We have been meeting for over nine years now, Georg and I. Nearly a decade. He has owned the plaid shirt he is wearing for eight of those nine years, the second-to-last button changing circumference and color as it falls off and is hastily replaced, by either Georg or his husband, Samuel. This, our tenth year, is our last together. Georg will miss me when I am gone. Maybe I will miss him, too.

Georg slides the sample of my spit into the machine and furrows his brow at his screen as if the machine can be shamed into speeding its calculations. *Machine*: the word comes from the Doric Greek by way of Latin by way of French, *makhana*, "device." The words that led to *makhana* meant something not mechanical at all, they meant a unit that functioned on its own, as in a body, that human machine. The machines at the testing facility are refurbished models bought cheap. Hence, they are slow. Georg tuts at the machine.

"How's Samuel?" I ask.

"Ha! Obsessed with the new Calla Pax show. Last night I caught him writing something on a fan feed. 'You are a fifty-year-old gay man,' I told him, 'not a teenage girl.' Samuel looks at me over his glasses—like this—and says, 'That is the same thing.' Ha! How is Elliot?"

"Fine."

"Fine? Good."

"Fine until I chopped him up and put the pieces in the freezer."

Georg sniffs. "I don't know why you make these jokes."

"What joke? I wrapped the body parts in waxed paper."

"Waxed paper," he repeats.

"You know." I shrug. "To prevent freezer burn."

Georg's brow smooths. My results have come up on his screen, and he has seen whatever he has wanted to see, or *not* seen whatever he has wanted to *not* see. He signs his name to a thick packet in my file and initials a slip of paper for me to give the front desk on my way out.

"Next month, I will bring you a cupcake," he says.

"What'd I do to deserve cupcakes?"

"One. I said I will bring you *one* cupcake." He plants a thumb in the center of my file. "What did you do? You finished your probation."

I stare at his thumb. It's a funny word, *thumb*, unpronounceable really. It's related to an Old Dutch word *duim*, meaning "to swell."

"You may want to check again." I indicate the folder. "I'm pretty sure you're stuck with me until the end of the year."

"Ten years from age of majority: April. Next month is April. Your birthday is in April, yes?"

"The eleventh."

"See? You're done." As he hands me the slip of paper, he pats my hand awkwardly. "Don't worry."

"Who's worried?"

"Valeria. I know you have a good heart."

"Yeah. In the freezer. Wrapped in waxed paper."

The teenager is still in the waiting room. She blinks a long blink as I pass so that she has only one set of eyes, crying ink.

The name Valeria means "to be healthy." It also means "to be strong."

THE WORD FOR SPELL, as in *casting a spell*, comes from the same root as the word for *narration*. This is evidence that ancient people believed language to be a sort of magic, the simple act of naming something akin to creating it, controlling it. If you know some-one's true name, you can destroy him, or so they say. In the old stories people hide their names from all but their most trusted loved ones. Supposedly, God hides His real name, even from those who worship Him. In college, I had a professor who asked the entire lecture hall to cover their ears before he whispered the real name of God. I left my ears uncovered and found myself disappointed by the syllables.

The meeting with the client goes on for over an hour. They want me to name their new eye cream, one of those tiny little pots containing tallow, perfume, and whatever manatee phlegm or pow-dered unicorn penis is supposed to make your wrinkles go away. They even have Calla Pax signed on as the spokesmodel. I'll have to tell Georg so that he can tell his husband.

I know immediately what the name of the product should be: Crone Cream. I also know the executives are not ready to hear this idea. They're off in the swan-feather, flower-petal, snowflake realm. But I can see her, the crone, waving from the window of her little house. I'll have to wait to suggest it. If I say, "Call it Crone Cream," right now, these men will all blink at me, then one of them will reply, "Sincerity is the new irony." As if they understand irony. They don't know that irony means God's laughter. *Yahweh's* laughter.

After the meeting with the eye-cream clients, I take the train downtown to meet Elliot and Rhett. On the train, I watch strangers' eyes, studying the wrinkles that curl from them like script, like talons. How much squinting, how much laughter to earn each of those lines?

Crone Cream.

I would like to wander down a wooded path to the sod house among the pine trees. I would like to stand at its window and ask the crone my three questions. No, that's not what I would like. What I would like is to be the crone, the answers hidden in the folds of my skin. The word *crone* comes from the word for "carcass."

THE FRENCH HAVE A TERM, *enfant terrible*, which we now use to mean a young person with preternatural skill, a prodigy. Originally, it meant a child who says something honest but impolite, for example asking, "Why are you so fat?" to your cherished dinner guest. *Cruel* is the word we use to describe children, as in *the cruelty of children. Cruel* comes from *crudus*, for "raw" or "bloody." What we mean is that there's something natural to a child's feral behavior, a curiosity untinctured by empathy or social rules. Think of the child bending sunlight through the magnifying glass to raise tendrils of smoke on the ants' backs. The child isn't acting unkindly. Kindness *does not occur* to the child.

To my mother I was an *enfant terrible* in the traditional sense. My behavior sent her to bed with migraines, then to longer and longer holistic retreats. My father would describe me as a spirited child, if you asked him, but he loved me too much to see me clearly. My mother knew what I was.

When I was six and discovered our little cat Sooty curled up and cold under the bushes, my mother took my chin in her hand and said, *What did you do to the cat? Tell me now, and I won't be angry.*

I wasn't sure what she wanted me to confess. I didn't remember having done anything to the cat. I had liked Sooty. I had named him. When I wore a certain sweater, he would knead his paws against it and suck the wool into wet tufts like he was nursing at his mother's belly.

What did you do? she asked again.

I had prodded Sooty's side when I found him curled under the bush—that's how I knew he was dead and not sleeping; maybe this was what she meant. But when I told her those words, *I only touched him*, her hand flew from my chin to her own temple. *I can't hear any more!* she said desperately, backing away. *Don't tell me what you did next!*

What I'd done next was stroke his soft gray forehead.

I feel a headache coming on.

When the cat we got after Sooty, Mister Stuffing, ran away, she said, *I don't want to know what you did to this one.*

We had no more cats after that.

Elliot and I have a cat now. Her name is Slip. She has perfectly spaced stripes down her tail and she'll eat the rind of your breakfast cantaloupe down to the pebbly green. When I stroke her, she arches her back to meet my hand, and I say, "Careful now," unsure if I'm talking to her or to me.

PALOOKA, ELLIOT TEXTS ME: the password to the bar I'm to meet them at, one of these faux-speakeasies that are constantly going in and out of style. This one has you enter through the back of a Chinese restaurant. You walk among the laminated tables and straight into the kitchen, past the string of dead ducks, and up to a hulk in a fedora to whom you announce the day's password. The password is always some Prohibition-era slang yanked from the Internet, something like *giggle water* or *bee's knees*. Prohibition! Everyone loves a flapper dress or a fake tommy gun, but who remembers the thousands of people who went blind drinking unregulated wood alcohol?

The bouncer looks like an enormous Georg, balloon Georg, like someone put their mouth to Georg's pinkie toe and inflated him. I consider asking the bouncer if he knows about the wood alcohol and the blind people, if he can imagine what it would be like to take a swallow from a bottle and find the world winking out (*wink, wink*) as if a bird had pecked out each of your eyes.

It's the kind of thing I'd say to Georg, and then I'd say, "That reminds me: I have a bottle of liquor for your next birthday. Home-brewed."

And Georg would tut and say, "Valeria. You do not scare me."

And I'd say, "You don't scare me either, Georg. Let's do a shot together."

And he'd say, "Yes, okay. Let's. *Nazdorov'ya!*"

Then he'd look at my results on his screen and his brow would smooth, and he'd hand me the slip of paper and tell me that I am all right. That I can go now.

"Palooka," I say to the bouncer, and he steps aside to reveal a little door. He opens the door to let me through.

This is not the real password. The real password is Georg's slip of paper.

THE LAWYER MY FATHER HIRED was expensive, his neckties in soft colors, like paint swatches selected for the nursery walls. The child psychiatrist he hired was expensive, too, the print of her dress silk Rorschach blots. I sat between them, not next to my father. Our seating arrangement was such because my father couldn't look at me without his face crumpling, which, the expensive lawyer cautioned him, could not happen in front of the judge. I was eleven.

My mother was there, too, though not really. Really, she was dead. All the same, I pictured her sitting at the end of the table. She waved at me somberly, her head aflame.

We sat not in a courtroom but a conference room reserved for family court with posters of weary lambs taped to the walls and the fug of spoiled milk rising from the carpet every time I shifted my chair. The meeting was a formality. The professionals my father hired (poised and filigreed) had already conferred with the state social workers (overworked and oxidized) and come up with a plan. Seven years in a private psychiatric hospital, until I turned eighteen, probation for five years thereafter. I didn't even have to testify. After all, I had already confessed. We watched as the judge put her signature to my plan; it was over in a moment.

The adults were rolling their chairs back, well pleased (except for my father, whose face I could not see), when I said, "Your Honor?"

I said it the way I'd practiced in the stall during my last bathroom break. No one heard me, so I said it louder.

"Your Honor?"

They all turned to look at me now. Except for my father, who flinched his head lower, as if some object had come flying at it. And except for my mother, who had never taken her eyes from me. The flames around her head turned blue and began to smoke.

"Your Honor?" I said once more. Three times. Like a spell.

The lawyer and the psychiatrist tried to shush me, the lawyer by speaking over me, the psychiatrist by gripping my arm in a pinching way. The judge silenced them both and gestured for me to continue.

"Could it be longer?" I asked.

The judge pursed her lips. "The sentencing is over, Valeria. Now we all go home." One corner of her mouth tugged down after she said this. She'd remembered that I would not be going home, that my father would go home alone; I would go to an asylum; my mother had gone in the ground.

"Not the sentencing," I said. "My punishment. Could you make it longer?"

She peered at me, again shushing my lawyer.

"Please."

Somehow it worked. She extended my probation, ten years past my eighteenth birthday instead of five. "You'll be twenty-eight before you're finished," she warned me.

"I'll never be that old." I'd felt so certain of that then.

At the end of the table, my mother's head singed the wall behind her. She smiled at me. And despite all the promises he had made beforehand, my father lowered his face into his hands and began to cry.

I FIND ELLIOT AND RHETT in a booth at the back of the speakeasy drinking potion-colored drinks. "Last Words," they tell me, meaning that this is the drink's name.

"Hey, kid, how'd you get in here?" I say. Rhett is only eighteen.

He jerks his chin, indicating his father. But of course I'd already guessed that Elliot must have sweet-talked someone or other.

"We're celebrating," Elliot says.

"Celebrating what?"

"Acceptance!"

"You don't say. Which one?"

"UC Davis," Rhett announces, quick, before his father can tell me first.

"Hey, congrats." I slide into the booth. I take a sip from Elliot's glass: gin and lime and other things. "Who's gonna order me one of those?"

Elliot begins talking about his new installation, *Midas*, which he will put up in Nita's gallery next week; his voice is stuffed with pride. I can tell by the set of Rhett's mouth that Elliot has been going on about this for a while now. I also know that Elliot will continue describing the piece until Rhett offers to see it. If Rhett doesn't offer soon, Elliot will have to outright ask him to come, but it'll be better for everyone if Rhett offers. Rhett is the only one Elliot really loves. This is part of my punishment, and I accept it. If Elliot doesn't love me, that means he's safe.

I find Rhett's leg under the table and nudge it. The boy comes to, blinking.

"I could come see it," Rhett says. I nudge him again. "Your show. *Midas*. It sounds really cool."

"Are you sure?" Elliot asks. "It's during the day."

"I have a free period on Friday."

"Maybe one of your teachers would let you do a write-up?"

"A write-up?"

"Of my piece."

"Um. I'm not taking an art class."

"Art is the universal subject."

"I guess."

"And besides, if your teachers aren't offering extra credit, they're not really doing their job."

Elliot turns to flag down the waiter for another round of Last Words, and when he does, Rhett catches my eye and shakes his head: *Oh, Dad.*

When I married Elliot, Rhett was fourteen and I was twenty-three. I was nervous around Rhett at first, not for the usual stepmother reasons, not because I was closer to his age than his father's, not because I was afraid he wouldn't like me. In fact, I'd *hoped* that he wouldn't like me. *I'm not good with kids*, I'd told Elliot when we first started seeing each other. So okay, he'd been warned.

The prefix *step-*, as in *stepmother* or *stepfather*, comes from an old German word meaning "bereft" and "orphaned," connoting a sense of great loss. And no wonder! Look how the stepmothers behave in fairy tales. Though to this I would say: Why should it be natural to love another person's child? Unnatural if you don't? It is unnatural to not love your own child; that much we can agree upon. We can tell my mother she's outvoted. We'll have to tell it to her ghost.

The first weekend Rhett stayed with us, he and I ran into each other in the hallway early in the morning, both of us in our pajamas. We stilled and stared at each other, both in unison. He raised his hand, a cautious greeting. I scuttled back to my room.

It turned out that Rhett liked me. He liked the colors I dyed my hair. He liked the hard things I would say. He began to come to me with carefully practiced stories of some little incident that had occurred at school, then with requests for advice. The more aloof I was, the more persistent he was.

I had told Elliot I wasn't good with children, but I hadn't told him about the rest: my monstrous birth; my mother's headaches; the unfortunate cats; the school friends who'd left our house crying because I was too fierce in my play; the hospital where I had passed my teenage years. All the people I had disabled or devoured. I hadn't told him about Georg and my probation. About the smell of burnt skin, a whiff of which remained permanently in my nose. I hadn't told him about that.

So when Rhett stopped eating, I knew it was my fault. I must have done something to make the boy wither. What I did, I did to protect us all, moving myself to the very edge of the scene. During Rhett's weekends with Elliot, I went on work trips or booked the day up with errands and lunches. Then Rhett was put in the hospitals, this facility or that one, and the weekend visits ceased. I was expected to visit the facility on family days, of course, but I kept to the back of Elliot's shoulder so that I was blocked from the boy's view.

I was familiar with this scene, the private hospital where desperation is girdled in luxury. Before our visits, I went through the boxes Elliot had prepared, plucking out the items I knew the intake nurse would remove—shoelaces, ballpoint pen, mouthwash. Finally, Elliot noticed.

"How do you know they won't allow mouthwash?"

I shrugged and said, "Common sense." My heart pounded.

I let the nurses do it after that.

At one of my appointments with Georg during this time, I pointed at the Apricity and said, "Too bad it can't give you a number. Too bad you don't have a machine that can do that."

"What number?" Georg asked.

"A number. Like they do for radiation in the air or toxins in the water. And if the number's high enough, you know it's not safe anymore. To drink. To breathe."

Georg coughed drily. "And this imaginary machine, it would assign a number to you?"

"I'm just saying it would be an objective measure."

He glared at me from under his formidable brow. "You think you are a toxin?"

I have not cried since I was a child. I must have cried when I was a child, though I cannot remember it. When Georg asked me that question, I felt the tears waiting there behind my eyes, like a person who holds his hand on the doorknob but dares not turn it and step through.

Just then, my results came up on the Apricity; I could tell by Georg's face, his brow smoothing. He started to turn his screen to show me, which wasn't allowed. Not that I care about rules. That's not the reason I stopped him. It's that *I* didn't want to see them, whatever things the machine said to him about me. I do not deserve happiness. I don't want to know where to seek it. When I grabbed his hand, Georg winced. When he pulled away, I saw that my nails had left tiny marks in his skin.

He turned his screen away and glowered at me. "It is an okay number."

"But it doesn't give you a number," I said.

"It is okay," he repeated, nodding to himself. "Valeria. You are not a toxin. You are—what? You are safe for public consumption."

AFTER WE WALK RHETT to the bus that will take him back to his mother's, Elliot and I go honey tasting. There is a shop in Bayview that sources their honey from an apiary out back. The walls of the shop are set with clear glass jugs beveled like beehives, spigots at the bottom, which the honey pours through. While the clerk assists Elliot in finding the sweetest honey, I wander to the windows at the back of the shop that allow customers a view of the bees. The actual hives are just stacks of screens; they look like old dressers. A beekeeper tends them, veil pulled over her face. The honeybee is the only species of bee that dies when it stings you. Its intestines release with the barb of its stinger, and it flies away gutted.

A spoon at my lips.

"Try this," Elliot says.

It is so sweet that a shiver runs through me.

"This is the sweetest one?" I ask.

"Nope." Elliot touches the tip of my nose. "That's you."

When I stick out my tongue in reply, he puts more honey on it.

Elliot doesn't know what I am. It is both endless salvation and an endless gutting that he doesn't know.

ELLIOT IS FRIVOLOUS. Elliot is charming. Elliot is harmless.

There should be some folkloric creature like Elliot, one that, when stabbed, does not bleed. The knife goes in and comes out silver, comes out clean.

I met Elliot at one of Nita's parties. I'd met Nita when I worked for a marketing firm that promoted her gallery. Nita liked the blouse I was wearing, so she invited me to her party. That was Nita.

The marketing job was my first out of college. When I left the facility, the doctors had warned me to prepare for a difficult adjustment. But college hadn't been difficult. I'd fallen in with the boarding school kids, my past imprisonment similar enough to theirs that my references passed without suspicion. At the end of four years, I'd claimed a degree in linguistics. Words were like me, shifting. My father visited me at school just once, for the graduation ceremony, still ducking his head, now over a slice of white cake. Do you know the origin for the word *father*? It's related to the Greek and Latin *pater*, from *pa*, one of the first sounds a baby can make.

At that party, at Nita's, that one night, Elliot came up to me with an extra drink. I have always attracted this type of man, the kind who approaches women with not the offer of the drink, but the drink itself. To make small talk, I insulted the large painting that Nita had hung over her mantel. *A scribble*, I believe I called it.

Elliot squinted at the corner of the canvas. "Can you read the artist's signature?"

But I didn't need to. I could already tell what it said by the way he smiled.

"Shit. It's you, isn't it?"

We ended up having sex in the spare bedroom on a pile of other people's coats. I knew he was older. Did I know he was married? A father? I must have sensed it, though he had, that night, removed his wedding ring before attending the party.

So when I say that Elliot is harmless, I know that his ex-wife would not agree with this statement. What I mean is that Elliot is harmless *to me*. Which is not to say that I don't love Elliot. Do I love Elliot? I do. As much as someone like me is capable of such an emotion. Maybe I do not feel it as you do. How would we ever know how our feelings compare? There is no origin for the word *love*. It is one of the first words and has always meant only itself.

ELLIOT AND I LEAVE THE SHOP having purchased a jar of honey so heavy that we cannot carry it out. It will be delivered to our apartment tomorrow. There is nowhere else we have to go, so we wander. The Bayview district was for years a shipyard, then during World War II, a laboratory used to test the effect of radioactive material on animals, after that deserted, after that government housing. Now the young, wealthy, and careless have reclaimed the neighborhood for their own. We wander past a shop that sells leather driving gloves; a restaurant that serves only wild-caught game; and two more speakeasies, one disguised as a florist's, the other as a bank. When, next, we pass a VRcade, I do something unprecedented. I suggest we go inside. Then I do something else unprecedented. I say, "Let's play."

"Play? Both of us?" Elliot blinks.

I nod.

He mimes a heart attack.

Elliot loves games. We don't have a VR system in our apartment, I keep saying no, so Elliot will sometimes go to a VRcade by himself or with Rhett. He never asks why I don't want to go. He explains me to himself: "Women only like games of their own making, everyone knows that."

The VRcade attendant is an old biddy with hair as pink as mine. She smiles to see me. "Cerise?" she asks, touching the top of her head. I know that she is referring to the color of her dyeing cartridge.

"Magenta," I say, touching my head in turn.

She leans forward and says in almost a whisper, "Do you know where that word comes from?"

In fact, I do. "A town in Italy. They discovered the color of dye there."

"But do you know this? The town had just suffered a battle. They named the dye after the blood-soaked ground."

I shake my head. I did not know that.

She hands us our masks and gloves. "You kids have fun." Then quick as a snake, she grabs my wrist and, with her free hand, wags a finger between our two faces, hers and mine. "It's like looking in an enchanted mirror."

The VRcade is well outfitted, our booth clean and the menu of games richly stocked. I scroll through the titles, half expecting it not to be there. It is an older game, after all. But there it is, slotted between *Alligator Alley* and *Anodyne Astronauts*.

"*Amusement?*" Elliot says when I bring it up on the screen. His voice sounds just this: amused. "Look at the date. It's practically vintage."

"Like you," I say.

"I'm better than vintage, baby. I'm a classic."

The screen shows an amusement park at night, the bright shrouds of the game tents, the piping music, the spindles of the Ferris wheel tipped with lights. I lower my mask and the park deepens and widens around me, as if I'm inside it, the world convincing enough except where it's pixelated in the corners. Even so, I feel it, that expansiveness specific to childhood, the breath filling you all the way up to the puff of your cheeks, the feeling that each breath is good. Elliot appears next to me. His avatar has been mistranslated, and in the game his hands are clumps of pixels, as if he holds two fuzzy bouquets.

His avatar turns to me with its flat smile. Elliot's voice booms in my mask's earpiece: "Your face!"

"What?" I lift my hands to it but of course feel only the plastic of the mask.

"It's all blown out. Pixels."

"Your hands, too," I say.

"You sure you want to play this one?"

"We have to get a candy apple to start the story. The booth is over there."

I begin walking through the crowds of doting parents and laughing children. The programming has been done on the cheap, and the same people appear and reappear at different points in the crowd: a woman wearing kitten ears, a boy pointing straight up at the sky, a man with a green balloon tied to his wrist.

"You've played this before," Elliot says, catching up.

"As a kid," I allow.

"I thought you hated games."

"What kid hates games?"

His avatar's face remains wanly smiling, but of course that is the only expression it can make. I spot the candy apple booth just ahead of us. I feel like I'm hiding a knife behind my back. I feel like I'm being led to the slaughter. Both at once. Because why did I suggest we play this game if I wasn't going to tell him? Is this it? Am I going to tell him now? And if I do will he turn away? Will he leave me? Will I be happy then?

We reach the booth. The apple purveyor has been given more detail than the people in the crowd. She has shaggy gray hair and a raised mole just beneath her eye, the kind that makes you wonder if she can see it all the time, sitting there in the corner of her vision, a blot on the horizon.

"Order one," I tell Elliot.

Apple is another word that has always meant itself. In fact, it used to apply to any fruit, vegetable, or even nut. All fruits were apples. The potato was the *apple of the earth* (and still is in French: *pomme de terre*). Dates were *finger apples*. The banana was, in Middle English, the *apple of paradise*.

The apple the old woman hands Elliot is the regular red kind, though redder than a real apple, heart red from its candy coating. Elliot lifts it to his face. His avatar's mouth stays closed in its smile, but there's a crunching sound, as if he has bitten into the fruit. The crunching sound reverberates across the park and comes back to our ears changed; it has become the whirr of propellers. And with that, men start dropping out of the sky.

Perhaps they aren't men. Perhaps they are women. Or monsters. There is no way to know what is behind their masks. This was a popular theme back when *Amusement* was made: masked killers. They were in all the movies, shows, and games. Sometimes they were sent from the government, as *Amusement* implies with its helicopters. Sometimes they were supernatural, slipping through a crack between dimensions. Pop culture scholars wrote that the trope represented fear of the establishment, a sense of disassociation from the self, and so on and so forth until all the modern-day problems had been properly aired. Most origins for the word *mask* come from the word *disguise*, but there is a Celtic origin that translates as "the dark clouds gather before the storm." And then there's *masca*, which means "witch."

In the game, the masked figures come out of the sky on cords so thin that it appears as if the men grasp the edges of the night and slide down them. When they reach the ground, they unsheathe their knives, slitting the throats of the people in the park. The throat of one of the men with a green balloon. The throat of the girl with two long braids. Even the throat of the apple seller. The blood arcs, red droplets becoming tiny squares, scattering into pixels in the air.

"This way!" I say to Elliot, and run away from the slaughter, away from the park, away from the game.

The game is called *Amusement* both for the sensation it's meant to engender and because it takes place within an amusement park. If you play the game as intended, you can enter the different booths, tents, and rides, hiding from the masked assassins, collecting weapons to fight and kill them. If you play through to the end, if you "win," you eventually kill the leader of the masked army, save a child trapped at the top of the Ferris wheel, and steal one of the helicopters, flying off to . . . where? Somewhere safe, I suppose. I don't know. I've never played it that way.

On the outskirts of the game, there is a narrow perimeter of space around the amusement park, dark fields bordering the bright tents and stringed lights. The masked assassins are here, too, but fewer in number. This space was created for players who become overwhelmed by the carnage in the amusement park, amateurs who need somewhere to go to recharge their health bar or practice basic moves. It was my mother who discovered the field. It was I who discovered the burning house.

MY MOTHER'S HEADACHES increased with my age. When I arrived home from school, she would meet me at the door with a description for the day's pain. *Like rocks grinding into my temples. Like a giant squeezing my skull. Like a swarm of bees in my brain.* Then she would stand back from the doorway, allowing me in, and shuffle back to her darkened bedroom. She never directly said that I was the cause of her headaches, but I knew. If I brought her tea, she would wince each step closer I took, and though she would accept the mug from my hand, she would raise it to her mouth and watch me over its edge, never taking a sip. She feared I would poison her. She never told me this, but I heard her and my father argue about it behind a closed door.

"She's just a little girl," he said. "She's your *daughter.*"

She said, "Yes. That's how I know."

I know now that my mother was ill in her head, and not with headaches. The doctors have explained it to me, and I am aware of their expertise. But there is knowing something and then there is feeling it. For adults, these are two different things. For children, they are one.

The game was a present for my eleventh birthday. After my mother opened the door for me—today's headache: *Like birds pecking out my eyes*—and in the hours before my father returned home from work, I'd play *Amusement*, keeping the sound down low so my mother could rest. Then one day the rasp of her slippers coming down the hall, stopping behind me. I didn't dare turn around for fear that the sight of my face would pain her. I held myself very still and kept playing the game.

For a week, the same. I began to play; she came and watched. By the time I had turned off the game, she'd gone back to her room. Then, one day, the rasp of the slippers, the soft settling of the couch cushion, and a new sound: the rustle of her hair as she placed the other mask over her head. And she appeared next to me, an avatar with my mother's face. She must have made it while I was at school. Still, I did not turn to look at her, not in life, not in the game. I could see her avatar, though, with its pleasant flat smile. I marveled at how her eyes looked when they were unpained.

She headed away, out of the amusement park, into the darkened fields. I followed her. For days we did this, traversing the fields together, allowing the masked assassins to kill us when they found us. Once she threw herself in front of me, sacrificing herself to the assassin's knife. A feeling rose up in me that I have not experienced before or since. No matter. We both died.

Then one day I saw the flicker on the horizon. I broke away from my mother's lead, running toward it, and when the screen did not split in two, I knew that she was following me. We came upon the burning house. I stood back while my mother entered it. A moment later she appeared at the window, swathed in flickering fire. She stood there and waved at me. I glanced over my shoulder and lifted my mask and saw through the clear plastic of her mask that the smile was on not just her avatar but her own real face. She didn't have to tell me that her headache was finally gone, as if the imaginary flames had burned it away.

"THERE," I SAY TO ELLIOT, and I can see it in the distance, the little house set ablaze.

"What's inside?" Elliot says, his avatar running after mine across the dark fields. "Weapons? A passageway?"

I don't tell him that the house is only a bit of throwaway programming, a little detail to make the game world feel real. I don't
tell him that there is nothing inside but fire. We reach the door,
close enough that if the fire were real, you'd be able to hear it
crackle as it ate up the wood. But it is not real, and so it dances silently, changing color.

"Stay out here," I tell Elliot. "Go around and look through the
window."

"You're going in?"

"Yes."

"Why do I stay out here?"

"You'll see."

I enter the house. My view flashes with the oranges and yellows.
There is no heat. The tongues of flame flicker and stutter at the
corner of my mask's frame. *Tongues of flame*, this is something we
say, as if the fire can speak, as if it taunts us, as if it scents the air like
a snake. I go around to the window, and there, outside, is Elliot,
standing where I've asked him to stand.

"What now?" he says.

It is easier to tell him with the mask over my face.

"We'd play the game after I got home from school."

"What? Who?"

"My mother and I."

"You don't talk about your parents."

"I am now."

He pauses, then nods. *Go on.*

"We'd do this. That's all I'm saying. She'd stand in the house, where I am. And I'd stand where you are, watching her. And she was happy there."

In the VR booth, Elliot and I stand shoulder to shoulder; in the game we stand facing each other. We wear masks; in the game we are barefaced, though my face is gone, blown out in pixels. Elliot is out on the cold dark plains. I am inside burning. He doesn't hear what I'm confessing, but also, I don't tell him. He waits for me to tell him. Forty amusement park–goers die in the time he waits for me. I count them off by their screams. I add them to my tally.

"Do you want to keep playing?" he asks.

"It's just that I don't know if she understood."

"Who?"

"My mother."

"Didn't understand what? How to play the game?"

"That she wasn't really burning."

HERE IS WHAT WAS SAID in family court:

That I was old enough to know what I was doing.

That I was too young to understand the permanence.

That my apology showed remorse.

That I had gotten the canister of white gas from the camp supplies and the matches from the drawer in the kitchen where they were kept.

That she must have been napping on the couch, her headache

medication so strong that she did not wake from the plash of gas, its wetness.

Slept still through the snick of the match.

HERE IS WHAT no one said:

That I was in the backyard when it happened, alone now that we had no cats.

That the smell of cooked skin and burnt hair came first, down the hall and out the back door, ahead of the smoke, ahead of the heat, ahead of her screams.

That she was aflame by the time I got there.

That she rose as she burned and pinwheeled round the room.

That she looked like one of the Catherine wheels from the amusement park.

That I don't remember getting the white gas or the matches, though I knew where both were kept.

That I don't remember doing it.

But I must have.

I must have.

Right?

That I stood there and stared at the play of the flames.

That I thought to hug her in an attempt to put the fire out but that, in the end, I was not willing to risk myself for her.

That when I told them, "I'm sorry," when I repeated it over and over, this is the crime I was confessing to. Not that I had set her on fire, but that I had watched her burn.

For a moment when she saw me there, she tried to stop screaming.
For a moment she tried to wave.

I AM NOT SUPPOSED to have Georg's address, but of course I do.
Back in the fifth year of my probation, he left his coat on the back
of his chair, and when he went to the bathroom, I looked through
his wallet and saved his address in my mind. After Elliot and I leave
the VRcade, I make up a forgotten appointment and take three
trains to get to Georg's house. When I arrive I find a bungalow,
almost as small as the burning house, its edges smudged with moss.
I sit on the stoop for over an hour before the curtain flicks aside and
flashes a man's face—not Georg's, so Samuel's. A moment later, the
door creaks open behind me, and Georg comes out and lowers
himself gently onto the stoop next to me.

"Valeria." He taps the lighter, a cheap bit of plastic, gripped between my hands like a bauble. "You forget your cigarettes?"

"I burned down the rest of your neighborhood," I lie.

"You did?" He makes a show of looking around at the houses,
still and sleeping.

"An orphanage, too."

"Oh?"

"And a hospital. The leukemia ward. All those bald kids. They
were gonna die anyway, right?"

"Valeria."

"I should be able to burn myself, shouldn't I?"

"Burn yourself? With this lighter?"

"Maybe not my whole self. Just part of my hand. A spot on my arm."

"Not your whole self?"

"I should. But no."

"Well, that is a relief. But why even a spot?"

"I told you, I can't do it." I shift on the stoop. "Not even a spot."

Georg is quiet and so am I. Then he reaches over and flicks the lighter so that the flame rises up between my hands. We watch it shiver. He lifts his thumb; the flame goes out.

"You did not burn those buildings," he says.

"I might have."

"You did not burn the little children."

"How do you know?"

"You are safe."

"Did the machine tell you that?"

"I am saying it: you are safe."

When he puts his arms around me, his shirt smells like whatever he has been cooking, something with garlic. I try not to shake too hard in his arms. I try not to let my tears and snot stain his shoulder. Because I don't want to harm anyone or anything, not even this shirt. Georg doesn't care. He wraps his arm around the back of my head and holds my face to his shoulder firmly, and when I am done crying, he releases it.

I sniff and touch my eyes and nose gingerly.

"Do you know the word *fire* has no origin?" I tell him. "It has always meant *fire*, never anything else."

"Hmph."

"That means fire was one of the first things."

"We were one of the first things also. Yes?"

"Who?"

"We. You and me. People." Georg glares at me. Past him are rows of houses, tiny and unburnt. "We were one of the first things?"

"Yes."

"Yes?"

"Sure." I sniff and wipe at my eyes. "We were here to say the word."

He nods, like I have proved his point. "We were one of the first things, and we are good. Valeria. We are good."

7

Screamer

Pearl didn't recognize the woman who answered her knock. Well, *woman* was overstating it. She couldn't have been much older than Rhett, low twenties, leaning on the door like they, she and the door, were in it together. Perhaps she was the daughter of the client Pearl was there to meet. Or the girlfriend? The nondisclosure agreement Pearl had signed was absent any name except for that of the anonymous client's law firm. Given all the secrecy, Pearl thought she might recognize the client on sight. As the car service had driven her hours from the city, and the Calistoga hills had unwrapped themselves to reveal this edifice of timber and glass, the door of which Pearl now knocked upon, she'd imagined the lupine grins of various actors, the taxidermied smile of a certain former governor, even the whey face of CEO Bradley Skrull. Pearl hadn't imagined this, though, this girl, this young woman, tiny all over except for her eyes and breasts, both sets inflated to full capacity. The girl was a Japanese cartoon. No, she was a Japanese cartoon of a woodland animal. When she opened her mouth, Pearl expected to hear a squeak.

The voice that emerged, however, was surprisingly husky, almost boyish. "Apricity! Right?"

"Yes. I'm from Apricity. I'm Pearl." Pearl extended her hand.

"Calla," the girl returned, with a sheepish note to her voice that Pearl took to mean, *But of course you already knew that.* But of course Pearl hadn't. So this was Pearl's client then, this nubile cartoon.

Instead of shaking Pearl's hand, the girl fastened on to it, yanking Pearl into the house. Pearl found herself tugged along through a series of professionally decorated rooms, the colors complementary, the throw pillows abundant, the knickknacks too quirky to be endured—traffic signs cast in mother-of-pearl, mobiles of dangling paper jellyfish, a bird's nest filled with toy soldiers. Calla kept up a bright stream of talk as they tripped along, the words coming so rapidly that when Pearl finally caught a sentence, she held on to its tail for dear life.

"—and then I sent everyone away so that we could meet, just the two of us."

As if on cue a voice from the next room called, "Calla?"

"Well, everyone except Marilee." The girl tugged Pearl into what turned out to be a faux-rustic kitchen, a witch's kitchen, complete with open brick oven and a dented copper pot large enough to stew a child. "But Marilee isn't everyone."

On the contrary, Marilee did appear to be everyone, or rather *anyone*, a composite of all middle-aged women, their weights averaged into a plumpness that wasn't quite fat, their hairstyles swirled together into a dusty brown wedge cut, their khakis and cardigans compiled into these two unremarkable specimens. However—Pearl blinked—there was something missing. It took her a moment to place it: no smile lines. Around Marilee's eyes and mouth there existed an eerie smoothness. Botox, she assumed, until she met Marilee's gaze, at which point Pearl revised her opinion, deciding that the woman lacked smile lines for that most obvious of reasons.

"I'm Calla's manager," Marilee said.

"She's practically my mother." Calla beamed with enough wattage for both of them. "I mean, she taught me how to use my first tampon."

"Don't be dramatic. You read the instructions on the box."

"Well, she *bought* me my first tampon."

"That may be true," Marilee allowed.

"You started young," Pearl said.

"What? My period?"

"Your work." Pearl fumbled for vagueness. "Your work in the industry."

Marilee's eyes cut to Pearl, then away, and Pearl could tell in that one glance that the woman had read her and read her correctly: Marilee knew that Pearl had no idea who her client was. If this offended the woman, she didn't show it, returning her cool gaze to Calla.

And it didn't really matter after all, Pearl supposed, not for the job at hand. Pearl could run the Apricity on a complete stranger as easily (maybe more easily) than a close friend. But then, there was the matter of politeness. Pearl would be staying in this house—"on premises," the contract had said—for the next two weeks, so she should probably figure out what dubious talent this girl claimed, this woman managed.

"I understand we'll be running daily contentment plans," Pearl said.

"Stupid, isn't it?" Calla replied.

"Um. Is it?"

"Phenomenally. I bet you've never had anyone ask for daily Apricities before. It's like asking for daily dental checkups! Daily . . . colonics!"

Pearl looked to Marilee for assistance, but the manager's eyes remained fixed on Calla. "I, uh, suppose it is a rather robust course of—"

"I mean, a person's Apricity doesn't change by the day!"

"Actually, your contentment report can change over the course of your life. As your idea of happiness changes, so may your path to it."

Calla didn't even blink at these lines from the manual. "But daily? Not *daily*."

"That would be unusual," Pearl admitted.

"Right? I *told* Flynn this was stupid, but he said it was either this or a therapist, and I do *not* trust those people. *They're* the crazy ones! Don't you think so?"

"Therapists?"

"Oh, all of them: psychologists, psychiatrists, counselors. I had a therapist once who told me that my personality type suggested that I would be likely to . . . never mind. Anyway, I said to Flynn, *No therapists*. And he said, *Yes, something.* So: you. You're our 'something.'"

"Flynn—?"

"One of the producers. Well, *the* producer really. He says we have to ensure my mental stability or whatever, which is powerfully unnecessary because, like I keep telling him, it's not a big deal. I don't know what they think is going to happen."

"Calla—" Marilee said, but the girl talked over her.

"I'm a professional, after all. This isn't my first time at the . . . what's the saying? Roller rink? Cat show?"

"Rodeo," Pearl said. "'This isn't my first time at the rodeo.'"

"'Rodeo'? Really? I like 'roller rink' better. Like I was saying, this isn't my first time at the roller rink. This isn't my *fifteenth* time at the roller rink. But they all act like I'm going to—"

"Calla," Marilee said, louder this time, and the girl stopped short.

"I wasn't going to tell her."

"It'll be daily Apricities," Marilee said to Pearl. "As per the contract."

"Would you prefer a particular time of day?" Pearl asked, sneaking a glance at Calla.

"We'll let you know," Marilee said.

"Not too early," Calla put in.

"And is there anything in the results that I'm . . . to look for?"

"We'll let you know," Marilee repeated, and Pearl knew enough to recognize when she was being dismissed.

———

PEARL WAS LED UPSTAIRS and left alone in what were to be her rooms, a guest suite done up in faux-Gothic finery. She circled the suite, fingering the upholstery and fixtures, and confirmed what really she already knew from the lawyers and the car service and the house in the hills. There was serious money here.

Though she'd grown up middle-class, the daughter of an insurance investigator and an optician, Pearl had, in her adult life, learned how to be among the wealthy. She'd had her first practice with Elliot's family and then nearly a decade more with Apricity's clientele. These were, after all, the people who could afford an Apricity reading, and these were the same people who wanted it most desperately, money having already ruled out the most obvious suspects for their unhappiness—toil, illness, and want—the real culprit still a mystery.

This time, however, instead of a self-assured executive or silvered socialite, the possessor of all this largesse was a girl barely out of her teens. Pearl called Rhett to ask if he'd heard of a celebrity named Calla.

"You mean Calla Pax?" Rhett had answered on the first ring. He answered all of Pearl's calls these days, an unspoken agreement to reassure each other (themselves?) that things were better now.

"I don't know. Young. Redheaded. Busty."

"She had blue hair the last thing I saw her in, but that doesn't mean anything, she's always changing it."

"She's an actress then?"

"*Mom.* You didn't even try looking her up, did you?"

"I prefer your synopses," Pearl told him. This was partly true, but it was also true that she had wanted the excuse to call him.

Rhett was away at college, UC Davis, his first year. And Pearl? Pearl was left at home worrying. She worried when Rhett's girlfriend, Saff, left for Northwestern, the status of their relationship unclear to Pearl, something Rhett described as, "We're talking." She pictured Saff meeting some Midwestern RA and breaking Rhett's heart. Pearl worried when Rhett was assigned an international student for his roommate. She pictured Rhett and this foreign boy standing in the middle of an enormous quad, blinking around in bewilderment. She worried about venomous professors and clubby frat boys and the balance on Rhett's meal card. She told herself firmly that she should not worry. Rhett was doing so much better. Pearl was superstitious and reverent, both, of this "doing so much better." She had to keep touching it, as if it were the belly of an idol. She knew she would have to restrain herself soon, before the patina wore away and Rhett started avoiding her calls.

"Look her up while we talk," Rhett instructed. "Last name Pax, P-A-X."

Pearl obeyed, searching the name and projecting the results into the room. And yes, there in a circle around the high bed upon which Pearl sat appeared holographs of the girl who had answered the door. An army of Callas. What Rhett had said about the hair was true: blue hair, blond hair, black hair, pink. But the differences between the girls wasn't what was remarkable. What was remarkable was the similarity.

"What's she so afraid of?" Pearl asked.

"What do you mean?"

"Each one, she's screaming."

And it was true. Each of these rainbow-haired, translucent Callas had her mouth stretched wide.

"Well, that's what she does. She's a screamer."

"Is that a type of music?"

"Mom. She's an actress."

"So . . . for horror movies?"

"Sure. *Skin Scythe*? *Skin Scythe II: Gently He Cuts*?"

"Sounds familiar," Pearl lied.

"But she's gone beyond horror. She's in a bunch of stuff: kidnapped-daughter movies, murdered-girlfriend-revenge movies, monster-destroys-a-city movies, terrorist-destroys-a-city movies, meteor-destroys-a-city movies. She's big in VRs. Oh yeah, and she has a ringtone."

"A what?"

"It's probably already on your screen. What's it called? A standard option."

Pearl tapped *Alerts & Sounds* on her screen. The Callas blinked out, replaced with a list, and there it was between *Beethoven* and *Clavier*, a ringtone called *Calla*.

"I found it," she told Rhett, her voice tinged with awe.

"Play it."

"No, they'll hear."

"Who'll hear?"

"I'm at the office," Pearl lied again. "Besides, I think I can guess what it sounds like."

"Screaming, yeah."

"So in these movies and games and things she just . . . screams?"

"I mean, she acts. She has, like, different characters."

"All in peril."

"Sure, yeah. I mean there has to be a reason for her to you-know."

"A 'screamer.' And she's famous for this?"

"Very. I kind of can't believe you've never heard of her."

"You know I don't watch those sort of movies."

"Mom, it's *every* sort of movie. Oh, and you'll like this, her fans are split into two factions: Calla Lives and Calla Dies."

"Pardon?"

"Calla Lives and Calla Dies." Rhett's voice had taken on an edge of enjoyment, the timeless pleasure of shocking one's mother. "It's like you said, she's always in peril, and so some of her fans like the movies where she *survives* the peril, and others like it better when she's snuffed."

"Snuffed," she repeated.

"Search 'Calla Pax Pie Chart.'"

"Do I want to see this?" But she told her screen to search it anyway, and suddenly a brightly colored wheel spun before her, a pie chart, and staggering within each wedge a tiny cartoon Calla with Xs for eyes. One of the Callas *oof*ed over the cartoon butcher's knife in her chest, another scrabbled at the rope twisting around her neck, a third's head popped off and rolled between its cartoon feet. The chart tracked not just how often Calla's characters lived or died, but when they died, and *how* they died. Pearl located the one wedge of the chart where a Calla stood unanimated and unmolested, her eyes dots instead of Xs. "She only lives twenty percent of the time?"

"Sounds about right. When a new Calla movie comes out, there's an actual betting line. Vegas odds."

"People put money on whether or not her character dies?"

"Yeah. It's a big thing. They lock down the movie sets. Leave pages out of the scripts. Make everyone sign something saying they can be sued if they leak."

"An NDA."

"What?"

"A nondisclosure agreement," Pearl said.

There it was, the reason for all the secrecy. The producers didn't want to squash the buzz around whatever movie they were making now, didn't want to ruin the betting line.

Pearl read from the chart, "She's stabbed thirty-six percent of the time, strangled eighteen percent, shot seven percent. What's 'death by eagle feather'?" That slice showed a flurry of movement, but it was too thin to make out what was happening to cartoon Calla.

"Oh yeah. That's a good one. See, she's camping with her friends on this, like, cliff, but there's an old legend . . . Wait. Why are you asking about Calla Pax? You're not giving her an Apricity, are you?"

"No no no," Pearl said.

"But you said you're at work."

"They're considering her for an endorsement." Pearl sat down on the edge of the bed as she repeated the cover story spelled out in the NDA she'd signed.

"Really? For Apricity? Weird. I mean, you guys are supposed to be all about happiness, right? And Calla Pax is about, like, terror and death and stuff. Unless maybe it's ironic?"

"Yes," Pearl said. She'd gone back to *Alerts & Sounds*, her finger hovering over the button that would play the *Calla* ringtone. She imagined that husky voice launched into a scream. "I think it's meant to be ironic." The wallpaper in the guest room, she noticed, was not actually classic Victorian scrollwork but human mouths open wide.

"I WATCHED SOME of your movies last night," Pearl told Calla. They were faced off on sofas in the sitting room off the foyer at their (not too early) meeting the next morning. The mobile of jelly-fish spun lazily over Calla's head, their tentacles waving; on the mantel behind her, the toy soldiers guarded their nest, rifles leveled at Pearl.

"Really?" The girl beamed. "Which ones?"

"The titles . . . let's see—"

"Were they action movies? Those ones all sound the same. *Final Bullet, Pure Vengeance, Death Drop*."

"*Death Drop*. I watched that one. And the one where you played the diplomat's daughter. In Japan."

"*Western Sunrise, Eastern Blood*."

"And the first *Skin Scythe*."

Calla raised her eyebrows. "Wow. Triple feature. Don't tell me you stayed up all night watching movies."

Pearl had watched not just three but *seven* Calla Pax movies; however, she only watched up until Calla's character died, which was usually no more than thirty minutes in and was often the opening scene. The only film Pearl had seen in its entirety was *Western Sunrise, Eastern Blood*, where Calla suffered kidnapping, beating, branding, and almost rape by the Yakuza before she was rescued by her diplomat father, a man who had to cast aside deeply held pacifist beliefs and embrace a violent form of martial arts in order to save his daughter's virtue and (secondary, it seemed) life. The final scene showed Calla reclaimed in her father's arms, the bodies of her kidnappers piled at their feet, the sun rising behind them, a red orb.

"You were good," Pearl said. "Very affecting."

Pearl wasn't lying. Though the movies themselves, especially watched seven in a row, were preposterous montages of bullet sprays and cleavage, serial killers and cleavage, airborne cars and cleavage, Calla Pax *was* affecting. When she was being chased through the woods (or through the serpentine streets of a foreign city or through the catacombs of an ancient race of human-bat hybrids), your breath caught in your throat. When she was finally cornered, you gripped the blankets. When she died, your hands flew to your mouth. When she screamed, that famous Calla Pax scream, it was your own release you felt.

"I try to make the characters real for me, so they'll be real for you," Calla said demurely. After having memorized pages from the Apricity training manual, Pearl knew a practiced response when she heard one.

"How old were you when you made *Skin Scythe?*"

Calla's eyes flicked up. "Pearl! You never ask an actress her age!"

"I'm sorry. I—"

Calla grinned. "I'm *kidding*. I was fourteen. Practically a fetus."

"And such an adult film."

In *Skin Scythe*, Calla played the plucky little sister whose skin the killer peeled off in one long, thin strip, hanging it from the tree branches outside the hero's bedroom window. There had been a lot of screaming in that one. It was, unluckily, the last movie Pearl had watched before going to bed. She had the lurking feeling that her sleep had been filled with nightmares, though she couldn't remember a one.

"Oh, it was boring really," Calla said. "*Hours* in the makeup chair. But not as bad as *SS2*. In that one I'm skinless the whole time." She pointed at Pearl and started giggling. "Your face!"

Pearl forced a smile, hoping to dispel whatever expression of shock or disgust had inspired Calla's laughter. "It's just . . . who thinks of these things?"

Calla leaned forward. "Middle-aged men with tinted screen specs and superhero T-shirts."

When, moments later, he entered the sitting room, Pearl realized that this had been a spot-on description of Flynn the producer.

Flynn perched on the couch's arm, ruffling Calla's hair. "Hi there, superstar. Up with the birds today, I see!"

"Hey, Flynn," Calla said.

Pearl opened her mouth to introduce herself, but Flynn got there first. "I'm Flynn and you're Pearl." He pointed at himself and Pearl in turn. His eyes did a quick scan, at first she thought of her figure, but then she realized he was reading whatever his screen specs were saying about her.

Before Pearl could respond—if a response was even called for after such an introduction—Marilee marched into the room and planted herself in front of Calla. "We said eleven."

"Did we?" Calla sniffed. "I thought ten."

Pearl hadn't seen either of them, or anyone else, since her arrival the previous afternoon. After her call to Rhett, she'd stayed in her guest suite for a couple of hours, unsure if she was welcome to move around the house. When dinnertime came, she'd wandered downstairs and found the first floor empty, though all the lights had been left on. On the kitchen counter she'd discovered a covered tray marked with her name, underneath its lid a salad of strange leaves, cheeses, and fruits, as delicious as anything she'd ever eaten. Also, bread and wine. When she'd finished, Pearl had washed her dinner plate in the sink and taken the remainder of the bottle up to her room, where she'd continued her Calla Pax marathon. During the opening credits of *Death Drop*, Pearl's screen had lit with a request from Marilee for a meeting the next morning at eleven, and then, during *Skin Scythe*'s infamous peeling scene, a second alert from Calla saying that they needed to move the meeting up to ten. When Pearl had come downstairs this morning at half past nine, she'd found Calla already waiting in the front sitting room, a coffee service and basket of muffins set out on the table before her.

"I think you know very well what time we said," Marilee told the girl.

Calla stared back, belligerent in her feigned innocence.

Pearl averted her eyes and busied herself with her Apricity case, taking longer than necessary with the clasps. Flynn, she noticed, feigned nothing, watching the disagreement with open interest.

"We were just talking," Calla finally said. "About my movies. Pearl likes them." Then, as if conceding a point, "Don't worry. I didn't *say* anything."

Pearl was careful to keep her head down, but her thumb slipped and one of the clasps on her bag released with a *click*, loud in the tense room. She might as well have popped her head up and asked, *You didn't say anything about what?*

Pearl straightened, polite smile on her face, Apricity machine in her hands like a silver platter. "Shall we get started?" she said.

"*You and I* will get started," Marilee replied. "*Calla* will join us at eleven. As planned."

Calla glowered at Marilee. She grabbed a muffin from the basket and bit off its top as if this were an act of defiance.

"Come on, darling." Flynn held out a hand to Calla, opening and closing it. "There's some music I need your opinion on."

Calla flicked a blueberry from her muffin onto the coffee table. She rose with a deep sigh, dragging her feet after him. However, the temper tantrum didn't last even the length of the room, Calla saying brightly, "You definitely need my help. Your taste is terrible. Remember last week when I caught you singing along to . . ."

"Usually it's all I can do to get her up before noon, and today she's downstairs making breakfast." Marilee took Calla's vacated seat and leveled her scowl at Pearl. "She told you an earlier meeting time, didn't she?"

"We really were talking about her movies," Pearl said, adding, "She seems a little lonely."

Marilee blinked. "Yes. Well. Great artists are."

Great artists? Fortunately, Pearl caught the smile before it rose to her lips. There was something in how Marilee had said it—*great artists*—that told Pearl she'd meant it, that Calla was one of those. One of the greats.

"You talked about her movies," Marilee repeated.

"That's all."

"What did she say about them?"

"Not much. That the makeup process for *Skin Scythe* was time-consuming."

"Yes. She complained about it bitterly for the entire shoot. What else?"

"You and Flynn came in just then. But, Marilee, I want you to know that my discretion extends beyond the Apricity results. Even without the NDA, I wouldn't reveal anything that"—Pearl gestured meaninglessly—"happened here."

Marilee watched Pearl for a long unsettling moment. "Calla's current project is confidential."

"I understand. I won't tell anyone about it."

"Yes, because you won't *know* about it."

Pearl dropped her eyes. "My son explained to me about the betting."

"Betting?"

"The Vegas odds. Calla Lives or Calla Dies."

Marilee dismissed this with a hand. "That's not a concern. That's not . . . anything. The current project is confidential for other reasons. It's a licensing issue, actually. Patents and certain approvals."

"For a horror movie?"

Marilee stared at her. "It's millions upon millions. Of dollars."

"Oh."

"I tell you this so that you understand what's at stake. Financially. Legally. Calla doesn't understand—rather, she *won't* understand. She likes to play willfully ignorant, which means she won't be as discreet as she should be. She signed an NDA too, you know. You can help her avoid breaching it and save her, and me, the trouble of a lawsuit."

"Of course. But . . . how?"

"By not asking her questions, by meeting at the times *I* specify, by doing your job and nothing more. If you review the agreement *you* signed, you'll understand why this is to your benefit as well."

Pearl didn't need to reread the nondisclosure agreement; the repercussions for any leaked information were severe enough that she remembered them quite well.

"I'll administer her contentment reports," she told Marilee. "Nothing more."

"And you'll share the results with me."

"All right. And Calla?"

"No. Not Calla."

"If she asks?"

"Become . . . imaginative."

"Can't I just tell her that I can't tell her?"

"You can try that." Marilee tilted her head, waiting for Pearl to arrive at the obvious conclusion: *But it won't work.*

"Shall I give you a report if—?"

"Daily. You'll give me daily reports."

"Like I told Calla, her contentment report is unlikely to change over such a short period of time."

"Yes, yes, like you told Calla and like the people at your company told me. I understand. All the same, a daily test for Calla. A daily report to me, even if you are telling me the same thing over and over again. I promise I won't be bored." She pressed her lips together, a stand-in for a smile.

"Is there something you'd like me to look for?"

"Any signs of unrest."

"You mean psychological issues? Anxiety? Depression?"

Marilee frowned. "We don't use those words. *Tabloids* use those words."

And doctors, Pearl thought, but she echoed, "Signs of unrest. Okay. Sure."

"She thinks I bully her, but she doesn't understand." Marilee reached forward and collected Calla's abandoned blueberry from the coffee table, popping it into her mouth. "This is how I protect her."

THE NEXT THREE DAYS followed the same pattern. Pearl woke early and took her breakfast tray (delivered by a posh catering service, she discovered on day two) to the garden out back and ate on the bench near the koi pond, attended by lacy trees, no neighbors in view. Marilee had told Pearl that she had the run of the first floor, but when on the second floor to keep to her guest suite. *And stay away from the east wing!* Pearl longed to joke with Rhett, but the nondisclosure agreement meant him, too. The rest of the morning Pearl spent catching up on paperwork that had been languishing on her screen for months. Otherwise, she was cooling her heels until eleven, when she met with Calla to run her daily contentment plan.

At these meetings, Calla was as loquacious as ever, though Marilee had surely had a talk with her, too, because the girl didn't again attempt to tell Pearl about any of her movies, certainly not the current one. Even if she had tried, Marilee was always nearby, in and out of the room on some task or another. Calla didn't even ask what was on her contentment reports. The answer would have been nothing, or at least nothing alarming. In fact, as contentment plans went, the list was charmingly straightforward: *Eat ice cream, take nature walks, adopt a dog.* As Pearl had predicted, the plan didn't change. There were no "signs of unrest." In fact, it was one of the least controversial contentment plans Pearl had ever seen.

Each noon, a town car came to pick up Calla and Marilee and take them to, Pearl assumed, the movie set. This left Pearl free for the rest of the day, free but restricted to the house and the garden. The first couple of days, she tried to scare up more work, but after spending two hours needlessly reformatting an Apricity intake form, she admitted that her time would be better spent in the garden rereading *Jane Eyre*. She wished she'd brought the model she was working on, a western bristlebird (*Dasyornis longirostris*), mud colored but for iridescent shimmers on the tips of its wings and tail.

No one came home for dinner, unless you counted the catering service with Pearl's tray. Pearl spent the evenings in her guest suite working her way through the Calla Pax oeuvre. Sometime after midnight, Pearl would hear Calla return, Marilee's voice on the stairs, shepherding the girl to bed. Sometime after that, Pearl would fall into a deep cottony sleep.

It was late in the third night that Pearl half woke to what sounded like Calla screaming. She thought it was her own memory of one of the movies and fell back asleep. In the morning, she remembered and wasn't so certain.

"Did you notice? We're both named after objects," Calla said at their next meeting, the Apricity swab still tucked in the pouch of her cheek. The girl looked tired, Pearl decided, a sallow tone under the cover of her makeup.

"Are we?" Pearl said.

"*Calla Pax*. Think about it." She handed Pearl the swab.

"'Peace lily'?"

"Well, technically, 'lily peace.' So *peace lily* backward. It's not my actual name anyway. I mean it is now. Marilee and I made it up."

"What's your real name?" Pearl asked.

"I don't even remember anymore!" the girl said, her eyes sparkling. And of course this couldn't be true, though it was, Pearl thought, a rather sad sort of joke.

"You know what?" Calla said. "I don't even like lilies. Peace is okay, as far as it goes. How about you? Do you like pearls?"

Pearl smiled. "Not really."

"When you told me your name, the first thing I did was check to see if you were wearing any. Pearls, that is." She leaned forward and whispered, "I was glad you weren't. Can you imagine if you wore, like, a pearl choker and earrings? Or strands and strands of those long pearl necklaces? Like: *Hi, I'm Pearl!*"

Pearl laughed.

Calla sat back in her chair. "You can't get too into it."

"Into what?"

"What they call you."

Pearl glanced at the hallway, where Marilee had passed by moments before.

"Calla," she said quietly, "are you all right?"

"Who? Me?" The girl gave a smile as loud, in its way, as her scream. "Of course I'm all right! What else would I be?"

PEARL WOKE AGAIN TO SCREAMING that night, woke entirely, and knew this time that it wasn't a movie. She rose and hurried down the hall, letting the screams guide her until she arrived at the door from behind which the noise issued. The screams continued, punctuated only by the breaths that fueled them. They didn't stop even after Pearl knocked. Marilee's warning to keep to her own room entered Pearl's mind briefly as she opened the door.

At first, she thought Calla was awake, for the girl was sitting up in bed with her eyes and mouth opened wide. But she didn't turn to look at Pearl, couldn't rightly be said to be looking at anything. Asleep still. Pearl knew you weren't supposed to wake a sleepwalker, though she couldn't remember if this bit of wisdom had an actual scientific basis. Besides, she could hardly let the girl go on screaming. Pearl went to the bed—a monstrosity set in the very middle of the room—gripped Calla's shoulder, and shook it.

The shaking wasn't necessary. The moment Pearl's hand made contact, Calla's mouth closed, cutting off mid-scream, and her eyes focused. She blinked up at Pearl, then murmured her name, and Pearl felt a swell of protectiveness, tender and fierce. Where were the girl's parents in all this? Did she have even a friend? Or was it just her, Marilee, and producers like Flynn?

"You were having a nightmare," Pearl said.

"Oh." The girl swallowed, rubbed her eyes with a fist like a child. "Was I screaming?"

Pearl wasn't going to mention this, but what else would explain her presence in the bedroom? She nodded.

Calla's mouth twisted to the side. "Marilee would call it rehearsing."

"That's awful," Pearl said despite herself.

"I'm just kidding. Please don't tell Marilee. About the nightmares. She'll start *sleeping* here."

"Is it . . . the movie you're making?"

Calla's brow wrinkled, then cleared. "I'm not supposed to talk about that."

"Right. Of course." Pearl bit her lip, aware that she was doing the opposite of what she'd promised Marilee, persuading instead of dissuading Calla to confide in her.

After a pause, Calla said, "You could sit down."

Pearl was still hovering. Calla shifted over and Pearl sat on the edge of the bed. The sheets were warm and smelled slightly metallic. *Ozone.* The word rose in her mind. It was the smell that came before a lightning storm. They didn't have those in San Francisco, lightning storms. In fact, Pearl realized, she hadn't seen a lightning storm since childhood, though she still remembered the smell.

"What are you afraid of?" the girl said suddenly.

"You mean now? Or in general?"

"You're afraid of something right now?"

"No."

"I mean, you know, your *fears.* Yeah, in general. I know it's a rude question." Calla lowered her chin. "Will you tell me anyway?"

"All right. I'm afraid of suffocating. And of snakes. I've been afraid of those since I was young."

"What else?"

"My son." Pearl hadn't planned on saying it, but out it came. "I don't mean I'm afraid *of* him. *For* him. I'm afraid *for* him."

"Why?"

"Because he was sick for a long time." Pearl took a breath, forced a smile. "But he's better now."

"You're afraid he'll get sick again?" Calla peered at her.

"Of course. And"—Pearl paused, then decided to go on with it—"I'm afraid of what happens now."

"To him?"

"And to me."

"Now that you don't have to take care of him anymore," Calla said, and Pearl looked over, surprised at the girl's insight.

Calla sat up on her knees. "Do you want to know what I'm afraid of?"

Pearl nodded.

"The ocean. Not of sharks or drowning, but just the ocean. Being in the middle of it. It's a type of agoraphobia. And I'm afraid of being operated on and the anesthesia wears off, but just part of it so that I can feel everything but I can't tell the surgeons that I'm awake. And I'm afraid of spiders and cockroaches and centipedes. And being buried alive. Being buried alive *with* spiders and cockroaches and centipedes. They say you're either afraid of animals with lots of legs or afraid of animals with no legs. You and I are opposites on that. It's an evolutionary fear. But really most fears are. They activate the amygdala, which is like the brain we had before we grew bigger brains."

"You're an expert on fear. But then I guess you would be."

Calla sank down in the bed, pulling the sheet up to her chin. "Doesn't keep me from being afraid, though." She yawned. "I'm going to try to sleep."

Pearl stood. She paused at the door. "No more nightmares."

Calla snorted. "A girl can dream."

MARILEE SAT IN ON THE ENTIRETY of the next morning's Apricity session. Neither Calla nor Pearl mentioned the night before. Despite Pearl's conviction that it wouldn't change, Calla's contentment plan now had a new item on it, the unambiguous command *Sleep*. Pearl showed it to Marilee while the girl was upstairs getting ready for the town car. Pearl did not, because she had promised Calla she wouldn't, mention the nightmares.

"You said for me to alert you—"

"It's her work schedule, that's all," Marilee said brusquely. "It's unavoidable but, fortunately, temporary."

"When a contentment plan changes, well, it doesn't happen often, so when it does, it reflects a substantial change in well-being."

Pearl paused, but Marilee didn't reply.

Pearl forged on. "Do you think it might be the film she's making? I mean the content? That it might be troubling her sleep?"

"Calla has been doing this from a young age."

"Exactly," Pearl said. The look Marilee gave her prompted an immediate, "I'm sorry." Though she wasn't, Pearl thought a few minutes later as the sound of the town car faded down the street. She really wasn't sorry at all.

Pearl called Rhett for the third time in as many days. She couldn't remember what they talked about, nothing forbidden. "Mom," he said at the end of the call, "are you sure you're okay?"

PEARL STAYED UP AS LATE as she could manage, but there were no screams that night, and after she fell asleep, no screams woke her. Perhaps Calla had forced herself to stay awake, too. At their session the next day, it certainly looked it. Her eyes were sunken and shadowed, her hair unwashed and unbrushed, and although she kept up her usual stream of chatter, she didn't seem to notice that she reran the same topics, and even the same sentences, over again.

That afternoon, Pearl got out her screen and called up the pie chart once more, watching the vivid wheel of cartoon Callas gasp, stagger, and fall over again and again. When she was Calla's age, she and Elliot were newly married and had just moved to the city; she was pregnant with Rhett. Pearl had taken a job as a night secretary for a broker who traded in foreign markets. Her boss's schedule meant that she had to walk five blocks through their run-down neighborhood in the middle of the night, her pregnant belly held out before her like an offering. It was, in retrospect, a shockingly foolish thing to do. One night a man approached her, blocking her path, and she'd thought, *Here it is.* But he hadn't attacked her. No, he'd laid his hands on her belly and slurred, "Bless you," beaming, "bless you." After he'd shambled on, Pearl realized that she hadn't been afraid, not even for a moment. How young she'd been! How fierce! And, she could see it now, how fragile that ferocity!

Pearl left a note for the caterers underneath the lid of her lunch tray. And that night, after Marilee left, Pearl knocked on Calla's bedroom door with the carton of cherry ice cream the catering service had brought her. Two spoons.

"I'm worried about dripping on your bedsheets," Pearl said, though they were already deep into the carton. "I just noticed this room is entirely white."

"It's a replica of the one from *Skin Scythe*."

"Oh, Calla."

"Bedrooms are always white in horror movies. For the blood."

"No wonder you're having nightmares."

Calla frowned. "That's got nothing to do with it."

"It must be a very scary movie, the one you're shooting. For them to have hired me, I mean."

The girl shrugged. "Flynn and Marilee are just overprotective." Her voice had grown aware, if not wary. Of course she'd have experience with people angling for something, would know the sound of a hidden motive.

"I thought you might be interested in hearing what's on your contentment plan," Pearl tried.

Calla put down her spoon. "You're not supposed to tell me that."

"I know. But I think I should anyway. It says you should sleep, Calla. Sleep. And now I think you should tell me about the movie you're making. I think it's bad for you and—"

"I'm fine!"

"—and that it would help to tell someone about it."

They stared at each other, the girl's chin set.

"When I first got here, I had the feeling that maybe you wanted to tell me."

"Look, it's not like I do everything Marilee says."

"Okay then."

"It's just if I tell you, she'll *know*. She'll fire you. She said so on the first morning after I changed the meeting time. And I don't want you to go. Not until . . . not until we're done shooting my scenes. Or I really won't be able to sleep. Okay? Okay, Pearl?" She reached out and laid her hands over Pearl's, her enormous eyes gathering up what little light there was in the room, shining with it.

"Okay," Pearl relented.

"So can we talk about something else?"

"Yes, okay."

They ate ice cream in silence.

"I could . . ." Calla paused. "I could tell you about my nightmare. Marilee didn't say I couldn't talk about that."

"Tell me."

Calla tilted her head. "I dream I'm in an experiment."

"Like a scientific experiment?"

"Yeah. In a lab. And all those things I told you I was scared of—the centipedes, the ocean, and all that—the scientist is doing them to me."

"And you scream," Pearl said.

"That's *why* he's doing it. That's the experiment. To make me scream." The girl spoke deliberately, her eyes fixed on Pearl.

"Calla? Is the scientist in the dream Flynn?"

The girl's mouth quirked.

"What?" Pearl said.

"Just, that's a little obvious, don't you think?"

AFTER RETURNING THE EMPTY CARTON and spoons to the kitchen, Pearl stood in front of the rack of keys next to the garage door. She knew the icons on the key fobs, had matched them to the actual cars on the other side of the wall. Pearl thought about what would happen a week from now, once this job was over. She would return to the city, to her apartment. Her empty apartment. Rhett was gone. Elliot was long gone. The last man she'd dated, David, had removed himself from her life perfunctorily, efficiently, like unplugging an appliance from the wall. Pearl couldn't blame him. Things had been terrible with Rhett. Pearl had been run through with fear, cantilevered like one of her models. But with fear came certainty. Fear winnowed down your options, gave you a clear course forward. Pearl had known what she had to do: save her son. She'd stood over his bed every night, just like she stood over Calla's.

With a thought, Pearl took a key from the rack and slipped it into the pocket of her robe.

THE ENTIRE AFTERNOON was like a sequence from a Calla Pax movie. Pearl borrowed (stole) one of the cars from the garage and, after her daily meeting with Calla, used it to tail the town car down through the hills, over to the 101, and to an office building a few blocks away from the Sonoma County Airport. She parked across the street and watched Calla and Marilee enter the building, watched until the town car drove away. Pearl looked up the address on her screen and learned that the building was empty space, typically rented out to shipping firms. A filming location was her first thought. Yet there were only a few cars in the lot and no sign of equipment or crew. She waited another hour, witnessing no other comings or goings, before crossing the street and entering the building herself.

The building was—and this stood to reason—as empty as the parking lot. The front desk was unmanned, the lobby vacant. The mounted directory was the old-fashioned kind with the stick-on letters, but they were all lying in a heap at the bottom of the glass case. Pearl didn't need their assistance anyway, because as she stood there wondering which way to go, the lobby began to ring with Calla's screams.

Moving toward the sound, Pearl was struck with a sense of déjà vu, but then who wouldn't be, running down a long unfamiliar hallway, featureless but for its doors, the sound of screaming in the distance? Everyone had had some version of this same nightmare.

The door, when Pearl reached it, wasn't even closed all the way, much less locked. Pearl slammed it open with her forward momentum and took two tripping steps into the room. She found herself in an office space, the cubicles pushed aside in a jumbled puzzle on the far wall. All the familiar faces were there. Flynn the producer stood in front of a large screen projection cast by one of the two strangers who flanked him. He'd turned at her entrance, but the tint of his specs hid his eyes, casting back two small slippery reflections of herself. Marilee sat a few feet away in an office chair, leveling Pearl with her most withering look. The screams still rang around them, preserving the moment and pushing it forward into the next moment.

Calla.

Calla lay in the center of the room, on her back in a glass tank. *A glass coffin*, Pearl's mind amended. The girl was a source not just of sound but also motion, her hands brushing frantically over her own face and body, scrabbling at the glass walls, dark flecks flying from her fingertips. She was, Pearl realized, covered in bugs. Just then Calla turned. Her screams stopped for a single moment of silence as she caught sight of Pearl through the glass. Their eyes met. Then the screams started again, becoming Pearl's name.

Pearl scanned the room again—Marilee rising from her chair, Flynn taking a step toward the door, the young man standing by Calla's tank with a Styrofoam cooler—and found that she didn't understand.

"Where are the cameras?" she said.

No one answered her.

Pearl started forward, evading Flynn, pushing past Marilee (pushing past her *hard* because the woman tried to grab her arm), before finally reaching the tank and yanking it open. Then Calla's arms were around her neck and coming with them the beetles and spiders, but Pearl didn't allow herself even a flinch as she lifted the girl out. She set Calla on her feet, helping to brush off the bugs that scattered every which way. The guy with the cooler took an uncertain step in one direction and then another, until Marilee strode forward, raised her foot, and set it down on a centipede with an audible squish.

She sighed. "We'll have to hire an exterminator." Looked at Pearl. "What did you think you were doing?"

"She was terrified!"

"Precisely."

Calla was shaking out the last bugs from her shirt, and now Pearl saw the suction cups affixed to the girl's chest, to her wrists and neck.

"It's not a movie," Pearl said, thinking of what Calla had told her the night before. She surveyed the room, slowly this time. "It's an experiment."

"We'll have some more forms for you to sign." Flynn was at Pearl's shoulder. "Should we just go ahead and bring her on?" he asked Marilee. "I mean . . . !" He gestured around them. "She's seen it. And we could use an admin."

"What is this?" Pearl said.

Marilee sighed again heavily. "*This* is how leaks happen."

"Don't worry. I'll sign your forms."

Flynn gestured in the direction of the two strangers. "Shall we have our scientists explain it?"

Scientists? Pearl thought. They looked like college kids in blue jeans.

"Can . . . can I tell her?" Calla asked softly. She'd stilled mostly, though her fingers still twitched at her sides. She looked between Flynn and Marilee.

Marilee nodded, *Go ahead.*

Calla turned to Pearl, tucking her hair behind her ears. They were large ears, stick-out ears. Endearing ears. The light shone through them, making them glow pink. "It *is* like a movie," Calla began. "Sort of is. You know how when you watch a movie, you kind of feel what the character is feeling? Like how in a horror movie, when they're being chased by the killer, you're scared, too?"

"Sure."

"Well, this is like that but more—" Calla's eyes widened and she jerked backward. She stuck a hand into her hair, rustled it, and a spider fell out. "That's going to be happening all day," she said to Marilee.

"If we hadn't been interrupted—"

"Just let me finish telling her." She turned back to Pearl. "It's like that same feeling but more *direct.* Flynn and them—the scientists—they make me afraid, and then they capture it."

"Capture? Capture what?"

"The racing heart, the tingling palms, the adrenaline—but it's more than that. They capture the feeling, the way I experience the feeling. And then they can, like, *project it* into other people. They can make people feel it." She put two fingers to the center of her chest. "My fear."

Pearl touched Calla's arm. "How?"

"Auditory is the most promising route," one of the scientists said. "And then auditory-visual, of course. We're thinking of laying the tracks over *Skin Scythe.*"

"Or sensors in a VR mask and gloves," the other scientist put in, "lined up with the pulse points."

"Guys, guys!" Flynn put his hands in the air. "Stop talking. She's going to have to sign *all* the forms now."

Pearl put a hand on Calla's other arm so that she was holding the girl out in front of her. "What else did they do to you?"

"You mean besides the bugs?" Calla shrugged and looked at her feet. "The other things I told you. Buried alive. The surgery where the anesthesia wears off."

"They didn't actually—"

"No. Just pretend. That's why it stopped working. Because I knew it was pretend, I stopped being scared. So this week we did the bugs. The ocean is harder to do—sensors, a diving team."

"They're traumatizing you."

"I'm *fine*."

"You're traumatizing her," Pearl said to the others. "You know you are. That's why you hired me, because you know you are."

"You signed a contract—" Flynn began.

"Would you *please* stop talking about paperwork!"

"I'm *fine*," Calla repeated. "I agreed to do it. I *want* to do it."

"But why?"

The girl's gaze was as steely as Marilee's. "Because it's art."

"Calla. This isn't—"

"It *is*. And I'm good at it. Better than anyone else."

"Better at being a victim?"

"But I'm not a victim. I choose it. I'm in control."

"You're screaming in your sleep."

"Well, that's what I do." Calla extracted one of her arms from Pearl's grip and lifted it in front of her face. A tiny bluish cellar bug ran the length of the limb. "I'm a screamer."

Pearl looked over, an appeal to Marilee, but the manager had her chin lifted, a small proud smile, unfamiliar on her face.

Flynn nodded to himself. "We can use *that* in the promo."

Pearl stared between these two professionals, two adults, waiting for one of them to step in and stop this. Then she felt a hand find its way into hers, fingers intertwining. Calla.

"Will you stay and help me?" And she was the girl again, not the actress. "Please, Pearl. Please?"

Pearl watched the cellar bug make it all the way up the girl's arm, disappearing beneath her sleeve. After a moment, she took the girl's hand and helped her back into the tank.

In a week Pearl will return home, the smell of her own apartment, after such a long absence, both foreign and familiar to her. She'll walk from room to empty room, ending up in Rhett's bedroom. The plaid comforter will be pulled up to the pillows, the sheets beneath unrumpled and unslept upon as she sits on the edge of her son's bed. She'll take her screen from its case, tell it what she wants, the list of sounds. With a fingertip she'll press it: Calla. As the girl's screams surround her, filling the room, filling the apartment, Pearl will lift her head, expand her lungs, and open her mouth wide. She won't make a sound.

8

Body Parts

The woman said, "Come here, dear, you have an eyelash on your cheek."

And Calla leaned forward.

Why did you do that? Marilee asked her after. And oh, the reasons Calla could've given! She could've said:

Because Lynley Hart, host of The Gray Hour *and winner of two Peabodys, asked me to.*

Because her white buzz cut is a national symbol of journalistic gravitas.

Because she told me she'd just become a grandmother. And what are you saying, Marilee, that you want me to become the type of person who doesn't trust a grandmother?

Whatever the reason, Calla did lean forward, eyes closed, stage lights hot on her face, expecting to feel Lynley Hart's stately fingers brush her cheek and send the stray lash soaring. Instead, the woman's fingers passed over Calla's cheek and fastened onto an eyelash *still attached* to Calla's eye. With an efficient snap of the wrist,

Lynley plucked the lash free. Calla yelped. Not her million-dollar movie scream, more the squawk of a bird being plucked, which, Calla thought later, was kind of what she was.

When Calla opened her teary eyes, Lynley Hart was already settled back in her chair, looking not the least bit embarrassed by what she'd just done. She produced a small plastic bag from the inside pocket of her blazer and dropped Calla's eyelash into it. They both stared at it, that little curl of Calla.

"You too?" Calla said.

She could hear the distant rumble of Marilee trying to push past the ring of cameras and crew, shouting for Calla's pretend boyfriend/secret bodyguard. The last time Calla had seen him, he was parked at craft services, eating square after tiny square of marbled cheese like Pac-Man eating pellets. Useless. But then, he'd probably say the same of her. After all, she was the one who'd leaned forward with her eyes closed, which was precisely the kind of thing she was not supposed to be doing.

Why did you do it? Marilee asked her after.

And Calla could've answered: *Because she called me* dear.

There in the circle of cameras and lights, Calla said to Lynley, "You don't believe it, right? I mean, you're a rational person, smart."

Lynley Hart's smile was a fixture installed in the brick and mortar of her face. Her lips didn't so much as twitch. And Calla knew right then and there that the woman was going to pretend that she'd done nothing, that what had just happened . . . hadn't.

"Are we still filming?" Calla asked. "Can you at least tell me that?"

"We stopped a few questions back."

Of course they had. Lynley Hart wouldn't want a video to exist of her plucking bits off a young actress. Her gaze rose off Calla and landed on a person at the edge of the circle, a producer or cameraman. Calla wondered if the crew was in on it, if after the shoot, they'd cut Calla's eyelash into millimeters, each one taking a piece for himself. Lynley nodded and over her shoulder a red light appeared, the one Calla hadn't noticed winking out earlier. They were recording again.

"Thank you for coming in today, Calla," Lynley said smoothly. "It's always a treat to have a young artist on the show."

Lynley slid her hand into the empty space between the chairs, the decisive handshake that ended each of her interviews. Marilee had fallen silent. Or maybe they'd carried her gagged and kicking out of the studio. Calla realized her palm was still cupped over her eye. She lowered it cautiously and stared at Lynley's proffered hand, the squared-off tips of her fingernails. Calla felt like she was extending her own hand into a trap. But Lynley Hart already had what she wanted from Calla; there was nothing more she would take. Calla plunged her hand into the circle of light. A dry shake and it was done.

IN THE GREENROOM, Calla and her pretend boyfriend occupied opposite settees and watched Marilee's fingers skitter across her screen, loosing a furious swarm of threats. Marilee wanted to call a doctor to look at Calla's eye, but Dr. Fleming was out of the country, and Marilee said they couldn't trust his fill-in. Calla agreed. A doctor could get anything. A doctor could get a vial of her blood.

"It was just an eyelash," Calla told Marilee. "I'm fine."

"Why on earth did you lean forward?" Marilee asked.

Calla could've answered: *Because over and over I play the part of the damsel, and the one thing about the damsel—her heart is always true.*

"I guess because she asked me to."

Marilee's lips pressed into a line, opening only to mutter, "Because she asked you to."

Calla could've pointed out that she was constantly doing things because Marilee asked her to, but she didn't. After all, Marilee could've called Calla a little twit, and she hadn't. A modicum of restraint keeps the world going round.

Since the doctor couldn't be called in, Marilee insisted on inspecting Calla's eye herself, holding it open and peering in. So close, the pores on Marilee's nose looked like seeds on a berry; her breath was a polite peppermint, sour coffee underneath. She called over Calla's pretend boyfriend for consultation. He leaned in obligingly. Calla could tell it made him nervous to get this close to her. He was only allowed to touch her in front of the cameras or if someone tried to attack her; it was in his contract.

"I can see it," Marilee said. "The spot where the lash used to be. See that little fleck? Right *there*."

"The follicle," the pretend boyfriend provided helpfully.

"What?" Marilee snapped.

"That's what it's called." He disappeared from Calla's view. "The little hole where a hair grows out of your skin. Follicle."

"My eye is drying out," Calla complained, and Marilee finally removed her hand, if begrudgingly.

"I'll see that woman ruined," she said.

"It's just an eyelash. It'll grow back."

Marilee frowned, unconvinced.

"And if it doesn't, I can get an implant, okay?"

Calla's pretend boyfriend snorted.

But as usual, Marilee wasn't in the mood for Calla's jokes. "This is Flynn's fault is what it is."

"Don't blame Flynn," Calla said. "He's a child. A forty-six-year-old child."

"A child who breaks all his toys," she decreed. "I should never have let him talk you into that damn VR job. You know who's into VR *and* mythology? Weirdos, that's who. A special little cross-section of obsessives and escapists."

"But that's *why* we did it," Calla reminded her. "Weirdos decide cult classics."

If you're lucky enough to do a cult classic when you're young, you can draw back upon it when you're old, revive your career when you reach what would otherwise be the gulf between ingénue and ingénue's mother. That was the plan, anyway. Marilee and Calla had discussed it. And that's why Calla had signed on to play the oracle in the VR game *Mount Mythos*. That's why she'd gone to the studio and let them dab her with paint that made her skin look like fissured stone, why she'd hiked up the heavy skirts they'd tied around her waist and climbed onto that plaster plinth. Why she'd recited her lines in stentorian tones:

Travel on a crooked road, your flag held high, and there you shall meet it.

Dip her head once in oil, her feet twice in the ocean, then hold her finger to the flame.

Beware the one who walks footlessly behind you. Beware the tap on your shoulder.

It had been two days reading lines, one day making facial expressions to be grafted onto the game's avatar, and one more day assuming postures for the different story lines the player might activate—head bowed to bestow favor, arms lifted to invoke the gods, shift pulled away to bare one breast, and a graceless topple off the plinth. The part in the game where the Calla-oracle shattered into pebbles was, of course, something the animators added in later, a special effect. A player could take a pebble from the shattered oracle and store it in their inventory. The pebble had magical properties that increased the player's accuracy, fortitude, and luck.

As best as anyone could tell, *this* was where it had started, the rumor that a piece of Calla Pax would improve your lot in life. Maybe it'd begun as a joke or a prank in some fertile little corner of the Internet, but as of that morning, a strand of hair pulled from Calla's head was for sale on the dark web for $3,000, a tampon soaked with her menstrual blood and stolen from her trash for $4,000, a scrap of fabric torn from a sweatshirt Calla was wearing (the event that had prompted the hiring of the pretend boyfriend/secret bodyguard) for $750. Everyone wanted a piece of her, literally.

"Enough!" Marilee said, folding up her screen and whatever message had just surfaced on it. "I'm talking to that woman's producer." She marched from the greenroom, leaving Calla alone with her pretend boyfriend.

They looked at each other. She shrugged. He shrugged back. He'd only been her pretend boyfriend for two weeks; they were practically strangers, even if his hands had been all over her. He picked up a dye wand someone had left, selected a strand of his hair, and began dyeing the tip of it. He hadn't even checked the color cartridge first, Calla noticed. The wand turned out to be loaded with a milky yellow.

"You could pull off blond, if you wanted," Calla said. And he could. He was nothing if not pretty. She hoisted herself to sit on the back of the couch and scanned the room for food.

"They took everything out to the soundstage," her pretend boyfriend said. The blond had crept halfway to his scalp. He put down the wand and extracted a bundle out of his jacket pocket: a napkin wrapped around coins of cheese the same color as his strand of dyed hair. He came over to the couch and offered this bounty.

"Thanks," she said, picking one out. "Need to refuel, you know. Grow that eyelash back."

His smile curled one side of his mouth and a nostril. Pretty with a sneer. Marilee had let Calla pick him. They'd auditioned fifty actors, half guys, half girls, all with martial arts or fight training, all of whom thought they were trying out for a featured stunt role in Calla's next movie. Forty-nine of them still thought that. Calla hadn't chosen this one because of his elbow strikes or *kiai*s, but because of his sneer. She knew a cultivated expression when she saw one, and she could tell that he had practiced the look in the mirror. And if you have to practice a sneer, she'd reasoned, you are not a natural sneerer.

"So you stash cheese in your pocket?" Calla reached for another. "Kind of like a mouse."

She grinned and continued to chew openmouthed, working cheese and saliva into a gluey paste. Sometimes Calla liked to do gross things so that she could see the battle on people's faces between their idea of her and the actual her of her. But Calla's pretend boyfriend didn't seem the least bit bothered by her mastication. He plucked up another piece of cheese and held it between his teeth.

"It's my policy," he said around the cheese, "to always carry a little food on me."

"In case of the apocalypse, huh?"

He opened his mouth; the cheese dropped in.

"The apocalypse or low protein. Good for either."

"I was in a movie about the apocalypse *and* I was in an infomercial about low protein."

"So you know how it is."

"Actually, I've been in five movies about the apocalypse."

"Long apocalypse."

She made a face. "Five *different* apocalypses."

"Like that Robert Frost poem. *Some say the world will end in fire, / Some say in ice.*"

"Some say the world will end in sea monsters. Some say the world will end in ten-foot-tall vampire bats," Calla ad-libbed.

She had been sixteen and not yet famous when she'd made the vampire-bat movie. Back then she used to bribe PAs to tell her what the casting agents said about her after she left the room. Two hundred dollars for the unvarnished truth—that was the deal. For the bat movie, Calla had been up for a supporting role, the lead girl's babbling friend who, at the midpoint, is vivisected in the catacombs.

"They said you weren't buxom enough," the PA had told her when they met in their agreed-upon corner of the parking lot.

"Buxom?" Calla asked. She didn't know the word; she was only sixteen.

"You know. Boobs." The PA arched a brow and indicated her own breasts, battened down in their sports bra. "They said you don't have them."

Calla looked down at her chest.

"Big ones, I mean. They say you have to have big ones for a vivisection. They say that's what the audience wants. To see the tits separate from the girl." The PA chewed the inside of her cheek. "Strangling deaths, too, they said. Got to see them heave." Her hand fidgeted at her side, ready to accept payment. "Hey. They liked your reading, though. 'At least this one can act.' That's what they said."

"Thanks." Calla passed her the bills. "That's, um, helpful."

And it'd turned out to be helpful after all, not the information so much, but Calla's modest décolletage, because instead of the vivisected friend, they'd ended up casting her as the lead. And by the time Calla's breasts had come in two years later (and come in *how*), she was famous enough to be slaughtered in whatever manner she so wished.

"I saw that vampire-bat movie," Calla's pretend boyfriend said. He lowered his voice and recited the tagline, *"Evil echolocates."*

"The director came up with that. He was a real doof. Instead of calling action, he'd shout, 'Batter up!' Get it? *Bat*-ter up!"

"That's not doofy. That's awesome." He retrieved the dye wand, saying over his shoulder, "You were good in it, by the way."

Calla knew the formula for compliments given to one's face: downgrade by one. If someone said you were great in a movie, in truth they thought you were good. If someone said you were good, they thought you were just okay. Calla considered herself immune to criticism by now, but she found herself rankled by this bit of faint praise. Who was this little pretender, this little scrabbler, to deem her just okay?

Which was why Calla said, "So you want to be an actor, huh?"

The question was unkind because you could want to be an actor all you liked, but you weren't an actor, not really, unless a casting agent and producer and director said you could be one.

The pretend boyfriend, however, looked impressed rather than insulted at Calla's comment, or, to put a finer point on it, he looked impressed *at having been* insulted. He opened his mouth and said— but whatever he was going to say was interrupted by the chime of Calla's screen. It took her a minute to find it tucked away in Marilee's bag. When she unfolded it, the face on the screen was a familiar one. Pearl!

Calla moved to answer but then paused, her hand stilled with a thought: What if Pearl wanted to take a piece of her, too? To reach out, fingernails sharpened, scissors hidden in her hand, and—?

No. Pearl was her friend. As if to underscore this, Calla jabbed fiercely at the center of Pearl's forehead, answering the call.

Pearl's eyes focused as Calla's face appeared on her screen—"Calla!"

Her usually tidy short hair was tousled, and her collar was crooked, as if she had been tugging on it. She appeared windblown, windblown with worry.

"Hey, don't look like that!" Calla said. "I'm fine! See?" She swung the screen down, a scan of her intact body, and back up to Pearl's now-startled face.

"Calla. What—?"

"You called about the thing, right? About how I'm like an elephant tusk or a monkey paw or whatever?"

"A rabbit's foot," her pretend boyfriend said from somewhere behind her.

"Like a rabbit's foot," Calla repeated. "You know, some good-luck charm?"

"Well. Actually." Pearl fussed at her collar. "In a way."

"As you can see, I'm totally and completely okay. You know Marilee. She hired muscle. Okay, sometimes the muscle is inattentively eating cheese." Calla cut eyes at her pretend boyfriend. "But the other day this guy on the street was going for my hair and he totally clotheslined him."

"Your hair?" Pearl pinched the bridge of her nose. "Oh, Calla."

"Didn't you hear me? Like flat out on the pavement!"

"I'm so sorry."

"Why are *you* sorry? I know, I know, it's a common expression of sympathy not necessarily an admission of responsi—"

"I'm sorry because it's our fault!" Pearl burst out.

"No, it's not," Calla said immediately, ignoring the hollow in her chest, which was suddenly empty and echoing as the vampire-bat catacombs. Not Pearl. She could trust Pearl. "It's some weird Internet thing."

But Pearl wasn't listening; she was speaking to someone off-screen. "No. I don't think— Fine. Stop. I said fine." She turned back to Calla. "My colleague wants to talk to you. Would that be all right?"

"Maybe I should get Marilee," Calla's pretend boyfriend said. Calla ignored him. She should've known he would have been given such instructions.

"Sure," she said loudly to Pearl. "I'll talk to whoever."

Calla heard the door open and close behind her as her pretend boyfriend scampered off to tattle. On her screen, Pearl disappeared and a hunched man took her place, his chin jutting forward, his shoulders nearly level with his ears. But no, he wasn't hunched after all; he was crouched, like he'd been cornered and was coiled to spring.

"Miss Pax!" he said, coiling tighter. "What an honor."

"Thank you."

"The first time I saw *Skin Scythe*, you know what I did?"

"Um. What?"

"I pointed at the screen"—he pointed at this screen now—"and said, 'Her. Her!'"

Calla glanced over her shoulder, finding herself suddenly hoping that her pretend boyfriend would return with Marilee after all.

"—director of special projects," the crouched man was saying when she turned back. He touched a hand to his chest as if this title was his name. "But you can call me Carter. I work with your Pearl—*our* Pearl—here at Apricity."

"Nice to meet you."

"You too, Miss Pax. You too."

"Um, Pearl just said that—"

"Miss Pax, Miss Pax, Miss Pax! If you, if you could just? If you could indulge me? I have something to tell you. To offer you, really. And if I could get—if you would be kind enough to let me get—through it?"

"Sure," she said. "Shoot."

Carter took the hand from his chest, made it into a gun, and pretend-fired at the screen. (Calla curbed the urge to pretend-die.)

"What I have to offer you," he said, and then paused, "is a job."

"What? At Apricity?"

Carter smiled slowly. "*As* Apricity."

"As?"

"As."

But before he could tell her any more, Marilee had marched into the room and lifted the screen from Calla's hands, Carter and his baffling offer sailing high above her head and out of her reach.

PEARL AND THIS CARTER would go through appropriate channels, Marilee told Calla after confiscating her screen. She was pissed that Pearl had contacted Calla *sneakily*, a word she kept using. Marilee had set up a meeting at Apricity the next day, for herself and Calla's agent. Calla would not be in attendance, a punishment for Pearl's presumption in calling Calla directly.

"And no chatting with Pearl in the meantime," Marilee warned.

They were in the elevator at the *Gray Hour* parking garage. Calla's pretend boyfriend stood at the buttons, acting like he wasn't listening.

"Don't blame Pearl," Calla told Marilee. Calla hadn't told Marilee what Pearl had said, about being responsible for the people trying to steal bits of her.

"Don't blame Flynn. Don't blame Pearl. Really, Calla, whom would you like me to blame for this predicament? You? Me? I suppose me."

Calla shook her head. "Not you. No one. Fate."

Marilee tsked. "You don't believe in fate."

And it was true; Calla didn't believe in fate. She knew celebrities who did, like some god had bent over their crib and made a chalky mark of future fame on their infant forehead. Calla had no such illusions. She believed in determination to the point of stupidity: lying in the pool of fake blood until it dried and stuck to your skin, practicing death faces in the mirror until you couldn't look at your reflection for days, paying PAs for insults that no one would deliver to your face. Calla also believed in luck, but luck writ small. Not the cascade of a slot machine, but a wink, a tip of the hand, a faint glimmer in the air. Like the luck of your breasts developing late, which landed you the lead role instead of the vivisected best friend.

The elevator dinged and the doors slid open.

"Photographers," the pretend boyfriend said, jerking his chin at the far end of the garage, where their car was parked.

Marilee swore, a filthy Shakespearean curse.

"No, wait." She consulted her screen. "I arranged these ones. You two"—she pointed between Calla and the pretend boyfriend—"get ready."

"How much?" the pretend boyfriend asked.

"Well . . . It's midafternoon." Marilee hemmed. "Let's say a four. Sweet, no groping."

"How's your breath?" Calla asked him.

"Cheese scented," he replied.

They exited the elevator, Calla's pretend boyfriend sliding up next to her, his hand in hers. The photographers caught sight of them, with flashes of light like dry summer lightning and shouts of "Here! Here! Calla! Look here!" But Calla didn't look at any of them, because her pretend boyfriend was already inches away, tipping up her chin and touching her cheek, and she hadn't even had to tell him to wear his sneer when he was about to kiss her, that it would photograph as intensity; he was already sneering. And behind the sneer, his breath was, as he'd said, of cheese, damp and custardy. It wasn't exactly pleasant and it certainly wasn't sexy, but Calla liked it somehow anyway. They opened their mouths for just a moment, and his hand wandered into her hair. They parted. There. That was a four.

As she walked past the photographers, Calla's fear unfolded like a sheet shaken out and lifted so that it caught the air. She clapped on a smile and searched out of the corners of her eyes for the hand that would snake out and grab her, the gleam of a knife, the first foot-shuffling of a stampede. She could feel the muscles in her pretend boyfriend's arm tense around her, ready for the counterstrike. As soon as they'd made it behind the car's tinted windows, Calla's pretend boyfriend retracted his arm from around her shoulders and scooted away. Calla slid down in her seat, hugging herself. Safe. It took her a moment to realize that, in her fear, she had forgotten to remove the smile from her face.

THE MEETING WITH APRICITY was scheduled in the morning, which left Calla an entire night to stalk the rooms of her house. She was restless, imagining the role she might inhabit. She pictured her own body, but dim-eyed and slack-jawed, pictured herself stepping inside it like a suit, bringing it to life and motion. *As Apricity*, Pearl's colleague had said. He probably meant a spokesperson. Calla was already the face of a perfume, a screen, a clothing line, and a children's charity.

As Apricity, Calla thought to herself as she wandered past her pretend boyfriend, who was sprawled on the couch napping.

As Apricity, she thought as she climbed the stairs to the bathroom, fumbling around in the vanity until she found the polish wand and nail clippers. She sat on the edge of the tub, using the wand to drain the color from her nails and then the clippers to cut them, letting the cloudy slivers of fingernail fall to the floor. She winced as she cut her thumbnail too low, the skin beneath a newborn pink. She swept the cuttings into her hand, thought, *A small fortune*, and sprinkled them in the trash under the sink.

Then she went back downstairs and touched her pretend boyfriend on his arm, which was dangling off the side of the couch. He opened one eye immediately, like an owl or a cat. So her pretend boyfriend had been pretend sleeping. He rose and followed her to her bedroom, though she hadn't said, *Come with me*, or so much as smiled. They stopped in the middle of her room and stood awkwardly facing each other.

"Like a six?" He raised his eyebrows. "A seven?"

She winced. "This isn't part of your contract."

"Hey. I was only kidding."

He took a step forward and, after a pause, touched her wincing cheek.

The sex was strange. Calla couldn't help but think that he was caressing her body parts in order, top to tail, like he had some sort of checklist in his head. And his sneer that she had so liked before? Now she wanted it gone. The sneer finally melted away in the seconds before he came, but his face without it felt like something she didn't have the right to see, so she closed her eyes, feigning ecstasy.

After, he stood naked at the end of her bed, his skin flushed with pleasure or embarrassment, Calla couldn't think about which. He balled his underwear in his hand.

"That was nice," Calla said, silently applying the equation of downgrade by one. Amazingly her pretend boyfriend seemed to accept this faint praise with a bashful smile. Then he shimmied into his jeans and returned to his couch.

Calla was certain she would have nightmares, maybe of leathery bat wings or a shelf with her body parts stored in a row of bottles. But she fell asleep and, a moment later it seemed, opened her eyes to morning.

THE APRICITY OFFICE was deep in the business district, where the height of the buildings made the midmorning shadows spiky. Calla watched the shadows stretch from inside the car, their edges sharpening by the minute. She watched the crowds of people walking along the grids of sidewalk like some elaborately coded machine. She turned sideways in her seat and put her feet against the car door, wedging her heels on the armrest. Calla could come on the ride to the meeting—Marilee had finally agreed to this much in the face of Calla's stubborn pleas—but she would stay in the car. Calla and her pretend boyfriend had been waiting curbside for over an hour.

Pretend Boyfriend passed the time by constantly changing the radio station; a singer couldn't finish a line without being interrupted by the flick of his wrist. Now that they were alone, Calla wondered if he would bring up the night before. She'd expected him to try to sneak things today: a kiss, a caress, even a shared look. But he'd stayed at the periphery, as usual, dutifully extending his arm around her shoulders in public, retracting it once the car doors slammed closed. Calla wasn't sure if she was relieved or disappointed by his inattention.

Mostly she was frustrated. Marilee and Pearl and everyone else were up there in that office building making decisions about her like she was some kind of product, some—Calla reached for the word—commodity. She kicked her feet against the door in a soft one-two, a tiny temper tantrum. Then she realized she didn't need to kick the door; she could simply open it if she wanted to. She sat up and did so.

Her pretend boyfriend whipped around. "What are you doing?"

"Going to the meeting."

She swung the door open the rest of the way and, despite his protests, launched herself out of the car. She landed on the pavement, nearly colliding with a passing bike messenger.

"Shit!" The messenger skidded to a stop. She was scabbed up and tatted up, so much so that it was hard to tell one from the other. "Don't you even look when—?" She caught sight of Calla's face. "You're Calla Pax."

Calla thought she should tell her pretend boyfriend that this was what being famous was like, people repeatedly telling you that you're yourself.

Just then, behind the bike messenger, Pearl exited the Apricity building and headed down the sidewalk at a fast clip.

"Pearl!" Calla called. No luck. "Pearl!"

Meanwhile, the messenger was fumbling for her screen. Calla darted around her and jogged down the sidewalk in the direction

Pearl had gone. She could see Pearl just ahead now, the swing of her green coat. She pushed rudely past a man in screen specs— "Hey!" he said—leapt over a small dog, grabbed Pearl's arm, and spun her around.

Pearl stared at her, then past her. Calla looked back, too. Her pretend boyfriend and the bike messenger were following after. The bike messenger had her screen held out in front of her, filming Calla.

"Can we talk?" Calla said.

Pearl, ever efficient, nodded once and scanned the area. "Let's—" She gestured toward a privacy kiosk at the end of the block.

They tacked toward it, the lunch crowd slowing them down, the pretend boyfriend and bike messenger still in pursuit. When they reached the kiosk, Pearl took her screen from her pocket. A few taps on it and the door swung open.

"What about them?" Pearl asked.

The other two had caught up.

"Him, not her," Calla said, grabbing her pretend boyfriend by the sleeve.

The three of them crowded into the kiosk. The bike messenger didn't try to follow them, just kept filming through the transparent kiosk door as it slid closed, her expression benignly startled. Luckily, the kiosk was free of litter and urine stink. The unlock price was high enough that the kiosks were usually pretty clean, but sometimes post-happy-hour business types considered it worth the cost to stumble in for a pee.

"Japanese garden, Edo period," Calla said.

The kiosk walls stayed clear; some of the passersby were now glancing curiously at the filming bike messenger.

"It's an older model." Pearl was checking her screen. "Basic options."

"Nighttime. Beach. Winter," the pretend boyfriend said.

The kiosk walls went dark, blocking out the messenger and the street. Behind them a black ocean turned, battering itself on the bone-white sand that sifted beneath their feet. Above them, a night sky pricked with stars. The regular pattern of the stars had been strategically scratched out, creating eyes and a mouth: a smiley face. Calla smiled back at the face in the sky.

"Was that woman chasing you?" Pearl asked.

"Kind of. Maybe. Yeah."

Pearl crossed her arms and rubbed her hands along them like she could feel the wintry temperature of the beach, though the kiosk was, if anything, overly warm. "Should we call Marilee?"

"No," Calla said. "You should tell me what's going on in the meeting."

Calla's pretend boyfriend began to say something. Calla touched his wrist to signal for him to be quiet, but he must've mistaken her intent because he took her hand in his. To Calla's surprise, she let him.

"'*As* Apricity,'" Calla said, the words that had been on a loop in her mind. "That Carter guy said they wanted to hire me 'as Apricity.' What does he mean?"

Pearl sighed. "He wants your voice. He thinks clients will like it better if the machine speaks to them."

"In *my* voice?"

"They'd record you saying a list of syllables, phonemes, common words, and then they have software that puts it all together so that it sounds like you're talking. Or rather, that the machine is talking as you. So"—Pearl gestured, palms up—"that's the job."

Calla tried to imagine it, those little silver boxes making their pronouncements in her voice. She opened her mouth, closed it, suddenly afraid to make a sound.

"There's something else," Calla made herself say. "Yesterday you said those people—" She indicated the patch of starry sky that used to be the kiosk door.

"Were my fault," Pearl interrupted. She bit her lip and nodded. "They are. It was us. Apricity."

"How?"

"When Carter first had the idea about using your voice, he needed proof people would like it. So I suggested—" Pearl put a thumb to her chest, repeated, "*I* suggested that he float it on the web, in certain forums. He couldn't ask about the idea directly and, well, it got garbled. That Calla Pax would be telling people how to be happy became that Calla Pax could *make* people happy. And it somehow—*somehow*—turned into this."

"But you don't know for sure that—" Calla began.

"I do, though. I went back and tracked what Carter posted, where it went. It was us. Me. And I'm so, so sorry."

"You don't have to be *sorry.*"

"Of course I'm sorry. I don't want you to be hurt. I was so angry at Marilee when I found you in that tank, that *coffin*, covered in bugs. And now I've done it to you myself." She threw her hands in the air. "Now we're in this goddamn clear coffin together."

She'd raised her voice, and when she said the word *clear*, the kiosk heard it as a command. The stars fell away. The ocean turned in on itself once more and rolled up into the horizon. The walls became transparent again, revealing the city street outside. Except now you couldn't see the city street or the city sidewalk or the city anything. All you could see were the people crowding around the kiosk.

The bike messenger was still outside the kiosk door, still filming. She must have simul-streamed on her feed or texted other bike messengers, or maybe she didn't do any of those things and word had spread however word spreads. Whatever the cause, there were now dozens of people out there, maybe a hundred. The entire kiosk was surrounded. And when the walls went clear, the crowd could see Calla.

They didn't scream or stampede. They didn't try to heave the kiosk on its side. They simply shifted, minutely and mightily. They shifted closer until their hands were pressed against the kiosk walls, until Calla could see the lines of their palms, a dozen forked roads of fortune.

"What do we do?" her pretend boyfriend said.

Pearl was saying Marilee's name into her screen over and over again. To Calla their panicked voices sounded small and far off, like she'd set down her screen in the middle of a call and begun to walk away.

Pearl had gotten through to Marilee. She was trying to explain the situation, Calla's pretend boyfriend piping up with extra information. And so the two of them were slow to notice when Calla slipped her hand out of her pretend boyfriend's hand and pulled open the kiosk door.

The crowd, however, was waiting for her. When Calla opened the door, there was a soft gasp that sounded strangely like an echo of the kiosk door unsealing itself. The people nearest the door edged back, ceding Calla the space to step out onto the sidewalk. She could feel Pearl and the pretend boyfriend at her back, trying to grab her and pull her in, but the crowd filled in behind them and blocked their grasping hands. Calla took another step forward, and again, the crowd let her make her path. She took another step, and as if she had decreed it, the hands began to pat her gently, so gently, marking out the boundary between her body and empty space.

9

The Furniture Is Familiar

nd so I am back. A year and a hundred years later. My room smells like it belongs in another house, a different family's oils and soaps. Is this how I used to smell? Only the lizardy stink of Lady is familiar. I tap the glass hello. She's in the back behind her branches. At my tap, she jukes her head and keeps me in her peripheral vision.

My bedroom walls are covered with an image of the algae bloom along the coast, fluorescent and scummy. I set them that way months ago, when I was home for winter break. I'd just finished an oceanography class and was all fired up about how we pretend we're not putting poison in our bathwater. The algae walls are ugly, but they're honest. I bet Mom's wanted to reset my walls every day since winter break. Of course, she could've just shut the door to my room, but she wouldn't be able to bring herself to do that. Mom. She'd have to leave the door open at least a crack.

The algae mills on the surface of the water, frilled with tiny bubbles. Being home from college for the summer is like sleeping over at a friend's house you've only ever visited in the afternoon. The furniture is familiar, but the light has gone funny on you.

Mom knocks on the door frame. I wonder how long she's been there watching me, but then what's she going to see? Her standing there, watching me standing here, watching the walls?

"What would you like for dinner?" She smiles bravely. "The cafeteria ladies at your dorm gave me all their best recipes—tuna noodle casserole, chicken Kiev, mystery meat."

The joke is awkward. The topic of food is still awkward, though we both wish it weren't. Which, of course, is what makes it awkward. All that wishing.

"Tuesdays were taco night," I say.

"Taco Tuesdays?"

"The alliteration makes them taste better."

She smiles, for real this time. And okay. I'm glad for it.

"But the lettuce was always wilted," I press on. "Did they teach you how to wilt the lettuce?"

Mom doesn't miss a beat. "They taught me all their tricks."

My screen chitters at me. I don't want to look at it in front of her, but I can't make myself wait. I slide the screen out of my pocket, unfold it, and glance. And yeah, it's from Saff. A picture I can't decipher. A fold of fabric? A burl of wood?

Mom is purposely looking past me while I check my screen, which is a sort of privacy, I guess? "Terrible," she sighs.

It takes me a second to figure out she's talking about the algae bloom. She reaches out and touches the wall, which flickers under her fingers, making it look like the algae is sinking and resurfacing.

It's not good for the wall to touch it like that, but I don't bother telling her. She already knows.

"Scientists engineered a type of eel to eat the algae overgrowth," I say, something I learned in that oceanography class.

"Did it work?"

"Kind of? The eel ate the algae. And then a couple species of fish."

"Poor fish."

"Hey, that's what you get for trusting an eel . . ."

She raises her eyebrows in a question.

"Everyone knows they're slippery," I say. Bah-dum-bum.

Mom smiles again. And again, I'm glad for it. Though mostly I want her to get out of here so I can look at my screen in peace.

SHE FINALLY GOES TO THE STORE. For taco ingredients. When the HMS announces her gone, I take my screen back out and study the picture Saff sent me, projecting it big on the ceiling so that I can try to make out what it is.

I'm pretty sure it's a picture of the opposite side of her elbow. You know, that little crinkly place on the inside of your arm that marks where it bends. It's hard to tell for sure, though, because the picture is taken up close and the lighting is dim and Saff's skin is already dark to begin with, but I think that's what it is. The opposite of Saff's elbow.

And I guess I should add that I only *think* it's Saff who's sending me these pictures. They come in from an unknown number. I got the first one in mid-January, a week after Saff and I decided that since we were at different colleges in different cities living different lives, we probably shouldn't talk or write to each other anymore. We shouldn't talk or write . . . then in came a picture.

The first picture was of somewhere crowded, the angle low to the ground, the blur of legs and shoe leather, everyone walking at a fast clip. A train station, I thought maybe. A few days later my screen lit up with another picture, a few days later another, and so on and et cetera. After a while, I started sending my own pictures back.

I can't ask Saff if the pictures are from her because of our no-talking, no-writing deal. Besides, this summer she's staying in Evanston with her new boyfriend. Or so she told Ellie, who told Josiah, who told me. Maybe Saff's boyfriend is the one who took the picture of her arm.

I snap a shot of the algae on my wall and send it back to the unknown number.

Before I even put my screen down, it chitters again. (My ringtone of choice: deathwatch beetle. Extinct 2029.) This time it's not Saff, but my roommate, Zihao. Well, ex-roommate, technically, since the school year is over and we now inhabit different rooms. Zi is at the airport. He wants me to know that he's tired and that the line for coffee is very long. This is communicated through emojis, Zi's preferred language. He argues that emoji is a more sophisticated form of communication than words alone, but I suspect the real reason is that Zi likes to watch the images wiggle and dance. After all, Zi is always in motion.

If I fall asleep in line for coffee will the people behind pick me up and carry me to the front? he texts. This idea actually requires some language; only half of it is in emoji.

I tell him no, that the people in line will fit a bunch of straws together to make one long straw. They'll put one end in the coffeepot behind the counter and the other in his mouth.

American ingenuity! he texts back. Which is what I told him to say whenever he is confused by something people here are doing.

I smile and toss my screen on the bed. As it lands, it chitters once more, as if in protest.

Zi again: *Golly gosh gee! I hope I have a good flight.*

Zi is fishing. He likes to say that if I teach him how to be American, he'll teach me how to be human.

I roll my eyes and send back, *I hope you have a good flight, Zi.*

MOM HAS, in fact, found a way to wilt the lettuce. I think she might have put it in the oven. I raise my eyebrows at the limp bowl of greens she sets in front of me. Usually Mom won't carry a joke beyond the telling of it, whereas Dad will carry it to the end of funny and sometimes a mile or two beyond. When I say this out loud, Mom looks annoyed.

"I haven't talked to your father in three days," she says stiffly.

"I didn't say he *told* you to wilt the lettuce. I said it was *like* something he'd do."

She busies herself assembling a taco. "He's coming for dinner, by the way."

"This dinner? Tonight?"

"Yes. Why not?"

"Uh, because we're currently eating it."

She shrugs. "I told him seven."

"HMS," I call out, "what time is it?"

"Seven-oh-three post meridiem," the HMS reports.

I give Mom a look, but she doesn't see it because she's focused on her taco. She's practically arranging every individual shred of lettuce and cheese like she's making one of her models. Mom is the same as my bedroom, familiar but cast in a funny light.

"Your dad's less reliable than usual lately. Though," she adds in a murmur, "he *keeps* coming around." She looks at me furtively. When she discovers me watching her, she says, "Sorry. I was thinking out loud."

Which is another way of saying that she forgot I was here. Fair enough. I haven't been here.

"Your father is always welcome to visit," she says.

"Yeah, I know."

"We're still friends."

"Yeah, yeah."

I take a bite of my taco, and I can see her shoulders relax an inch now that I'm eating, like her shoulders are on the same hinge as my jaw. I don't think she even knows she's doing it. And I feel guilty about that, sure, but there's also a little voice inside of me that roars, *Stop caring about me!*

"Did he call you?" she asks. "You know, at school?"

"Every once in a while."

"I didn't tell him to." She takes a bite of her perfect taco. It fissures and falls onto her plate. "I mean, I didn't remind him. If he called, it was because he wanted to."

"So I assumed."

She's fussing at her wrecked taco, moving her hands this way and that, trying to figure out the best approach to the salvage. "Did, um, Val ever call?"

"Did Val call *me*? No."

"I thought she might have."

"Uh, *why*?"

"To see how your first year of college was going." She looks at me meaningfully. "She was your stepmother, after all."

"I guess." But I'd never really thought of Val that way. Even when she came up in a story I was telling someone, I wouldn't refer to her as my stepmother, just *Val*. I'd miss her, sure. But honestly? When Dad told me she'd left, the news was a quick throb and fade, the emotional equivalent of hitting your thumb with a hammer. I guess I never really expected her to stick around.

"She *was* your stepmother," Mom repeats. "She never even told you goodbye."

Mom called every three days while I was at school. *As much as you can stand, as little as she can*, was how Saff summed it up (before Saff and I stopped talking). Zi was delighted by Mom's calls. If she called while I was in the bathroom or down the hall, Zi would answer. Once I came back to the room to find my screen angled on

Zi's desk so that he could show Mom his footwork. His feet squeaked on the flecked tile, the ball bobbing between them, a planet in wild orbit. Mom's face in the screen was a tiny picture of delight. I think she might have even been clapping.

Most kids at school assume Zi is another rich international student whose parents are making him get an American business degree, but really he's here on a soccer scholarship. *Footie money,* as Zi calls it. He's really good. He was recruited and everything. Zi keeps his hair just long enough to make a stubby ponytail so that it won't get in his eyes during a game. His legs are like something someone carved out of wood, an archer's bow or a cello, beautiful in the shape of their function.

"My mom thinks you're a nice boy," I told Zi one time.

"And I think she's a nice mom." We were in our twin dorm beds with the lights out. A moment later, "Did she really say that?"

"Would I lie?"

"Of course. So does she really like me?"

"Sure. Why do you care?"

"Why do I care if your mom likes me?" Zi repeated my question as if the question were, itself, the answer.

Mom finally manages to collect the pieces of her taco and take a bite.

"Did Zi get packed up okay?" she says, mind-reading.

"He's at the airport. In line for coffee."

He's not, though. Not anymore. By now Zi is on his flight, sailing somewhere above us, fidgeting in his seat and annoying the passenger next to him. But I picture him still in line at the coffee kiosk, yawning and shuffling an invisible ball between his feet, taking his screen out to tell me all about it.

MOM WAS RIGHT not to wait on Dad, who misses dinner altogether. In fact, I'm in my room, toothbrushed and pajamaed, when he finally shows. The HMS doesn't announce him; there's just suddenly Dad's voice down the hall booming, "Aaannnd, he's back!" I don't know who the *he* is supposed to be: me or himself.

By the time I hoist myself up on my elbows and force my eyes open, Dad is already leaning in my doorway, head and shoulders in the room, the rest of him back in the hallway. Val calls Dad "the friendly lamppost." Well, *called* him.

"Lights out, huh?" he says.

I blink up at him. "Tired. Lots of packing today."

"*Pack up all my care and woe,*" he sings softly.

To tell the truth, I've been avoiding Dad lately. I purposely miss his calls and return them with clips or memes. I keep it light and glancing, a *Hey, old man!* and a *Ha, ha, ha,* just like he does. Look, I'm sorry Val left him. But it's hard to feel totally and completely sorry after he left Mom and me.

"You really are beat, huh?" Dad tilts his head, assessing me.

I'm pretty sure he knows I've been avoiding him, but he won't push it, won't fret or hint like Mom would. He'll just tilt his head and set his mouth in a line that's neither smile nor frown and wait me out. And it's hard to know if he's giving me space or if he just doesn't care that much.

"So much packing," I say. "My dreams are going to be delivered in moving boxes."

He chuckles.

"I'll let you get to them then."

My screen stops him, a flash of light in the dark room like someone has snapped a picture of us. It's another image from Saff. Light glancing off the surface of an accumulation of water—a pool? A fountain? A puddle? Something about the water and light makes the picture look subterranean. Is she underground?

"It's from Saff," I say, without thinking.

And then, also without thinking, I project the picture to show Dad.

He steps toward it, the image reflected in his glasses. "Huh," he says. "Interesting framing."

See? This is what you get with Dad. You tell him your ex-girlfriend sent you a mysterious, possibly subterranean photo, and he says, *Interesting framing.*

"Maybe she took a photography class or something," I mutter.

"Tell her she has an eye."

"I can't tell her anything. We don't talk anymore."

Dad tilts his head another few degrees and says not a thing. But to be completely fair, what is he supposed to say to that?

You killed the conversation, Zi likes to say to me. *You strangled it. You shot it with a gun. You ax-murdered it.*

Dad retreats to the doorway. "Glad you're home," he says. And I don't point out that it's not his home anymore. That it's not even really mine.

IN THE MORNING, I climb the mountain. The grass is uncut, whispering at my calves, and every few strides a flock of tiny yellow birds rises from it in a puff. The higher I go, the steeper the climb, until I have to grasp the honeycombed bark of the pine trees to pull myself along. After a while, the grass grows sparse and turns to drifts of crystalline sand that shift under my feet, then the sand becomes a deep powdery snow that sucks at my steps and dampens all sound. At the summit, there's no grass or snow or sand. The peak is bare rock, smooth and shiny gray, as if someone put the top of the mountain through a rock tumbler. At one edge of the peak sits a vinyl chair, the kind you might find in a small-town diner. I sink into it, winded from the climb.

Even though I'm not expecting them, I don't flinch when a pair of hands comes down to rest on my shoulders. I can't feel the hands, only see them, flickers in the corners of my vision. I can imagine the weight of them, though, the fingers dancing along the crest of my scapula. I turn and Zi's avatar smiles steadily at me.

Zi and I spent a lot of time on our avatars. We even let each other make final adjustments, working off the theory that other people see you more accurately than you see yourself. The result is that Zi's avatar is essentially his doppelganger, if you ignore the fox ears and gold eyes he insisted I add. But mine? Zi made me about twenty-three degrees handsomer than I am, even if he swears he didn't.

I stand and turn so we're facing each other. Zi reaches up and flicks my cheek. Again, I can't feel it.

"I chased you all the way up here," he says. "Didn't you hear me calling your name?"

"Nope. Sorry. Must have had a big head start." And I must have, because Zi can outpace me any day of the week.

And it is any day of the week, or rather *every* day of the week, that we climb the mountain. We've been doing it every morning since October. It all started because Zi's coach assigned him the mountain to improve his stamina on the soccer field, but Zi was embarrassed to VR alone, masked and marching in place in the center of our dorm room. So he made himself into a total pest, worse than usual, begging, guilting, and bribing until finally I agreed to climb the mountain with him. Typical Zi. I warned him I wouldn't be able to make it to the top, and I was right. The first few times, I barely made it to the trees, gasping. By the second week, I'd made it to the sand. The morning I finally got to the snow, we whooped and kicked it up over each other in swirls and flurries, temperatureless and unmelting.

That's the day I realized something important about the mountain, something I didn't tell Zi: To get to the top, I needed energy. I had to eat.

Everyone—Mom, Saff, Josiah, everyone—worried I'd have a relapse when I went to college. Hey, even me. I was worried, too. It's what all the literature said could happen. Be vigilant. Avoid triggers. No gateway behaviors. Hell, it's probably why Saff didn't break up with me immediately after graduation. For the first few weeks, I was okay. The dorm food was bland, doughy, and inoffensive. But then, slowly, I started making rules again. Only vegetables. Twenty chews before I could swallow. A sip of water between each bite. And I knew that this was how it had started before, little rules that led to bigger ones. No food before dinner. Five hundred calories a day. Five hundred calories every *other* day.

But then Zi talked me into climbing the mountain.

"You really didn't hear me?"

I am on the mountaintop. Zi is still going on about chasing me up here.

"I was like, 'Rhett! Rhett! Don't you give a damn?'"

One of the nice things about Zi's being from China is that, unlike nearly every other person I've ever met ever, he didn't know about Rhett Butler and *Gone with the Wind*. Until a couple weeks ago, that is, when a girl on our hall told him about it.

"Just so you know," I say, "I'm rolling my eyes right now."

"And I'm grinning big at you," he says back. His lips don't twitch out of his fox's smirk. His golden eyes twinkle as programmed, every couple of seconds. Zi touches my shoulder again. I can almost feel it. "Have you seen your friends yet?"

"Nope. Last night was dinner with the folks. Well: folk. My dad missed it. Actually, they're being kind of weird." As I say it, I realize it's true.

"Are you seeing your friends today?"

"Hey, Zi? *We listen with our ears, big and round.*"

This is something Zi says when he feels I'm not paying attention. It's from one of the kids' shows he watches while I'm at my morning classes. What Zi doesn't realize is I'm always paying attention to him.

"And, no, I'm not seeing *Saff* today. I told you, she's in Illinois."
I don't mention the pictures she sent.

"How far away is Illinois again?"

"Dear god. How did you get into college? You must be very
good at soccer."

"Come on. I know it's in the middle somewhere." His hand
slides from my shoulder and taps me on the chest. "I just meant: it's
a lot closer to where you are than Beijing."

I take a step back. In my room, I come up against the edge of
my bed. On the mountain, I'm at the precipice, but you can't fall
or jump off or anything. Zi's hand is pointing at the center of my
chest.

"I should get going," I say.

"Huh, gee, wow!" Zi replies, fake bright. "It was pretty cool of
me to come meet you here on the mountain!"

I smile behind my mask. "Huh. Gee. Wow. It was pretty cool of
you to come meet me here on the mountain, Zi."

"Okay. You can go now. Have a nice morning, Rhett."

"Yeah, you too," I say, and it's not until I take my mask off, the
mountain disappearing and Zi with it, that I realize it's not morning where he is. I ask the HMS the time in Beijing and learn it's
actually the middle of the night.

I FIND MOM in the living room with a bowl of cereal. Another
oddity. She used to say eating on the couch was slovenly. She'd let

me do it (she'd let me eat *in the shower*), but I've never seen her do it before. She's got the bowl balanced in her lap, one hand resting on the Apricity next to her.

"You're working from home today?" I nod at her hand on the machine.

"No, no." She slides the hand back into her lap. "Just running late. Did you sleep okay?"

"Like it was my childhood bed."

She smiles briefly, a flash of lip and teeth that looks almost startled on her pale face.

"Did *you* sleep okay?" I say. I know better than to tell her she looks tired.

She looks tired.

"Of course. How else would I sleep?"

"Wracked with nightmares? Waking in a sweat?"

"Stop! I slept." She cocks her head. "Did your father wake you? I told him to tiptoe, but you know how he likes to thump around on his heels."

"My alarm woke me. Did Dad stay late or something?"

"No, no." She looks down at her hand on the machine. "He left just after he said goodnight to you." She brings the hand to her chest. "Shortly after."

"Are you mad at him?"

"Of course not." As she says this, she shifts her knee, causing her bowl of cereal to tip and nearly spill. She catches it.

I squint. "You seem like you're mad at him."

She pauses, then says, "Your father doesn't have the power to make me mad anymore. People talk about marriages 'making it'; well, that's when your divorce has 'made it,' when you can get past the pissed off."

"'Past the pissed off,'" I repeat.

She smiles. "Taco Tuesdays."

"The alliteration makes it taste better."

After she leaves for work, I check the HMS box in the hallway. When I scroll through the log, I see that Dad left the apartment this morning, just an hour before I woke up.

I SPEND THE MORNING inspecting the apartment I've lived in most of my life, walking to the center of a room and spinning in a slow circle, guessing the contents of cabinets and drawers before sliding them open to see if I'm right.

Mom has made a few new models since the last time I was home. I set them out on the coffee table: some kind of bird, some kind of weasel, some kind of anemone. The last I recognize; it's a death-watch beetle. Same as my ringtone.

I haven't told her yet that I've decided to major in environmental science. I haven't told her about Zi and me. Zi says I'm being chicken (he regularly sends me emojis of a chicken—just a chicken), but it's not that I'm scared, at least not of her reaction. I wasn't kidding when I told Zi how much she likes him. It's hard to explain. It's that there's the me who's there at college with Zi, and the me who was here in this apartment, who's here again.

I take a picture of the deathwatch beetle and send it to Saff. The reply is almost immediate.

The picture Saff sends is of a whitewashed brick wall marked with a graffiti scribble that was maybe supposed to be a heart, but the canister slipped partway through.

This time I recognize it.

That graffiti, that not-a-heart, is on the side of the corner store at the end of the block, the one where Mom and I go to buy what Mom calls "our little forgottens," by which she means necessities suddenly depleted, lightbulbs, batteries, soap. It's also the same store where Saff and I would go to buy her snacks, and sometimes on the way out of the store, Saff would pause and trace the not-a-heart with her finger.

Is she there now? I go to the window, but even pressing the side of my face to the glass, I can't see the corner store from here.

I get my shoes.

SAFF ISN'T OUTSIDE THE CORNER STORE. No one is. I project Saff's picture over the wall. It matches. My heartbeat is chittering away like a deathwatch beetle ringtone. The cashier is peering out at me from behind the counter. He's new. I don't know him; he doesn't know me. It's pretty obvious he doesn't like me standing here outside the store.

I take my own picture of the not-a-heart graffiti, trying to line it up just the same as Saff's. I send it back. Just as I'm telling myself she won't reply, my screen chitters in my hand.

You're there.

I stare at the message, waiting for the words to coalesce into another picture.

My thumbs twitch as I type, *Where are you?*

"Hey!" the cashier calls from inside. "Hey, you!"

The reply comes: *Not there.*

"What are you doing?" he shouts.

"Nothing. Just taking a picture." I lift my screen as if to show him.

He comes out from behind the counter. "You can't take pictures here!"

I nod—*Okay, okay*—and back up, hands raised, and head toward home. But when I get to our building, I keep going past it. I don't know. I can't stand to be up there right now with Mom's fake animal models, the images of algae floating across my bedroom walls, the bathroom scale splotched with the exact same soap stains that have been there for years. There's a bus stop two blocks over. I get on the 28, which goes to Dad's apartment. I've only been there once since he moved in, but I'm thumbed into the locks.

As I ride, I snap pictures: the scratched-up bus window, the slicked-down back of the bus driver's head, a gray brain of chewing gum stuck on the side of the seat. I send them to the unknown number one after the next—five, ten, dozens—so many they could be frames in a movie, so many you could use them to follow my trail.

Dad's apartment is on the third floor of his building, but I take the elevator all the way to the fifth, which is the top. I take a picture of the five button and its nimbus of light. Send it.

The roof is a cement plateau with industrial fans and a waist-high stone lip. The building's garden boxes are filled with cacti, someone's idea of a joke or just an easy way to comply with the green-roof regulation. I pick a particularly wicked-looking cactus and take a close-up shot of its needles; then I go sit at the edge of the roof, not up on the edge, but at the base of the cement lip so that I can lean my back against it.

I try to think of Saff. I make my memories of her into still pictures—there and there and there. There was a time when she was so important to me, and now she's gone. Maybe it's just that we've known each other the exact amount of time we're supposed to know each other. I don't send the picture of the cactus needles after all. I'm not feeling prickly anymore. Not sad either. More empty, like a wind is blowing through and fluttering the edges of me.

My phone chitters. Poor Saff. I must've sent her over a hundred pictures. She must think I'm crazy. I make myself look at the message.

I'm sorry I didn't say goodbye.

I blink at the words.

She did, though. Saff did say goodbye. We both did, back in January.

I needed to get away.

I know you're someone who can understand that.

The screen is shimmering, which means another message is about to come through. I stare at it, waiting.

I didn't want you to think I'd forgotten you.

Or didn't care.

And then I get it.

Val? I almost say into my screen, but don't. I don't want her to know I mistook her for someone else.

That's okay, I say instead. *I'm okay. Thanks for the pictures.*

You're welcome.

Goodbye, I say.

Goodbye.

After a little while, I stand back up and take a picture out across the city, other rooftops, taller buildings, patches of better-tended gardens, and there's surprisingly no fog today, so also the horizon.

"Rhett?"

I turn and Dad is at the rooftop door.

"The HMS said you were in the lobby. I couldn't figure out where you went."

"Oh. I didn't think you'd be home. I came up here."

"And I found you!" He points at me. Dad. More delighted by the solution than worried about the mystery. "Did you want to come downstairs? Hang out for a while?" He reorients his finger so that it points straight down.

I try to picture him and Mom together again. I used to wish for it when I was a kid. So much. In fact, even now when someone talks about wishing for something, I think of that: being thirteen in the bedroom of the apartment Mom and I had just moved into, in a room that I could almost pretend was my old bedroom when the lights were out, except even in the dark I could somehow sense that the bed was against a different wall, that the furniture wasn't where it was supposed to be, wishing—wishing to the point of whispering—that everything would go back to how it was before. Wouldn't it be funny if my parents got back together now? Now that I'm grown and gone?

"Let me guess," Dad says. "That expression on your face means, *Yeah, sure, Dad. Sounds like a fun afternoon.*"

I look at him, and suddenly I'm not mad at him anymore.

"Yeah, sure, Dad. Sounds like a fun afternoon."

He is visibly pleased.

"Just—let me send this."

"To Saff?"

"Someone else."

I send Val the picture of the rooftops, the horizon.

IT'S 7:42 P.M. IN SAN FRANCISCO, which means it's 10:42 a.m. tomorrow in Beijing. My bedroom window is darkening dusk, but on the mountaintop it's always midmorning. I get up from the vinyl chair where I've been sitting for a while now. I walk to the head of the trail and look down the mountainside. Past the snow and the sand, there's a figure just emerging from the trees. In a second, he'll raise his head and see me here, tiny at the top of the trail. In a second, he'll come to meet me.

10

Tell the Machine Goodnight

Pearl couldn't identify precisely when she'd begun talking to her Apricity. Sometime in the past year, after Rhett left for college and she was living alone once again. Once again? No, the past year was the first time she'd ever lived alone. She'd grown up with her parents and older sisters, had bunked with roommates through college, and had moved in with Elliot directly after graduation. When Elliot left, Rhett had remained. Once Rhett left, it was at last only her, only Pearl. And somehow the small murmurings one directs at one's machine—the *Where are you?*s, the *Hurry up, will you?*s, the *Stupid thing!*s—had become full sentences, had become conversation, had become confession. It was now routine that when Pearl returned home in the evening she would slide the machine from its case, set it out on the kitchen table, and talk with it while she prepared dinner.

"This garlic smell is going to be on me for the next two days." She'd pause mid-mince and give her fingertips a sniff. "I don't know. I kind of like it."

After dinner was made and eaten, the machine would take its place on the couch cushion next to hers, where they would count out the hours until bedtime, the opposite wall flickering with a movie and Pearl's glass of beer sinking in on itself. "Ach!" Pearl would cry with a gesture toward the actress on the screen, the one everyone was saying would be the next Calla Pax. "She's going to do it, isn't she? She's going to open that door. She is. Just you watch."

At the end of the end of the day, the machine would come to rest on the nightstand, where, if she wished, Pearl could turn her head and see it, a sleek rectangle, distinct in the dim light. She did not go so far as to tell the machine goodnight.

NOW THAT RHETT was back for the summer, Pearl made a concerted effort not to talk to the machine, at least not out loud. After all, she was not dotty. She spoke to it silently, even now, as she walked toward the bar and the man she'd arranged to meet there, the machine in its case brushing against her hip in the rhythm of her stride, as if nodding along with the conversation.

One drink, she promised the machine. *No matter how good or bad it is. One drink and then goodnight.*

Pearl could not linger even if she wanted to. Rhett would notice if she stayed out late. The thought came with a swell and a sigh. She was elated to have Rhett home, though a tiny part of her would miss her lonesome routine.

Not "lonesome," the machine spoke. *And not "lonely." "Lone." Your lone routine.*

The machine did not speak aloud either. Apricity was, despite Carter's best efforts, still voiceless. The plan to have it deliver its reports in Calla Pax's voice had fizzled when, at the last minute, Calla had refused to sign the contracts. Of course, Pearl was called in to persuade. A few days earlier, Pearl had seen the girl swallowed by a crowd so dense they'd had to dispatch Apricity security guards to fish her out. Calla had emerged from the press of flesh unscathed and, it seemed, with a new purpose.

Pearl hadn't recognized the girl who approached her in the Apricity lobby yesterday. Only when she'd said Pearl's name in that famously husky voice did Pearl look closer at the shorn hair and translucent brows and lashes.

"Calla?" she asked, and the girl put a finger to her lips with a conspiratorial smile.

"Not anymore. I get to pick a new name." She glanced around the lobby at all the people walking by unstopping and unstaring. "I'm thinking Gert."

Pearl marveled. It wasn't just hair and makeup; even the line of Calla's posture, even the bones of her face, looked different.

"I'm leaving the business." Calla said it lightly.

"You are? And Marilee—"

"Agrees. It was her idea."

"What are you—"

"Going to do? Travel for a while. With a friend."

"That was scary the other day." Pearl put her hand on Calla's arm. "I'm glad you're retiring."

"Oh, I'm not *retiring*!" She smiled and her nose crinkled, amused at Pearl's naïveté. "I'm just disappearing for a year. Creating buzz. For my comeback." She snatched Pearl's hand from her arm and pressed the palm to her lips for a quick kiss, then blended anonymously into the crowd. After a few steps, she turned back and called across the lobby, "Sorry I can't be your machine!"

When the machine spoke to Pearl now, she wasn't sure whose voice it used, but it wasn't Calla's.

Your lone routine, the machine repeated.

Her lone routine. Yes. Why was she going on a date tonight anyway?

Elliot, the machine supplied.

Right. She'd scheduled the date because of Elliot.

Even though the bar was filled to the brim with the after-work crowd, Pearl spotted the man, her date, right away. He was at a table in the back corner, seated so he faced the door, with one of those folding bicycles curled up at his feet like a dog. His hairline was ceding ground to his forehead, but the wrinkles looked like the right kind, made by smiles, not frowns.

The machine reminded her of his name: *Mason*.

When she reached the table, he stood. *Is that nice? That he stood?*

Yes, the machine replied. *In this overcrowded, underwhelming world, any gesture, no matter how slight, expressing that one person recognizes another person is a nice thing indeed.*

But if he pulls out my chair, Pearl thought, *that will be too much.*

Pulling out your chair would strike the tin note of insincerity, the machine agreed.

Mason did not pull out Pearl's chair, merely shook the hand she'd made offer of and asked if he could fetch her a drink.

"Vodka martini," she told him, "with a splash of olive juice."

"Splash of olive juice," Mason repeated, and disappeared into the crowd.

"Dirty" was the way you were supposed to order this preparation, but Pearl did not want to say the word *dirty* in the first sentence of her first date in however many years.

Three, the machine supplied, *it's been three years since you've gone on a date. Three years and five months, to be precise.*

Three years (and five months) ago she'd dated David, and him only briefly. David the divorcé. David the orthodontist. David the good citizen, who devoted one weekend each month to a different cause in need. Pearl was intimately familiar with David's altruism, emphasis on *intimate*. During sex, David liked to wear the thank-you T-shirts he'd gotten for his volunteer work. "Homeless Youth Food Drive" on the top and naked on the bottom. "Skin Cancer Fun Run" on the top and naked on the bottom. Pearl began to think of these sessions as "charity fucks." Suffice it to say, it hadn't been love.

You had a date last week, the machine said slyly. *If you count Elliot.*

No, Pearl did *not* count Elliot. Nor did she consider the nights he stayed over to be dates. Elliot didn't know Pearl was here at the bar. Didn't know that she'd created a profile on Spark Stats, a process that the app had informed her would take thirty to forty-five minutes but had taken Pearl a mere ten, her hastiness a performance of her nonchalance. For her favorite movie, she'd written the title of the last one she'd seen. For her profile picture, she'd used the photo from her work badge. UV light and her bangs all funny—who cared? Not Pearl.

"Olive juice," she muttered like a curse.

Did you know that if you mouth the words olive juice, *the machine said,* it looks like you're saying I love you?

We used to do that when we were kids, Pearl replied.

Who did? Not you and I. I was never a kid.

I meant me and the other kids in my neighborhood.

Did you ever notice how people do that? the machine asked. *Use* we *to mean the people they were children with, without any names or other reference?*

I hadn't noticed, Pearl admitted. *But you're right. People do that.*

A glass was set in front of her.

"Vodka martini, splash of olive juice." Mason slid into his seat, lifting his heels back up on his bike and tenting his hands over the small pooch of his stomach.

"When we were kids," Pearl told him, "we used to mouth the words *olive juice*. Then when the other person said, 'I love you, too,' we'd laugh and tell them we hadn't said, 'I love you,' we'd said, 'Olive juice.'"

Mason raised his eyebrows, the lines on his forehead rising in accordance. "Don't tell me you're saying 'olive juice' on the first date."

So he has a sense of humor, the machine observed.

An hour later, despite earlier promises to self, Pearl stayed for a second drink. And the machine joined them, sitting within a proscenium of empty glasses Mason arranged for it, shining and sober. She'd only gotten it out of its case because Mason had asked if he could see it.

"I went to a palm reader once. I've been to a therapist"—Mason shielded the side of his mouth in a mock whisper—"more than once. My ex-wife hired an interiority designer who changed all our light fixtures, which was supposed to *fix*ture all our troubles." He tapped his heels against his bike. "I exercise. I've done a lot in the name of happiness—"

"You're going to say that you've never sat for an Apricity," Pearl interrupted.

"That's right. That's what I was going to say."

"And then you're going to ask if I can do one for you now. But I can't! I don't have my swabbing kit, and besides"—she touched the edge of the machine—"they keep track at work."

"No freebies, huh? I get it. Bad for business."

This wasn't strictly true. Pearl could've done the assessment. She knew how to get around the tracking software. And it was tempting, the idea that she could discover Mason's secret desires right here and now, instead of years later when he left her for a pink-haired twenty-something and then, done with that, returned to her doorstep, head hanging from his neck at the same dejected angle as the bottle hanging from his hand. And she'd let him in! Like a fool, she'd let him in!

"But maybe—" Pearl began. *I could make an exception*, she was going to say.

Bad idea, the machine cut her off. Adding, *You're drunk, you know.*

And she was, Pearl realized, or at least tipsy, her typical nightly beer no match for the two martinis she'd sipped to nothing. She planted her hands on the table and pushed herself to standing. "Excuse me," she said.

The bathroom was single occupancy, and of course there was a line. When she finally gained entrance, Pearl sat on the toilet and then sank forward, her chest pressing against the tops of her thighs. Her ears rang in the sudden silence. What the hell was she doing? She wished she had a machine designed to answer *that* question. She'd told herself that she was signing up for Spark Stats as a gesture of independence, but she could see now that the gesture had been an empty one, that she'd expected to go on a bad date or two with horrible men and then return to Elliot feeling she'd somehow balanced the scales. But that wasn't independence; that was spite. And anyway Mason wasn't a horrible man. He was here to find companionship, connection, happiness.

Someone knocked on the door.

"A minute!" she called.

No, she, Pearl, was the horrible one.

She pushed through the crowd, intending to tell Mason the truth, or to tell him goodnight, or to tell him she'd go home with him; she didn't know which. And she didn't get to find out because when she got back to the table, she discovered that Mason and the machine were both gone.

PEARL'S THUMB JABBED AT THE LOCKPAD, missed it. Before she could try again, the door was opened from the inside, ruining Pearl's plan of creeping to her bedroom so that Rhett would not see her drunk (and tease her forever and ever). But it was, in fact, Elliot, not Rhett, who stood in the doorway.

Here again, the machine would've observed.

What is it that they say about bad pennies? Pearl would have replied.

That you'll have luck for the entire length of a day!

That's a lucky *penny. I said a bad penny.*

How can a penny be bad? the machine would have asked. *Aren't they all the same?*

But the machine wasn't there to say any of that.

Elliot was in his reading glasses and sweats, a pair of needle-nosed pliers jammed in the waistband. He'd been at her kits again then. He liked to mess with them, mixing up the parts of different animals—wings and scales with furred haunches. *Making chimeras*, he called it. And judging by his clothes, he assumed he was staying the night. Pearl sagged against the doorjamb, too tired to lather up even a little irritation.

Elliot took her in with a twitch of an eyebrow. "Had a few, kitten?"

Kitten, lamb, duckling, dove: she listed the nicknames Elliot liked to call her. *It's like I'm a one-woman petting zoo.*

But the machine was no longer there to hear it.

"What are you doing here?" she said.

"Gave Rhett a ride home from my place. He's not here, by the way. He's staying over at Josiah's. Hey, you all right?" He took her by the shoulder, guiding her into the apartment. "You gonna be sick?"

Pearl gave up and leaned into him, pressing into the place on his chest, the meeting point of joint and muscle, where, perfectly, *annoyingly*, her face fit.

"I lost my machine." She muffled her voice in his shirt, half hoping he wouldn't be able to understand her.

He heard anyway. "What? Your screen?"

"My *machine*," she repeated.

"Your Apricity?" Elliot was silent. He knew what it meant. After all, when he'd borrowed her old Apricity to make his *Midas* series, he'd had to sign all the same severe and forbidding forms she had, "personal liability," "complete and full responsibility," "damages in excess of," and so on. He cupped a hand on the back of her head. "We'll find it. We'll retrace your steps."

It was hardest when he was kind to her. It made something within her bristle.

She ducked under his hand and took a step back. "We *won't* find it."

"If we look—" he began, but she barreled over him.

"No. It's not lost. It's gone."

The words seemed to echo around the room, or maybe just around the inside of her skull. Not lost. Gone. *Gone.*

Elliot's hand was still lifted, his palm curved to fit the shape of her head. "It's not your fault."

"It is, though." She made herself look up at him. "They're going to fire me." And damn it all, she was crying, not for herself and not for her job and certainly not for her sham of a date, but for her machine.

AND WASN'T IT ONLY A MACHINE after all? Pearl asked herself an hour later, her spine pressed against the headboard, her knees folded to her chin, the sound of Elliot's shower through the wall a white noise shushing her murkiest thoughts. She would have to go in to work tomorrow and report the machine lost. She might be fired, but probably not. She'd been at the company for years. She was loyal. Carter would take up for her, and he was back in favor with the VPs. Most likely, they'd issue her a stern warning and a new machine. Even the thought of this new machine felt like a betrayal. Pearl's eyes spilled over. The shower shut off.

Elliot came from the bathroom, towel wrapped around his waist.

"What's this?" he said upon seeing her face.

Pearl brushed her cheeks with the backs of her hands to hide her tears, but she could have done that before, couldn't she? She'd heard the water turn off, had warning of his return.

When they were first married, Pearl would make a performance of her tears, working them up in another room and then emerging with them dripping off her chin like diamonds. It'd been her only recourse, she'd told herself, the only sure way to end a fight with

Elliot without completely giving in. But then Rhett had gotten to the age where he'd begun to use tears to get his way, and Pearl had recognized it for what it was: a child's tactic. So she'd matured. She'd dried up. Instead of forcing amnesty, she'd learned how to avoid the fight in the first place.

"Oh no no no no no," Elliot said when he saw her. He belly-flopped onto the bed and wriggled forward, leaving the towel behind. He began to dot her cheeks with kisses, taking up her tears with his lips. "Not allowed."

His comforting soon became sex, as it often did with Elliot. Laughter became sex. Boredom became sex. A bad day became sex. But it'd become something else altogether, having sex with him now. Now again. Sex with Elliot used to be a lark. Now it was like being left and returned to, over and over again.

When Elliot had first come back to her, Pearl had looked for evidence of the years that had passed and found it in the high ridge of his clavicle and the stringy muscles of his arms. Pearl's own body was older than it had been, too, of course. Was older, certainly, than Valeria's. In her mind, Pearl composed the questions she could ask Elliot about Val's body—*Taut skin? High breasts? Tight pussy?*— but held them in her mouth until they softened on her tongue, until they slid down into her stomach, her soft middle-aged stomach.

Sick on her swallowed questions, she'd started to spit them out to the machine, who'd said, enthusiastically and unhelpfully, *How beautiful to have a body!*

That's not what I asked, Pearl said.

How beautiful when two bodies touch! the machine replied.

PEARL WOKE IN THE MIDDLE of the night, her dreams picking their fingernails at the edges of her waking mind. Though once she opened her eyes, she couldn't remember a one of them. She knew her machine wouldn't be there even as she turned to the nightstand to look for it. She had a moment of panic when she turned the other way to find Elliot sleeping next to her; then she remembered that Rhett was at Josiah's. She didn't want Rhett to know about her and Elliot.

"Not just yet," she'd told Elliot.

Not just ever? the machine had whispered.

Pearl observed her ex-husband's face, soft in sleep, mouth half-open, hands sandwiched palm to palm between his thighs. It used to be precious, Elliot's sleeping face unclothed of its ceaseless charm, like a peeled lychee, something pale and vulnerable only she was allowed to see. That feeling was gone now. Lost. Stolen. Maybe if he'd only fucked Val, married her even, but not slept beside her each night. Maybe then Pearl could forgive him.

Where are you? she called to the machine.

She knew it had all been pretend, the machine's responses only Pearl talking with herself. Still she listened for its reply.

Nothing.

Pearl slipped out to the living room, gathering her screen and a glass of water on her way. She put Mason's name into Spark Stats, fully expecting his profile to have been erased. Not only was his profile still active, he had sent her a message.

> Pearl,
> I'd like to see you again, if only to explain.
> Would you be so gracious?
>
> —Mason

Pearl thrust the screen away and gulped down the entire glass of water while staring at the note. It was like an evil haiku. *Would she be so gracious!* She was so angry she could have spit. So she did. The glob landed on the coffee table, where she left it for as long as she could stand before wiping it away with her sleeve.

She had to respond. What other choice was there? She wished she could talk it through with Elliot, but she hadn't told him about Mason or Spark Stats. Not that she'd done anything wrong, not technically. She and Elliot didn't have a commitment, not even an arrangement. He'd shown up at her apartment three months ago, a mess after finding out that Valeria was leaving town entirely. First Val had left him; now she was leaving her whole life. Pearl almost admired her. The woman had quit her job, cut ties with friends, and was moving out of state, as if her marriage were an entire city that had been sacked. And here Pearl stood among the bombed-out buildings and smoking chunks of mortar.

It would've been one thing if Elliot had told Pearl that it had been a mistake, leaving her for Val. It would've been one thing if he'd promised her he'd still been in love with her the entire time.

It would've been one thing if he'd said he was sorry. But it was not any of those things. Not a one. All Elliot had had to do was touch her cheek and say, *Dove*, and Pearl had let him in.

She pulled the screen back into her lap, typing a flurry.

> Mason,
> I will meet you so that you can return my property.
> The bar opens at 2 pm.

Pearl read it over again, silently apologizing to the machine for referring to it as *property*. Other than that, she was pleased with the firmness of her message. Though her hands had shaken as she'd typed, and still shook. She reread, then added one more sentence before hitting *Send*.

> Do not mistake me for gracious.

PEARL WAS WAITING ON THE STOOP when the bartender un-locked the door at five past two. He seemed both surprised and annoyed to find her there.

"Come on in," he said.

She stepped across the threshold, somehow expecting Mason to be already inside, but of course the bar was empty. The design of the tile on the floor was beautiful, she noticed, without all the people standing upon it.

"Do you have coffee?"

"I can make a pot," the bartender said begrudgingly.

She sat in the window so that she could see Mason coming, which he did soon enough, no bike this time, a carryall slung over his shoulder. Was her machine in there? Mason paused when he saw her in the window, then tilted his head and smiled sheepishly, a shrug of a smile. A smile Pearl did not return. Would she be so gracious indeed?

He came in and ordered a beer. At the look on her face, he pushed the pint glass to the center of the table and said, "I'm not drinking it. I only ordered it so the man could do his job."

"How considerate of you," she replied, barbed. Usually Pearl took pains to be pleasant—she knew how sour women were seen—and it was an unexpected pleasure to act the bitch.

Her eyes went to his carryall.

"It's not in there," he told her.

"Then where is it?"

He took a breath and then, as if stepping off the precipice, said, "At my office."

And suddenly it was not Mason but Pearl who was falling, falling, with no ground below her. She had thought him a petty thief; she had thought him a bored narcissist; she had thought him a kleptomaniac. But she had not thought—*why* had she not thought?—of this option, which was worse, far worse. She could be more than fired; she could be sued. Even so, the image that rose in her mind was not of lawyers or courtrooms but of her machine in pieces on a table. She spoke the words aloud: "Corporate espionage."

Mason's mouth twisted to one side. "That's dressing it up quite a bit."

But it wasn't. The Apricity technology was proprietary and

zealously guarded. CEO Bradley Skrull was on public record promising the machine was to be used for only one purpose: to help people achieve happiness. The lawyers had buttoned this down in all the contracts. Pearl and her coworkers were given quarterly trainings about what to do if approached by a rival company. The first step was *Secure the machine.*

"You targeted me," she said, "on Spark Stats."

Mason looked away.

"What did you do to my machine?" she asked.

She imagined it dismantled, tiny screws strewn like chips of bone. A violence. Pearl bit the inside of her cheek.

"We're exploring new applications for the technology." But this was not answering her question. "You've heard about palm screens. A screen in—*in*—the palm of your hand? After those hit the market there's going to be a wave of bio-embed tech."

She stared at him. "You want to put Apricity *inside* people? And it would . . . what?"

"Do what it does. Tell people how to be happy, day to day, minute to minute. And the commercial possibilities are off the charts. A new spin on direct marketing, right? Companies would be climbing over each other to . . . Why are you shaking your head?"

"It's a perversion," she said, loud enough that the bartender looked over.

Mason appraised her. Then he asked, "Do you know what the name means? *Apricity?*"

"Of course I do. 'The warmth of the sun on one's skin in the winter.'"

"And just think if you could feel it"—he slid his hand along the table so that the tip of his finger touched hers—"right there."

She jerked her hand away, had the impulse to slap the back of his.

"I want my machine back."

"And we want you." He had a tab in his hand. He touched it to her screen, which flashed with his business card: *Apex Analytics, 218 Townsend Street.*

"Me? What for? You want a coder. I'm just a technician."

"We already have coders."

"Who?"

But of course he wasn't going to answer that. He simply smiled in reply.

"We want you," he repeated.

"Well, you can't have me," she said, and what a joy these words were to say out loud. She repeated it in her head: *You can't have me!*

Mason's eyes changed, and he was something else again, not the middle-aged bachelor, not the petty thief, not the corporate spy. He smiled at her, and if it was an unkind smile, she could not tell.

He said, "But you're not happy."

She met his gaze. "I want my machine."

SHE DID NOT RECEIVE it. What she did receive was a job offer as a "consultant" at triple her current salary. Her response to this offer was to reach down and pull Mason's carryall into her lap. He watched her gamely as she picked through the contents. As he'd said, her machine was not within it. She deposited the carryall at his feet and left the bar without paying for her coffee. A bad date indeed.

Pearl had called in sick to work that morning, so there was nowhere to go but home. Rhett was still at Josiah's, but Elliot was there, and he was all action. He ushered her through the door and sat her down in the living room, not even asking where she'd been. He'd synced his screen with the HMS (and of course he knew the HMS password; he'd set up the damned thing) and projected its display onto the wall: a map of downtown San Francisco, a bright green line zagging through its center.

"Here's where you were yesterday." He ran his finger along the line. "Or at least where your screen was."

They'd downloaded the tracker app when Rhett was in elementary school to help coordinate drop-offs and pickups and after-school lessons, the busy schedule of a young family. It'd been years since they'd needed it, though the app had clung on through software updates and device transfers. After Elliot left her, Pearl had found a new use for the app, opening the city map two, three, many times a day to trace the vector of Elliot's movements, until one day his line had traveled to a lawyer's office, and Pearl had known that he was requesting divorce papers. At which point she'd locked herself out of the program and into the bathroom with both the sink and shower running, making sure to pitch her sobs below the sound of the water so that Rhett would not hear them. When Elliot had shown up with the papers the following week, Pearl had experienced the strangest feeling, like she'd had not foreknowledge of his arrival but a premonition of it.

"My guess is you lost it somewhere here." Elliot pointed to a segment of the line. "Maybe at this bar. Do you remember having it there?"

"I don't know where I left it."

"Maybe Izzy remembers."

She didn't correct him that she had not been at the bar with Izzy. In fact, a soft "I could ask her" escaped her lips.

"All we have to do is follow the line," Elliot said.

"But if it was stolen . . . ?"

He shrugged. "If it was stolen, it was stolen. But we don't know that, so we can at least look, right?"

"I suppose. I—" She bowed her head, touched her fingers to her temples. "I don't know."

Elliot stepped close to her, an inch away. She waited for him to ask, *What's wrong?* And she knew that if he did, she would be brave enough to say, *Why did you leave me?* Or *Why did you come back to me?* But Elliot didn't ask that or anything. Instead, he pulled her fingers from her temples and replaced them with his own, rubbing small circles there. Pearl pictured the tracery of the movement like the green line on the map, a person turning round and round in a circle, and she felt despair open up in her chest. And she hated him. And she longed for him. And she craned up until her forehead rested against his.

EVENTUALLY, FOLLOWING THE LINE, she ended up at the same bar for the third time in two days. This time with Elliot in tow.

"Back again?" the bartender said when he saw her. He didn't seem angry; Mason must have paid for her coffee, then.

Pearl glanced at Elliot, who'd donned an easy smile, chin slightly lifted, like he and the bartender already had an inside joke running.

"Glad you remember. She thinks she left her hard drive in here yesterday." This was the lie Elliot had come up with on the train. Pearl had sat next to him and practiced her responses, unsure why she was letting it go this far, unsure if she was keeping the truth from him out of stubbornness or shame.

Elliot pantomimed the dimensions of the Apricity machine. "About like that."

The bartender sucked his teeth. "Big hard drive."

"It has an entire library on it," Pearl said, her contribution to the lie. "Medical books. For my job."

"You can see why we need to find it." Elliot bounced on his heels. "She'll get in trouble. Her boss is a real prick."

The bartender smiled as one is obliged to do at this comment and flashed his empty palms. "Sorry. Not here."

"Do you have a lost and found?"

"Yeah." He reached under the counter and set two items on the bar: a rolled-up umbrella and a marabou-tufted tiara with the word *bride* spelled out in rhinestones.

Elliot plucked the tiara from the counter—"Hey. I've been looking everywhere for this"—and fitted it atop his head, perfectly centered between the gray streaks at his temples.

The bartender snorted, charmed, as they always were, by Elliot's antics. And it seemed to Pearl a type of violence, that much charm continuously wielded, a blade that severed you from your own good sense.

"How do I look?" Elliot asked her.

"Beautiful," she said.

"And here I was hoping for 'virginal.'" He placed the crown back on the bar. "After all, it is my wedding night."

On the ride home, they caught a nearly empty train car. They sat facing each other, Elliot stretching his legs across the gap so that his feet rested on the seat next to hers. His screen chimed and he glanced at it.

"Rhett just got home."

"He texted you?" Pearl asked.

"No. The HMS did." He waved his screen at her. Right. He had the tracker app on there now. "So what do you say we go home and tell him?"

"Tell him . . . ?"

He cocked his head. "About us."

The train rattled. Pearl stared at Elliot's sneakered feet, sole-down on the seat. He shouldn't do that. People sat there. Little old ladies sat there. Children. She resisted the urge to push his sneakers off the seat. Her insides rattled with the train.

"I really can't think about that right now," she said.

"He's definitely going to roll his eyes and say *ew*. Brace yourself. There will be an *ew*. But you know that's just for show. You know underneath it all he's going to be happy for us. All three of us."

"I really can't think about that now."

Elliot showed his palms. "Okay. No hurry."

She watched him warily. He was always gracious in defeat. Because it was never truly defeat, was it? Only a slight delay in Elliot's inevitable path toward getting whatever he wanted. The train slowed, and his foot shifted, revealing on the seat an imprint of dust in the pattern of his sneaker sole.

The train stopped, and suddenly Pearl was standing.

"Not our stop, dove," he said.

Which Pearl already knew. She strode to the doors, pushing past an embarking woman so roughly that the woman exclaimed. She didn't pause to apologize.

"Dove!" she heard Elliot call behind her, but she was already out of the train and working her way through the lattice of people on the platform.

"Pearl!" he cried.

Run! the machine said.

Pearl ran.

THE ADDRESS ON MASON'S business card, 218 Townsend Street, housed a Chinese bakery, closed hours ago. A few blocks from the water, it was mostly businesses in this neighborhood, the streets empty at night, the windows lit with security lights that winked on and off by their timers. Behind all of it, the dark spread of the bay, a void.

The bakery doors were speckled with peeling yellow *hanzi*, only a few of which Pearl could read: *sweet, dozen, luck*. Maybe there was an office above the bakery, or maybe this bakery was where Mason met his poached employees before taking them to the real location of his company, of her machine. The shine had worn off the middle of the door handles. Pearl imagined their silver transferred fleck by fleck to palm after grasping palm and borne away. She gripped the handles herself and pulled, expecting the firm reminder of a dead bolt. Instead she stumbled back as, miraculously, the left-hand door swung open. Someone must have forgotten to lock up. Pearl waited for the alarm, waited so long that the silence itself became its own sound. When no alarm rang she stepped inside, closing the door gently behind her.

The air smelled faintly of both cleaning solution and cooking oil. Chairs were inverted neatly on tables, the pastry cases empty, save for a rag wadded in one corner like a collapsed cake. A faint light glowed off the tiles and glass. Pearl peered over the counter and into the pass-through window; the light came from a room at the back of the kitchen.

"Hello?" she called out, her voice wavery.

Silence.

Then:

Hello, the machine replied.

You're here! Pearl said.

Silence again.

No, the machine said, *I'm not.*

But—

You're alone now.

But I can hear you.

I'm alone too, it added, as if for comfort.

Pearl stepped around the counter, into the kitchen. The room at the back was a little office, jammed-in desk, screen hidden by a sleeve of to-go cartons, chair cracked and spitting its stuffing. And there, on the seat of the chair, was Pearl's machine. In a moment, it was in her hands.

As soon as she lifted it, she knew something was wrong—too light, much too light. She thrust the machine into the desk lamp and turned it round. There. The invisible seam where the halves of the case joined together was now visible, a thin line, a whisker. Pearl shimmied her nail into the crack, then her finger. The machine split open. Inside? Nothing. The machine's guts had been removed. She held only the shell. Pearl rummaged among the to-go cartons and in the desk drawers, already knowing she would not find what she was looking for. Eventually, she stopped and pressed the empty case to her chest.

I'm sorry, she said.

For what?

For losing you.

But you found me!

She walked back slowly through the darkened rooms, across the kitchen, around the far end of the counter, picking her way among the tables, the machine still pressed to her chest. A movement through the scrim of peeling *hanzi* on the doors caught her eye. Elliot. He was standing in the pocket park across the street, staring at his unfolded screen with a furrowed brow. He turned around in a circle. The green line of the tracker app would have led him here, but he wouldn't guess she'd be in a closed-up bakery.

Pearl stepped back into the shadows. She reached into her pocket and powered down her own screen. A moment later, Elliot flinched, and Pearl felt a small stir of satisfaction, knowing her green line had just ended dead. Elliot murmured a few commands into his screen; when those didn't work, he began to walk, retracing his steps. Once he was out of view, Pearl slipped from the bakery and hurried down the street in the opposite direction, the Apricity casing still clutched in her hand. It felt like a brick she might throw through a window.

"DAD CALLED!" Rhett shouted down the hall as Pearl closed the door behind her.

She stuck her head in his room. He was standing in the center, VR mask and gloves in one hand, hair sticking this way and that, barefoot. He must have been playing a game.

"How's Josiah?" she asked.

"Shorter than Rosie now." Rhett smirked. "And both of them miserable about it. Did you hear me say Dad called? Twice, actually. Did your screen die or something?"

She patted her jacket pocket, the bump of the empty Apricity. "Must have."

"He wanted to know if you were here."

"What'd you tell him?"

"That you *weren't*." Rhett gave her a suspicious look.

"Well, I am now." She reached to ruffle his hair in a way she knew would make him duck. "Play your game. I'll call your father."

He watched her for a moment more, then shrugged and slid the mask back over his face.

INSTEAD OF CALLING ELLIOT, Pearl simply turned on her screen, which would make her green line light up on Elliot's tracking app. Sure enough, half an hour later, the HMS announced his entering the lobby. She was sitting at the center of her bed, weighing the empty Apricity on her palm, when she heard him in the hall. She lifted the machine to eye level and studied it up close. There were no scratch marks along the seam. Whoever had opened the case must have had the proper tools.

"You found it!" Elliot stood just outside her bedroom door, fingers grazing the frame and toes at the threshold, as if following some imaginary protocol. "See there? I told you you'd get it back!"

"Your optimism wins the day once again, El."

He watched her with his eyebrows knitted together and a small frown. He said softly, "Does it?"

Pearl turned and spent time arranging the machine on her nightstand.

"Rhett's asleep," Elliot said. "His door's closed."

"He's playing a VR game."

"Same difference. Dead to the world."

She cut her eyes at him.

"I didn't mean . . ." He didn't say *dead* again. "I just meant since you don't want him to know about . . ." He also didn't say *us*.

"It's fine, El."

Elliot ran a hand through his hair from nape to crown, ruffling it. He used to do this when they were younger, when his hair was longer and thicker and would stick up in crazy shapes like a mad scientist's. He looked like Rhett. Actually, Rhett looked like him. It was one of the more unfair things about life, that your child had to look like your ex-husband.

"Can I . . . ?" He gestured at the foot of the bed. Pearl thought, then nodded, and he came forward and sat down on the very end of the mattress. After a moment, he lifted his chin and indicated the pillow next to hers. "Can I . . . ?"

She snorted. Incorrigible. "Why not."

Elliot settled in next to her but kept his hands clasped on his stomach and did not reach for her. They lay there, silent and parallel, until sometime later Pearl opened her eyes and realized she'd fallen asleep. On the pillow next to hers, Elliot's eyes were closed and his breathing was even.

"HMS," she murmured, "lights off."

Dark.

"It's been a hard time for me," Elliot said.

"I know."

"Do you?"

Pearl reached over and rested her hand on his chest. He exhaled. Her hand rose and fell with his breath.

She was almost asleep again when she heard him say, "I'm glad you found your machine."

When she woke, she was lying on her back, the ceiling etched with morning light.

He's gone, she told the machine, without needing to turn her head or reach out to the other side of the mattress to know it.

That's okay, she told the machine. She thought a moment and decided that it was.

THE MORNING WAS A HASH. Pearl hadn't set the alarm and so had woken late. She tried to call in sick again, but Carter said no way, *no way.* They were already behind on the pitch for whoever or whatever was supposed to replace Calla Pax. So Pearl showered and dressed and stumbled into the kitchen to find a creature squatting in the center of her table. One of Elliot's chimeras, horned and winged and many-eyed.

What do you think it's supposed to be? she asked the machine.

The machine didn't say.

She left the chimera there next to the salt.

By the time the coffee was made, Pearl had resigned herself to her tardiness. She said goodbye to Rhett, still darling while shaking off his sleep, and stowed the empty Apricity casing in her coat pocket, feeling very much like an empty casing of herself.

On the train, the hand wrapped around the bar in front of her caught her eye. It was missing the tip of its index finger, the second joint ending in a smooth surgical nub. She looked up to the face. She knew the man. She couldn't remember his name, but she remembered his contentment report. *A desk by the window, tangerines, the tip of a finger,* she recited to the machine. *You told him that.*

He must've felt her eyes because he glanced down.

"Morning," he said, then considered. "Do I know you?"

"Pearl," she said. She wasn't allowed to mention his Apricity assessment, not here on a crowded train. "We met through work."

"Hmmm." He nodded, and she couldn't tell if he'd placed her or not. "Melvin," he said.

"How are you doing?" She kept herself from glancing at his finger.

"Oh, good. You know. Getting along. As one does." He inclined his head. "You?"

"Yes," she said.

"Yes?"

"Getting along."

He smiled at this. The train slowed and stopped.

"Mine," he said. "Nice to see you again."

He offered his hand, and they shook briefly. Pearl waited to feel the missing fingertip against her palm. Couldn't.

SHE WALKED INTO THE OFFICE with the empty casing in her hand, ready to turn herself in, but Carter was lying in wait by the elevators.

"Put that away," he said as he hustled her into a conference room. "Izzy is covering your appointments today." For her part, Pearl let herself be hustled.

The VPs had created a new position for Carter: director of special projects. This role and its boundaries remained largely mysterious but apparently included handing off Pearl's work to her colleagues so that he could pull her onto this project or that, which he did nearly every week.

The conference table was stacked with materials for what Carter kept calling "the post-Pax pitch."

He keeps saying it, she told the machine, *like a tongue twister. Post-Pax pitch. Try saying that five times fast.*

The machine didn't.

Carter had filched everyone's interns, like the Pied Piper with his parade of children, who merrily asked Pearl question after question and got little accomplished. Pearl made a bunker of work at the end of the table and lowered herself into it and didn't report the stolen machine . . . and didn't report it. The empty casing sat next to her on the table, just there. She half hoped someone would pick it up and realize it was missing its guts.

"You're a little addict, aren't you?" Carter said.

Pearl blinked up from her screen. Her eyes were tired. She'd been working for hours without pause. She realized all the interns were gone and vaguely remembered their leaving for lunch.

Carter nodded at her hand. "Look at how you fondle it."

She lifted her hand from where it rested on the machine.

"Here. Let's give you a fix." Carter bent down and came up with his collection kit. He extracted a swab and stuck it jauntily in his mouth.

"What are you—?"

He held the swab out to her. "Go on. Test me."

"What? No."

"Why not?"

"This is silly."

"Pearl." He took her hand and wrapped her fingers around the swab. "I'm invested in your happiness. In fact, it'll probably be the first thing on my con-plan, that's how invested I am."

Now. Now was the time to tell the truth about the machine. She could confess to Carter, and he could help her figure out what to say to her manager. Hell, if Carter's own history was any indication, instead of being fired, she'd be promoted. But instead of speaking, Pearl found herself going through the motions she knew so well: unwrapping and swiping the chip, fitting it into the machine, and waiting for the results. Though this time, she was only pretending to wait for results she knew would not come.

"In a moment," Carter said in a smooth voice, "Apricity will deliver the results of your assessment . . ." The script from the manual. He pointed at her.

Pearl shook her head, but Carter pointed again and, despite herself, she began to recite along.

". . . what we call your contentment plan. It is up to *you* whether you'll follow the recommendations Apricity has made for your increased life satisfaction. Keep in mind, Apricity boasts a nearly one hundred percent approval rating. That is why we can say with confidence: 'Happiness is Apricity.'"

They finished their ragged chorus.

"Well?" Carter said.

"Let's see." Pearl made a show of scanning her screen.

She was waiting, she realized, for the machine to speak. She shook her head and said, "Learn the clarinet, write in cursive"—

Pearl paused, trying to come up with one more—"and take a long trip. Alone," she added hastily.

She knew it was a mistake when Carter's face changed.

"Really?" His voice had changed, too. He was staring at her.

"Yep," she managed.

He looked surprised . . . upset? Pearl repeated the list in her mind. She'd tried to pick harmless things. *What have you done?* she asked the machine, but of course it was she who'd done it.

"Does that not sound right?" she asked.

Carter spun his chair in a slow circle, stopping when he'd completed a rotation and was facing her again. "It's just, I always get the same thing. For years I have. It never changes." He spoke quietly. "Until now."

And then his face broke into a grin.

"You're glad?"

"Yes." Carter beamed. "*Yes.*"

"Oh. Okay."

"Okay, okay, okay!" He pulled another swab from his kit. "Let's do you."

"No! I—" Pearl stood, fumbling for the empty casing. She dropped it and looked down aghast, half expecting it to have popped open. But it sat on the carpet, a perfect rectangle. She kneeled down and swept it up. "I need to . . . I'll be right back."

She'd gotten as far as the door when Carter called after her.

"Pearl!"

She paused and looked back at him.

"How about a smile?" he said.

PEARL QUIT. Just like that.

Well, not just like that. There were forms and more forms and questions and more questions. Her manager brought in a VP she'd never met before, who brought in the head of security. Pearl presented them with Mason's business card and also the empty machine casing. When they lifted it from her hand, she hardly felt it go, like she'd held nothing in the first place. She gazed at her empty palm, then smiled and thanked them and left.

THE STAIRWELL WAS DARK when Pearl climbed to her apartment. She had the feeling of traveling through a tunnel rising from deep underground. Rhett's door wasn't latched, and Pearl's knock swung it open. Her son stood at the center of the room in his VR mask and gloves, marching in place. Each footfall landed with a small jolt, as if he were trudging down a slope. He wouldn't be able to see or hear her with the mask on, but he must have sensed her, or maybe he'd simply reached his destination because he stopped marching and lifted the mask from his face.

"You're home," he said.

"What's that game you keep playing?" she asked.

He looked down at his gloved hands. "It's not a game. It's a mountain. You don't play it, you just climb it."

"Did you get to the top?"

"I did."

"How's the view?"

"The view from the imaginary mountaintop?" He was teasing her. "Amazing. You can see for imaginary miles and miles."

He smiled at her.

She smiled back. How could she not?

"And the imaginary sky?" she asked.

"Blue."

ACKNOWLEDGMENTS

The author's Apricity report would list the following people: Ulysses Loken; Sarah McGrath; Doug Stewart; Kate Beutner; Kris Bronstad; Sarah Beldo; Kate Hagner; Jim Sidel; Phoebe Bright; Mike Copperman, Caroline Comerford, and their workshop full of talented writers; James Hannaham; Kirstin Valdez Quade; Judy Heiblum; Danya Kukafka; Lindsay Means; Helen Yentus; Grace Han; Geoff Kloske; Jynne Martin; Kate Stark; Cara Reilly; Szilvia Molnar; Danielle Bukowski; Caspian Dennis; Rich Green; and Beth and Frank Williams—happiness machines one and all.

The poem quoted in "The Happiness Machine" is "Lines for the Fortune Cookies" by Frank O'Hara. The word origins in "Origin Story" are from *The Oxford Dictionary of Word Histories,* edited by Glynnis Chantrell, and *Fantastic Worlds,* edited by Eric Rabkin.